THE
Nearness of You

Lena Hampton

Cover art: Canva.com
Cover design: inDEWstyle
Manuscript Edit & Review: Lori Draft
Copyright @ 2015 Lena Hampton
All rights reserved.
ISBN: 978-1-941639-16-0
Second Edition

This book is a work of fiction. All names, characters, and incidents are derived from the author's imagination. Any resemblance to actual persons, living or dead, is entirely incidental.

To Angee

prologue

Last Year

RYAN CLARK DIALED THE NUMBER again. She had to pick up. She had to answer the phone soon. After four rings, her voice came on the line, but it wasn't her—it was the voicemail again. He ended the call and dialed again, getting the same result. He knew she was probably nowhere near her phone. It was move in day. She was probably hanging her clothes in the closet next to his or adding feminine touches to his former bachelor pad. Either way, she wouldn't have her phone at the ready to answer his call.

"Ryan, you're going live in five," his producer said as she passed by.

He tried calling again, hoping against hope she would pick up this time, and he'd be able to tell her something in those few minutes that would keep her clothes in dresser drawers next to his. The plan had been to show his prowess in the kitchen, followed by a display of the same in a much more intimate room which would lull her into a love-induced state, making the news more palatable and her more understanding. He was well-prepared to plead his case, but there was no chance for that now.

The news story—the one that would make his career and cause his marriage to crash and burn before takeoff—had to air today. It had been originally planned for tomorrow, but the national higher ups had gotten wind of it. They wouldn't—and didn't want to—sit on it until then. This wasn't just Chicago politics as usual. It was national news.

With one minute to air time and still no answer from his wife, he sent a text. He had a mere one hundred and forty characters to explain. "Amara, you are more than my wife, you are my life. I need you to breathe. My world was incomplete without you. Please remember that I love you. I forever love you, Mrs. Clark," he wrote. He prayed that would be enough until he was able to beg and plead.

AMARA WALKED INTO HER new home. Boxes in various stages of being unpacked were scattered throughout the space. It was still early afternoon, but she was exhausted after a day of moving most of her belongings into a storage unit and then coming to the apartment and trying to find appropriate places for the rest of her stuff amongst her new husband's things. Manual labor was hard, but directing those doing the manual labor was a lot harder, she thought.

She kicked her stocking feet up on the oversized ottoman and noticed both the remote and the notification light blinking on her phone. She clicked on the television and began to scroll through her phone. There were several missed calls from husband Ryan (she so loved the way those two words fit together) and her boss Senator Layton. It was her day off, so she opted to call her husband first.

Before she could dial the number, the "breaking news" graphic flashed across the screen followed by her husband's face. She sat up to pay attention to his story. His voice filled the room with words that prompted her to stand and then left her immobilized. The phone vibrated in her hand. She raised the phone to eye level, unable to tear her eyes away from the TV. Senator Layton was calling. She tapped accept and raised the phone to her ear.

There was no time for her to greet her boss because his agitated voice on the other end of the line was already barking out questions. "Isn't that your boyfriend on Channel 7 telling the world something you promised wouldn't go beyond you? How could you do this?"

"I didn't do it. I didn't tell him."

"Are you seriously trying to act as if you are not the source 'close to the campaign'? Did a little pillow talk lead to this breaking news? Is that why you're off today?

You said it would be a slow news day, and nothing would be happening. Was that for maximum impact? You said it would be slow today, a lull in the campaign, and you needed a personal day. You just didn't want to be here to deal face to face with the fallout from screwing me over."

"I didn't do this. I didn't..."

"Well, it's done, and so are you."

And with that, the line went dead. She opened her hand, and the phone fell to the ground, landing with a soft thud on the thick carpet. Amara's knees gave out, and she sank to the floor. Her heart plummeted, landing with a crash that shattered it into a million pieces. *How could you do this?* she asked an absent Ryan over and over again in her head.

She couldn't bear one more moment of his handsome face. She turned the TV off and began stacking boxes on a dolly. What had taken three men half a morning to unload into the apartment took her an hour to load in her SUV. She gave the apartment a cursory glance to be sure she'd gotten everything. Her phone vibrated on the granite countertop, and she flipped it over without looking at the display, took the back off, and removed the battery so she wouldn't be tempted to answer if it were Ryan. As she disassembled her phone, the ring on her finger glistened in the glow of the pendant light hanging overhead.

The ring slid off her finger with ease. She took that as a sign that leaving was the right decision. For a moment she thought about leaving a note, but decided there was no need. There were more important things to think about, like where she was going to go. She no longer had an apartment. Even if she did, she no longer had a job and may not for a while, and she didn't want to deplete her savings on rent. There was one place to go. Her real home. Her parents' house. She needed to be with people who she knew loved her.

RYAN HAD RETURNED TO the apartment first. He hadn't expected her to be there, but he was going to look everywhere until he found her. He looked everywhere. He'd checked her apartment and looked for her car at the campaign office. He'd even made the brief drive to Gary, Indiana to see if she'd gone to her parents. After inviting him in, her mom smiled and said she wasn't home. There was nothing in her manner or cadence to hint to the lie she was telling, so he returned to the apartment he'd given up hope of sharing with Amara. He checked all the rooms again, looking for any trace of her.

A throw pillow rested next to the stuffed chair in the bedroom. It was hers. It had the soft scent of flowers, spice, and vanilla that her old apartment always smelled of. He carried it with him as he checked the rest of the house. Had it been there before? Or had she come in the hours he'd been out looking for her? There was no way of telling. As he walked back into the kitchen, he knew it didn't make a difference.

He sank to the floor and leaned against the base of the island, hugging the pillow to him and breathing in the scent that reminded him of Amara. The engagement ring and wedding band lying on the counter above his head told him that if she had been there, she wasn't coming back.

chapter 1

Present Day

AMARA TOSSED HER KEYS ON the entry table and kicked her shoes off. She liked the four-inch heels much more than they liked her feet. She shrugged out of her coat and hung it on the coat rack then flipped through the mail as she walked to the kitchen. Most of it wasn't for her, and what was, wasn't important, so she tossed it on the island for later. She pulled the stemless bistro-style wine glass off the drying mat and pulled a bottle of Riesling from the refrigerator. She lifted the lever on the wine stopper and paused. It had just struck her that the mail had landed on top of something. But it couldn't be.

She sat the wine down and slowly approached the mail on the counter. As cautiously as someone facing a bear, she lifted the edge of the stack of mail with one finger. There was only one way her wedding band set could be there. Her hands flew to her mouth with a gasp. She jumped back, afraid of the circle of metal and stones on the counter. The sudden movement was halted, causing her to lose her balance.

Two familiar hands steadied her. "Honey, you're home."

She went rigid. Her body was torn between pulling away, leaning into the feel of the man behind her, and using every self-defense move she'd ever learn. Not knowing what to do, she just stood there. "Ryan? What...what...why are you in my home?"

"As of this afternoon, this is officially my house, but I'm hoping to make it into a home with you."

She turned in his arms, glared at him for a moment, then pushed away from him. She walked back to the front door, stuffed her aching feet back into her heels, and grabbed her keys. Not bothering to put her coat back on, she slammed the door on her way out. This called for more wine than she had in the house. Perhaps a martini— or twelve.

Amara drove out of the subdivision where she'd been renting from her friend Magnolia, Noli for short. The word "renting" was being generous. Her friend hadn't asked for any money and hadn't cashed a single check Amara had sent. Selling the house to Ryan could explain that. Ryan and Noli were cousins, and blood's thicker than water. Also, Noli knew nothing of the shambles that was her marriage with Ryan. But Amara was still grateful because when she first relocated to Indianapolis, she had been sleeping on her cousin Serenity's couch.

She sat in the parking lot of the liquor store with the two bottles of Riesling they had chilled. It was cheap, and she'd have a headache in the morning, but that would be fine. A migraine would distract from the resurfaced pain in her heart. She pulled out her phone and dialed Noli.

"Hey, Amara, what's up?"

She didn't bother with greetings. She needed to get to the bottom of this. "Ryan's bought the house."

"I told you about that."

"No. You didn't." She was fighting to keep the hostility out of her tone.

"Well, I meant to tell you. Being a new mother killed whatever brain cells being pregnant didn't take. I'm so sorry it slipped my mind. It's not a problem, is it?"

Amara mumbled a string of profanity before saying speaking. "No, it's not a problem. I didn't know you were selling."

"Ryan really liked the house when he was there to help Jack get the baby furniture for me and asked if I'd planned to keep it. When I told him I didn't really need it, he said he was moving to Indy and offered to buy it."

"Didn't you tell him I was already living in it?"

"Yes, but he said you're like family."

"I'm sure he did," Amara bit out.

"You don't sound too happy. Did I do something wrong in letting him buy it?"

"Sorry, Noli, it's not you. It's Ryan. He's a ..." her voice trailed off. She couldn't think of anything decent to say, so she said nothing and just took a deep breath.

"Is there something wrong?" Noli asked, concerned.

Was it considered wrong that the only man she had ever loved continued to turn the knife he'd put in her back?

"Everything's just peachy. I'm sorry if I got upset. Ryan moving in just caught me off guard at the end of a long week."

"I apologize for forgetting to tell you."

"Forget it. I can deal with Ryan. I was also calling to see about renting the space at Cooper's bar for a fundraiser. Can you have him give me a call?"

"Actually, I'm the one to talk to about that. We're business partners now."

"Business partners and co-parents...interesting." At least someone was pulling their love life together.

"Amara don't you start too."

"Start what? I just said it was interesting. Cooper must be special—this is the longest you've stayed put for a while." After the death of Noli's parents, she had started traveling the world to run from the pain. But an unexpected pregnancy followed by an early delivery and a father who refused to be absent had Noli planting her roots. "I'll contact you about the fundraiser when I have more details. I thought it would be a good idea to have it at The Smithery because it would show support for an Indiana small business while running for State Senate."

"Who are you working for again?"

"Ethan Bedloe."

"The governor's son?" Noli asked.

"That sums up my problem—trying to get people to see Ethan as his own person while still benefiting from the name recognition."

"I'm so glad you got this job after what happened on that last campaign," Noli gasped. "Amara, I'm such a horrible friend. I totally forgot that Ryan was part of what ruined that. I'm so sorry."

"Don't worry. With all that's going on in your life, I totally understand you forgetting how messed up mine is and that Ryan shoulders the bulk of the responsibility."

"Your life's not a mess. You've picked up the pieces."

Amara had picked up the pieces, and it seemed that Ryan was trying to scatter them again. "It is a mess, and it's about time I actually cleaned it up and stopped shoving everything under the bed."

"Tell me about it. I'll talk to you later."

It had taken a few months of outright rejections and many unanswered phone calls for her to land another job managing a campaign. It meant moving from the nation's third largest city, the city she loved, to Indianapolis. At first she understood why it was sometimes purposely mispronounced Indiana-no-place, but it had begun to grow on her.

The quiet neighborhood she ran through in the morning helped her clear her head. Occasionally there was another black woman about her age running, but usually just her and the chirps of the birds. There was no such solitude in Chicago. She'd gotten accustomed to the slower pace and loved the lack of traffic jams. She'd even found favorite local spots to eat, drink and shop. The best thing about the city was that she could turn on the TV without seeing Ryan.

It was difficult enough to heal a broken heart, and the difficulty was definitely compounded when the handsome face you were trying to forget was constantly on the screen. How was a woman supposed to move on when the voice that had once whispered sweet nothings to her was constantly coming from the speakers? Well, perhaps he wasn't constantly on. Maybe it was more like she had recorded some of his shows to watch when she missed him.

Amara had missed Ryan to her core since they'd been separated. For a while, there wasn't a day that went by that she didn't miss him deeply and then hate herself for it. And then when she'd finally gotten to a place where he wasn't on her mind and the prospect of rebuilding her career was real, the real test had come—she'd been forced to see him face to face. Ryan wasn't just her estranged husband, he was also the brother of her best friend, Diane.

When Diane got married this spring, they were both there. He looked so handsome in his tux. He was charming, and he laughed and smiled with ease while she had to do all she could to keep the tears from flowing. If she started crying, she'd have to reveal to her best friend that she was stupid enough to marry a jerk that had been using her to advance his career. Then she'd have to tell her that said jerk was none other than her brother. He had pursued her for the entire weekend, and she avoided him for fear of the tears. Or worse, that she'd end up in bed with him again. She needed a Ryan rehab, or a twelve-step program, but neither existed—she'd Googled it in a moment of desperation.

Then she'd had to see him again when Noli, who happened to be his cousin, unexpectedly became a mother. Seeing Ryan beaming over his cousin's baby crushed her broken heart into a fine dust because she'd fantasized about him holding their child with that exact look of adoration on his face. But she'd survived that.

Could she survive them living in the same house? She was about to find out the answer to that question because she thought maybe it was time she took a page from Noli's book and stopped running.

Ryan stood up from the couch when she came through the door. His hands were shoved deep in his jeans' pockets. He looked at her for a moment then focused on something imaginary on the floor. If she didn't know any better, she'd think he was nervous.

"You want some wine?" she asked as she walked by him toward the kitchen.

"That would be nice."

She uncorked the bottle like a professional then poured a glass and pushed it toward him across the counter. Handing it to him brought with it the risk of touching him, and that was a risk she didn't want to take.

"Aren't you going to have some?"

He raised the glass to his lips but didn't take a sip. He was watching as Amara wrapped her lips around the bottle and drank. When she lowered it, there was a third left. "This is mine," she said wiping wine from her mouth with her index finger. "So is that," she said, pointing to the bag from the liquor store. "But you can have what's left in that bottle."

"I don't think you should drink that much."

"I don't think you should advise me what to do." She raised the bottle back to her lips.

"No person should drink that much."

"Ryan, why did you buy this house?"

"Drastic times call for drastic measures." He stepped closer. "I've missed you, Amara."

"None of that explains why you've bought a house in Indy when your job is in DC last I heard."

"When I found out you were moving here, I convinced the network to take a different spin on the show and base me here."

"So this isn't temporary?" He shook his head. "Then I'll move back in with my cousin. Or find a refrigerator box and set up camp down by the White River."

"Amara, why do you keep running from me? Running away from us?"

"What 'us' is there to run from?"

"The husband and wife us," Ryan said.

"Ryan, you married me to get information, to advance your career."

"I married you because I love you. I've been trying to tell you the entire time that I got the information from someone else."

"If not me, then who?"

He looked at the floor. "I can't tell you that."

She chuckled. "Protecting them is more important than us, more important than me." The pain had finally begun to dull so she could discuss this without tears threatening to fall.

"Nothing's more important than you," he said, bringing his eyes back to hers.

"My name is mud because of you. I barely have a career. I'm working for scraps on a long-shot US senate campaign. I can barely afford rent, which is the only thing that's keeping me from going upstairs and packing right now. If I were important to you, you'd clear my name."

"I can't do that."

"Then prove you didn't manipulate me and tell me who your source was."

"Is that what it'll take for you to forgive me?"

"Ryan, I've forgiven you. The problem is I don't trust you. Love without trust is just lust, and I want more than that in a marriage."

"And you have that. I love you. All I've ever wanted to give you is my love. That's all I have to give you."

"No, you could give me the annulment I've requested and let me move on."

"I'll sign the papers."

She thought those words would make her happy, but they didn't. They did the impossible and broke a heart she thought couldn't break anymore. Amara turned so he couldn't see her tears.

Before she could respond, his hands had slipped around her waist, and he rested his forehead against the back of her head. "I'll agree to an annulment. I'll even pay alimony and give you this house, but you have to give us a year to try and make it work."

She tried to squelch the hope that rose inside and bury the desire that flared from the feel of his arms around her. Despite her tough facade, she wanted this to work. She wanted him to keep trying because she knew she'd eventually let go of the hurt and anger, and the love she still felt for him would thrive again. "I'll give you three months."

Ryan let out a long breath. "Nine months."

"Six."

"Six months." He brushed a kiss on the tender skin of her neck. "Thank you, Amara."

"Don't thank me yet. There are other conditions. Like I'm keeping the master suite and you can sleep in one of the other bedrooms, or on the couch, or even in the garage for all I care." Her words were harsh, but she leaned into the embrace she'd longed for. It frustrated her that the person who had caused the pain was the only one who seemed to make it better.

"Okay." He tightened his arm around her waist and pulled her closer.

"And there has to be a Chinese wall. A complete barrier so that no information is exchanged between us. You can't ask me any questions about my work."

"I can't even ask you how your day was?"

"You can, but my answer will be general. And you have to stay away from my laptop, any papers I bring home, my cell phone, and anything else even remotely related to work. You go near any of it, and you sign the papers right then."

"Okay." He placed a hint of a kiss on her neck.

"And you have to take me on dates. We've never actually dated, and I want that."

"I'll do whatever you want, Amara." He nibbled on her neck.

She pulled away from the temptation of his lips. "And no sex," she demanded, pointing a finger at him for emphasis.

He took her hands into his and traced his thumb along their backs. "No sex," he agreed, but there was a glint of mischief in his eyes as he pulled her to him. "But I can't promise you that we won't make love at some point over the next six months."

"We won't."

"You know you want to. I'm pretty certain you want me as much as I want you. You'll give in."

"You are nowhere near as irresistible as you believe yourself to be. Remember, we won't be sharing a bed."

He hunched a shoulder in disregard to her statement. "Can I take my wife to dinner?"

"I can't go anywhere. Guzzling almost an entire bottle of wine in minutes gets you pretty drunk pretty fast."

"You relax, and I'll take care of dinner."

chapter 2

IT DIDN'T TAKE LONG FOR the wine to take over and for her to doze off on the couch. She was beautiful. Her dark hair was pulled back into a chignon with her long bangs swept to the side, framing her face. Her long eyelashes rested on the top of her cheeks. Her pencil skirt had moved midway up her thigh as she adjusted to a new position on the couch. He loved her retro style that accentuated her curves to perfection. It made her unbelievably sexy without putting every inch of her flesh on display.

He was tempted to go caress her exposed skin, but he wouldn't give in. After over a year of trying, he'd finally gotten a chance with her, and he wasn't going to ruin it. He remembered the pain of watching Amara walk down the aisle as a bridesmaid for his sister, looking not quite her vibrant self. The wear and tear of stress was apparent in her weight loss and in the slight shadows under her eyes. Most probably didn't notice—she hid it well with makeup and a pasted-on smile that authentically imitated happiness. But he noticed. He knew her too well to not notice. The most painful part of it all was knowing she blamed him.

He'd thought it would take much longer to convince her to give them a chance. Her easy agreement could mean a couple of things—she either missed him as much as he missed her, or she had something up her sleeve. While he hoped for the former, he thought the latter was more likely. Any love she had for him was likely buried under a mountain of negative emotion, topped by doubt. Did she agree to try in the hopes of finding out his source?

It had been his plan to tell her everything, including his source, before the story aired. It hadn't happened that way, and she hadn't given him a chance to afterward. By the time he'd seen her again, his source had threatened to ruin Amara even further if he opened his mouth. His wife was tenacious and wouldn't stop until she got her answer. He was just as determined to protect her by protecting his source.

If Amara had agreed so quickly because she wanted this marriage as much as he did, he knew she still wouldn't make it easy. He would have to prove himself to her. After four years of limited to no contact with each other while she was in school, they'd found themselves moving in the same circles. What had always been there was still there. They finally gave in during a fundraising event in Vegas. The weekend had ended with their impromptu marriage in the wee hours of a Monday morning.

He'd thought the dance around their feelings had ended that night and that their life together had begun. A week later, it was their relationship that had ended. This night was the first time he'd had hope. He'd imagined them preparing dinner together, but her lying there while he fixed dinner was good enough.

Once the food was in the oven, Ryan joined her on the couch, lifting her legs so that they would rest on top of his lap. He began to massage her dainty feet. She loved shoes, and the higher the heel, the better. She was compensating for her lack of height, trying to better fit into a male dominated profession. She thought being taller would make her intimidating, and she thought the heels made her more intimidating, which they did, but they also made her incredibly sexy. It was one reason he didn't want her to wear them. He hated the thought of any other man thinking she was sexy. The other, less selfish reason he hated her wearing them is because they hurt her feet. He didn't want her to hurt.

Her phone vibrated across the coffee table with a picture of a man about his age and the name Ethan underneath. He suppressed his jealousy and the urge to answer. Is this someone she'd been dating? She'd left him months ago. Maybe she'd moved on. Maybe she'd agreed to a trial period to get the marriage over with so there'd be nothing impeding her future with Ethan. The guy looked familiar, but he couldn't place the face through the green-eyed monster in the way.

The sound of the phone dancing across the table woke her out of her light sleep. She looked at him through hooded eyes. Her lips drew back over clenched teeth as she pulled her feet from his hand and swung them to the floor. The phone had just stopped vibrating when she picked it up. When she saw who the missed call was from, she immediately dialed.

"Hey Ethan, you called?" She paused while the man on the other end spoke. Ryan could make out a voice, but not the words. Whatever it was, she found it funny and laughed. It was a real laugh, too, not one of her fake courtesy laughs. It had been ages since he'd heard her laugh. His jaw tightened knowing another man was the source.

Playing it cool made him hot. The road to her forgiveness was hard enough without any added obstacles. He used the many minutes of her phone call to plate dinner and set the table.

"Dinner looks great," she said.

"Thanks. Who was that on the phone?"

"No questions about work, remember?"

That was why he'd recognized the name. It was Ethan Bedloe, the son of Will Bedloe. "I didn't realize it was work-related."

"It was. Do you mind if we eat on the couch? That brief nap didn't counter the effects of that wine."

"Let me get you some water, and I'll bring everything over."

Amara took a bite. "This is good. Where'd you learn to cook like this? We both know you didn't learn this from your mother."

"My dad learned to cook so we wouldn't starve. Sometimes he'd watch me hide my food to throw away, so later, he'd sneak to the kitchen and cook something for me. He didn't want me to go to bed hungry, but he didn't want to hurt my mother's feelings, either."

"I didn't know that. Did he do that with Diane too?"

"Once or twice, but it was usually just him and me. Diane was so gracious that she ate what my mother tried to pass off as dinner."

"She didn't eat it. Diane used to call it the Catherine Clark diet. She said she stayed slim because she'd push food around on her plate until it seemed gone. I didn't know that about you and your dad. I guess there are still things about you for me to discover."

"Our dates will be a good time for you and me to get to know each other."

"We've never been on a real date. We went from friends, to lovers, to nothing, back to lovers, then to husband and wife, followed shortly after by estranged spouses."

"We've gone out."

"We've never gone out together. We'd see each other out and spend time together. Diane and I would have plans, and you'd tag along. But we've never dated."

"I guess you're right. We don't even have a 'how we met' story."

"We do so. Well, I have one. I remember the first time I saw you, it was love at first sight. I thought you were perfect." Ryan smiled. "Of course, I was five and lacked any real skills in judgment," Amara continued.

Still smiling, he grabbed his chest as if her comment had caused him physical harm. "Why'd you have to ruin a sweet moment?"

"I can't have sweet moments with you anymore. I don't know if I'll see them on *Good Morning America*. You only think it's sweet because I called you perfect."

"That's what made it honest."

"If we're being honest, why don't you just admit you snooped through my stuff and found out Senator Layton was gay?" Amara asked.

He was no longer smiling. "Because that would be a lie. I didn't even know you knew. I had a source."

"Then be honest and tell me who told you."

"I would if I could, but I told you I can't."

"Can't? Or won't?"

"Can't. Did you agree to try because you want to know my source?"

"Maybe it's still the five-year-old girl in me, or my inner nineteen-year-old, but no matter how hard I've tried not to, I love you. I agreed to try because I've never felt more joy than those few days I was foolish enough to believe I was Mrs. Ryan Clark because you loved me."

"I do love you, Amara."

"Let's be honest—that's not why you married me. I'm tired. I'm going to call it a night."

"What about dinner?"

"I drank mine."

THE NEXT MORNING, AMARA woke up with a headache worse than the one she'd had when a stray softball pitch was stopped by her forehead. She sat up slowly so as not to make the room spin from right under her. Eventually, her eyes came mostly into focus, and she saw on her nightstand two aspirin, a glass of water, a folded piece of paper, and her wedding ring set.

The rings brought it all back. The massive amount of wine she'd consumed in a brief amount of time and the reason for it. Ryan Clark was back in her life and would remain here because in a moment of weakness she'd given in to the persuasive feel of his lips on her neck. She was grateful for the aspirin and swallowed them down with the water, but she ignored the rings and the note.

She shuffled into the bathroom. The reflection in the mirror startled her. Yesterday's clothes were rumpled and twisted. The makeup that had been perfectly applied yesterday was smeared like a surrealist had painted her face. Her immediate thought was to fix herself before Ryan saw her. Her second thought was that maybe if he saw her this way, he'd sign the annulment papers and leave. Then she realized that he must have seen her tragic state when he brought the stuff up and sat it on the nightstand. She hated that he'd seen her this way. She hated that she cared.

Confusion couldn't begin to describe the conflicted chaos in her head. She loved him and wanted to give it a try. She hated him and wanted him to go away. She hated herself for feeling both ways. She needed to run this confusion off.

Amara washed the smeared colors off her face, pulled her hair the rest of the way down so she could put it back up, this time in a ponytail, and layered on her running clothes. It was February and dark outside, so it was probably below freezing. Hopefully, the cold would help her organize her thoughts quickly. She bounded down the steps and almost ran into Ryan.

"Good, you're up," he said. "I was just about to bring you breakfast."

For the first time that morning, she noticed the smell of food. He was holding a plate with an omelet and French toast in one hand and juice in the other. Most Saturday mornings, that would be a breakfast she'd eat and gladly ask for seconds or thirds. But not today. Between the alcohol still in her system and the upcoming anxiety of the next few months, she couldn't imagine taking even one bite.

"No, thank you, I'm going to go for a run."

"You're going for a run? It's freezing out there."

"I've run in colder weather. These are insulated for running in the winter."

"You have? Since when did you become a runner?"

"College. I was trying to keep off the freshman fifteen."

"I've never seen you run."

"I do it every morning."

"I've spent some mornings with you, and I don't remember you getting up to run before the sun was up."

"I've been more diligent since my recent unemployment. I can't afford a gym membership or to buy a new wardrobe if I gain weight."

She turned toward the front door, and she could hear him mumble something on his way to the kitchen. Then there was the sound of ceramic hitting metal then glass hitting ceramic as he threw the breakfast into the sink. She could tell he was frustrated because he was trying and not getting anywhere. He had to understand that she was also trying as best she could. He wanted things just to go back to the way they had been as if nothing had ever happened. But something had happened that made it impossible for her to turn off her resentment toward him.

"Ryan?"

"What?"

"Maybe we could have our first date tonight?"

"That's fine."

"Thank you for breakfast. It was a sweet gesture, but you shouldn't do things to woo me that you won't do years from now. A girl could get used to home-cooked breakfast on Saturday mornings."

"I'd cook you breakfast in bed every day for the rest of your life as long as I get to share it."

"The breakfast or the bed?"

"Both."

chapter 3

T HE RUN DIDN'T HELP HER decide how she felt, but she hadn't expected it to. It did help her remember that she was a woman of her word, and she'd said she'd try, so she would. She'd put on her big girl panties and try to make this relationship work. She wouldn't sabotage it, but she wasn't going to make it easy for Ryan because it wouldn't be easy for her. It was far from easy to let go of the pain his dishonesty had caused. Actually, the pain was more repressed than let go, but that hadn't been easy to do, either.

The bitter yet inviting smell of coffee greeted her as she came back in from the cold. A shirtless Ryan was leaning against the kitchen counter, reading on his tablet while the Keurig finished brewing his cup of coffee. Her memory had diminished the perfection of his chest. Her fingers tingled, not from the cold but because they wanted to reach out and run over every hill and valley of his abdomen.

"See something you want?"

Until he spoke, she didn't realize she was staring. "Yeah, can I have that cup?" she asked, acting like that was what she was ogling.

"Of course." His smile told her he didn't believe it was only the coffee she wanted.

When he handed it to her, his fingers brushed hers, heating her skin more than the hot cup of liquid she was holding. He turned and began to prepare another cup. Even his back was magnificent. A memory of digging her nails into those muscles in a moment of pure pleasure flooded her system, causing her to sigh from the sensation. "I've missed the Keurig. I was so mad at myself for forgetting it," she said to cover up her true thoughts.

"You could have come for it anytime you wanted. I'm glad you didn't, though. I discovered what I'd been missing. I never drank the stuff because my mother didn't allow caffeine. She said it would stunt our growth, or it was a gateway drug and we'd end up on crack, or gave us some other Catherine Clark logic."

His mother was unique, but it was obvious to Amara that she loved her family. "You and Diane need to give Catherine Clark a break. Sure, her horrible cooking could start a hunger strike, and a military regime has fewer rules, but deep under the frigid layers of her persona is a heart that wants the best for her children."

"I'm glad you've already qualified as suitable enough for Diane. That means you may pass the test to be my wife."

Amara took a sip of her coffee. "Your mother does like me. You know, she hugged me once."

"What?" He put a hand over his heart in exaggerated surprise. "She made affectionate physical contact with someone who doesn't share her last name? What did you do? Win a Nobel Prize for curing the common cold?"

"It was when I got a scholarship for college. I got a hug and a smile. She even said she was proud of me."

"That's another reason for us to be together. My mother likes you."

"Your mother also liked Diane's ex-fiancé."

"She liked that Alan was a doctor. I don't know if she actually liked him."

"It doesn't matter if she approves or not. I love you, and that's all that matters."

The time on the clock caught her eye when she looked away from him. "I need to go get dressed." She took a last long sip of her coffee. "Ethan and I have some things to go over, and I'm supposed to be there soon. Thanks for the coffee."

She attempted to sprint up the stairs before he could make another declaration of love, but he snagged her arm. His eyes studied her face for a moment. There was an emotion in them she had never seen before and couldn't figure out.

He pulled her by the hand until she was just an inch away from him. He ran his fingertips up her arm and across her shoulder until his hand spread out across the back of her neck. He pulled her mouth that final inch and lowered his lips to hers. The kiss began soft, his lips gently pressing against hers. His hands moved to cup her face as he deepened the kiss. His mouth coaxed then demanded. A fire sparked at her mouth and set her entire body ablaze. When he pulled away, she felt like a part of herself had withdrawn. That kiss made her understand that the look she'd seen in his eyes was jealousy, and his lips had just told her she was his.

"I'll see you after work for our first date," he said, confirming her hypothesis.

A FEW HOURS LATER, Amara sat on the floor of Ethan Bedloe's living room with a slice of pizza in one hand while clicking the wireless mouse on the coffee table with the other. She slid the mouse too far, knocking over the open bottle of berries and carrot juice she was drinking. The contents soaked some of the papers before pouring off the edge of the table and landing on Ethan's tan slacks and the ecru carpet.

"Shoot, shoot, shoot," Amara said, grabbing napkins. She dabbed at the papers.

"I'm all for the second amendment, but a gun isn't necessary over a little spill."

Amara smiled up at him and shook her head. In the couple of months that she'd been working for Ethan, she'd discovered his corny sense of humor was bottomless.

"Why aren't we at the campaign office?"

"Because the office is as big as my coffee table. I could budget for a bigger space, but I'd rather spend my limited campaign funds either getting my message out there or on a brilliant yet clumsy campaign manager."

"Campaign manager. Is that my title?"

"It's one of them. You're doing everything but being the actual candidate."

"I would be a candidate, but the name Adams hasn't had much pull since 1829." She shook her head at herself. "Your lame jokes are rubbing off on me."

"My jokes aren't lame." She gave him a look out the corner of her eye that said 'stop lying' without her having to say a word. He smiled at her. It hadn't taken long for him to decipher her various looks. There was a specific look she had when she was amused but didn't want to laugh. She donned it often to discourage his 'lame' jokes. What she didn't know was that seeing that cute smirk on her face only encouraged him.

"You're right, if your jokes were lame, that would be an improvement."

"Ouch," he said, clutching his chest as if wounded by her words.

"And you called me clumsy! I'm not clumsy."

She was right. She was one of the most elegant and poised people he knew. But today she was off. Even her normally meticulous clothes and hair weren't up to her usual standards. "No, you're not, but today you're a bit off. What's going on?"

"I indulged in a bit too much wine last night, and the effects haven't fully worn off."

He believed she was telling the truth—well, at least part of it. Growing up with a politician, he was good at picking out half-truths and could tell she had just told one, but he wasn't going to press her on it. "I'm going to change these pants."

Though Ethan had name recognition as the son of the current governor, fundraising had been slow going. His party quite obviously wanted his opponent to win the primary. The reasoning was that the other guy had a better chance of winning in the general election. The more likely reason was that Ethan wasn't willing to be in anyone's pocket or be someone's puppet. That's why he'd turned down his father's offer to help fund raise.

Ethan had had to reach into the trust fund set up by his grandfather to hire Amara. She wasn't his first choice. The meager salary he could afford to pay was laughed off by everyone but her. He'd been hesitant about hiring the campaign consultant with the tarnished reputation, but he was glad he had. She was brilliant and managed to get his fledgling candidacy off the grain, and it was now gaining traction. On top of her excellent political mind, she was beautiful and funny. He had to keep reminding himself that right now he needed to focus on his political career and not following in his father's footsteps of chasing tail all over the state from Lake Michigan to the Ohio River.

He threw his stained pants in the laundry basket and grabbed a pair of jeans. When he got downstairs, Amara was on all fours, cleaning the stain out of his carpet. He had a perfect view of her black skirt hugging her behind, and the split allowed more than a glimpse of her thigh. All thoughts of not following in his father's footsteps left him as he enjoyed the view for much longer than appropriate.

"YOU DON'T HAVE TO do that," Ethan said from behind her.

She raised up so that she was just on her knees and turned her head to look at him. It took her a moment to respond because the sight of him in his fitted jeans threw her off. They sat low on his hips, in a comfortable, relaxed fit. They hugged his thighs just enough to hint at the muscle beneath but weren't tight like skinny jeans. He'd always looked handsome in his suits or dress shirts and slacks, but he was downright sexy in those jeans.

"Is everything okay?" he asked after a few moments, looking down at himself.

"I've just never seen you in jeans. I didn't even think you owned a pair."

"Do I look that bad?"

"You don't look bad at all. They just make you look human."

"I *am* human."

"Well, this is the first sign of it. I wondered if you were a political android sent from the future to take over the government in preparation for the computers taking over and enslaving mankind."

He spread his arms wide and shrugged his shoulders. "You think I'm the Terminator?"

"That's ridiculous. The Terminator is more military than political. Anyway, that movie was about artificial intelligence trying to annihilate the human race, not enslave us."

"And you call *me* lame." He knelt next to her and took the sponge from her hand to finish cleaning up the spill.

"I did not call you lame," she said, sitting on the couch. "I called your jokes lame. Furthermore, there is nothing lame about the Terminator. Well, maybe the accent. It's not plausible that AI life forms would have an Austrian accent."

"You're still drunk from last night, aren't you?" asked as he left to return the cleaning products to the kitchen.

"I'm quite sober, and you've given me an idea. I'm planning a fundraiser in Southern Indiana, and I think we should get some campaigning in first, with you in jeans. It would make you seem more relatable than the elite son of a politician and an heiress. Also, it would help distinguish you as Ethan Bedloe, your own, not only the son of good ol' Will Bedloe. He's never been photographed in anything more casual than a suit jacket off and sleeves rolled up."

"If you think it'll make a difference, I'm game."

"Good, then we need to get you a new wardrobe that makes you look like a thirty-year-old guy."

"I am a thirty-year-old guy."

"Yeah, but your clothes say at least forty-seven-year-old man."

"There's nothing wrong with my wardrobe."

"I didn't say there was anything wrong with it, it's just the wardrobe of a slightly stylish man seventeen years your senior."

"You haven't even seen my entire wardrobe. Let's go take a look."

His frustration at her observation was humorous to her. She hadn't meant to offend him, but she had. She thought he'd been purposefully trying to dress older to make people forget he was so young. At thirty, he barely met the age of candidacy for a US senator, but he had experience on his side, and his platform was solid. Plus he was truly in politics to be a public servant. He wasn't doing it just because his daddy had, or for the power. He thought he could make a difference in this world.

Hanging and neatly folded in his customized walk-in closet was a wardrobe she was surprised to see—much hipper than anything she'd seen him in. He even had a few suits with a slimmer, more modern cut. She selected one and a matching tie and handed them to him.

"Try this on." They stood there for a moment without him moving. "Please," she added belatedly, trying to soften the command.

"Do you want me to change in front of you? I will. I don't mind." He began to unbutton his shirt while maintaining eye contact full of sexual suggestions.

"No, I'll step out." She shut the closet door behind her and waited for him to come out. This was her first time in his room. Somehow it was decorated just as she expected. The walls were the same khaki color as the rest of the house, the only difference was that the trim had been painted black. The comforter was a solid cream color with a black trim. There were four pillows on the bed, but no extras. The room was sensible and boring, just like the man who slept here.

Ethan came out looking anything but sensible in a suit cut to make his shoulders appear broad. Maybe they really were broad and she just hadn't noticed because his clothes normally hid his physique. She straightened his tie and rested her hands on his chest.

"This is a much better look. Why haven't you worn this?"

"This is more of a date suit than a business suit."

"I didn't know categories of suits existed. Wait a minute, you've been on a date? Do you know how much more electable you would be if you were married or even engaged?"

"Maybe if I found the right running mate."

She hadn't noticed her hands were still resting on his chest until he took them into his and held them close to his body. He lowered his head, raised one hand and placed a kiss on it, and then did the same to the other before placing both hands back on his chest. He put his hands on her waist and pulled her to him. His mouth descended to hers for a brief moment before pulling away slightly. When no objection was voiced, he joined their mouths again.

His tender kiss turned sensual. Her hands instinctively glided up his body until her arms encircled his neck. He slid a hand from her waist to the small of her back as he dipped down further to better reach the depths of her mouth. He wrapped his arms around her to lift her off the floor for better positioning and was thrown slightly off balance, causing them to bump into the bed. He trailed kisses from her mouth down along her jawline before stopping at the base of her neck. Her hands slid into his hair and she pulled him closer.

Her leg trailed up his side. He placed a hand under her thigh and lowered her to the bed, his mouth reclaiming hers as his hand explored the curve from her thigh to her hip, and then back to her enticing bottom. She arched her back, moving into his touch and pressing her body to his.

There were sparks of excitement throughout her body, but they couldn't match the flames that erupted when Ryan spoke her name or looked at her. The thought of him made her remember the look of jealousy he'd had when he learned she was coming here. The embers of passion were being squelched by a downpour of guilt. The more heated she became, the worse she felt about not stopping this before it started.

"Ethan, we can't."

chapter 4

H E STOPPED WITHOUT ANY FURTHER prompting, but he didn't want to. That was apparent from the sigh he released and the fact it took him a moment to roll away from her and into a sitting position. They sat on the bed next to each other for a few minutes. The only sound in the room was that of their still somewhat heavy breathing. She covered her face with her hands. He pinched the bridge of his nose. Each of them tried to pull their thoughts together and compose themselves, feeling bad about what had just happened for different reasons.

"I'm sorry," he said.

At the same time, she said, "This is so bad."

"I'm sorry," he repeated. "I shouldn't have kissed you."

"So very bad," she said again, her hands still covering her face.

"It's not a good thing that we kissed, but it's not that bad."

She slouched her back, giving in to the weight of what they had done and the pressure from carrying her secret for so long. Finally, she lowered her hands and looked at him. She wanted to see his reaction when she told him the truth of why she stopped. "Ethan, I'm married."

His eyes narrowed, and his face scrunched into a look of confusion. He stood up from the bed and studied the ceiling. "You're what?"

"I'm married."

He looked at her sitting on the bed. Her hair had come undone in places, and her dress was still raised to about mid-thigh. Her lips were swollen from their kiss.

"We should probably have this conversation somewhere else."

He left the room and went downstairs, and she joined him a couple of minutes later. He was seated in one of the chairs instead of in his usual spot on the couch. She sat in the chair opposite him. Neither of them thought it a good idea to sit next to each other. Things between them had changed upstairs in his bedroom.

"So you're married?" he asked after several minutes of silence.

"Yes, I got married a little over a year ago, a few months before I started working for you." Amara sat curled in the chair, her feet folded underneath her and her arms wrapped around her.

"If I had known, I would never have done that," he said, pointing upstairs. "I would never have even let myself think of you in that way. Why did you keep this a secret?"

She took a deep breath. She hadn't talked with anyone about this. Not her parents. Not her best friend. No one. She'd locked it so deep away that it was hard to let it out even now.

"While I was in Las Vegas for a fundraiser, I ran into this guy that I'd been," she pursed her lips trying to look for the correct term for her and Ryan's relationship, "dating for lack of a better term." One thing led to another, and we ended up married. Shortly after returning home, I realized it was a mistake and left him. I've seen him about twice since."

"Have you filed for divorce?"

"I filed for an annulment, but he refused to sign because he doesn't believe the marriage was a mistake. That was until last night. He agreed to sign, but only if I give our marriage a real shot for the next six months."

"So are you quitting to go back to Chicago?"

"I'm not quitting—he's moved here. In case I didn't tell you before, you need to work on not using 'so' all the time in conversation. You don't use it in speeches, but in conversation you do, and I don't want you to use it in an interview."

He smirked at the fact that she was always trying to polish him up for maximum appeal. "So...I mean, what's his name?

"Ryan Clark." She said it and hoped that somehow he would not make the connection. The flesh between his eyes wrinkled in dismay. He'd made the connection.

"The journalist?"

"Yes."

"The one that outed the anti-gay marriage, often times homophobic Senator Layton?"

"Yes."

"And you were the campaign manager for his presidential bid."

"Yes."

"Did you know he was gay?"

"Yes."

"Did you tell your husband?"

"Not knowingly."

"What does that mean?

"I never told him. I was as blindsided by the story as everyone else."

"Then how did he find out?"

"He says he had a source, but he refuses to say who it is. I think it's more likely that he may have seen something on my phone, or laptop, or in a file or something, but I never told him anything."

"If you think he, in a sense, stole the info from you, why are you giving the marriage a chance?"

She sank back into the chair, searching the air for words that could possibly explain her emotions. "When I agreed, I had just downed the better part of a bottle of wine in minutes, so I was slightly less than sober. And the reason I drank that much was because seeing him and being near him, I knew I still loved him. It's always been him, and it always will be. As deep as the hurt is, it's still not as deep as my love for him. I fell hopelessly and irrevocably in love with him when I was five because he could read the big words, and he was taking the time to read them to me."

Ethan was kneeling in front of her. It wasn't until he reached up and wiped a tear away that she knew she was crying. She wrapped her arms around him and cried on his shoulder.

As her tears began to subside, he said, "The good news is...I'm not gay."

She pulled away from him in confusion. "What are you talking about?"

"I'm not gay, so he can't out me and ruin my career. But the question is, do you still want to work with me after the advance I made on you?"

"You still want to work with me? That whole scandal doesn't bother you?"

"I knew about the scandal when I hired you. Selfishly, I'm kind of glad for it. If it hadn't happened, I could have never afforded you."

"You trust me? Even knowing my connection to Ryan and the fact I have no proof I didn't give him the information?"

"You said you didn't tell, so I believe you didn't tell. Plus I don't have any skeletons in my closet that would ruin my candidacy."

"You trust me because there's nothing to trust me with."

"I trust you because I think you're the woman who will get me to be the distinguished gentleman from Indiana on Capitol Hill."

"Thank you. You don't know how much it means to me that you gave me a chance and that you're keeping me."

"Thank you for taking a chance on me. I'm such a long shot to win. I do wish you'd trusted me enough to tell me, though."

"I apologize for not telling you earlier, but I didn't think it would come up. We hadn't seen each other in months until his sister's wedding, and then again when his cousin gave birth. We didn't exchange more than a few words both times. Then last night, he appeared out of nowhere and announced that we're roommates."

"You're going to really give it a try?"

"I am."

"Then we should forget about the kiss."

"We should."

"That is, unless things don't work out with him. I'm a patient man."

"Ethan, you don't want me. I know you think you do, but you don't. I'm pretty messed up. I still love him, and even if the marriage doesn't work, I'll probably always be hung up on him even after all he's done to me. Inexplicably, I will always love him."

"The heart has its reasons, whereof reason knows nothing."

"Did you just quote Pascal?"

"Did you just know I was quoting Pascal? Amara, stop being so awesome before I go against everything I believe in and try to steal another man's wife."

"You're a great guy and a pretty spectacular kisser—you don't want to be second fiddle. You deserve someone who thinks you hung the moon. Somewhere out there, there's a woman—probably a sweet and sensible kindergarten teacher—who's perfect for you. I'm not that woman, but I hope you will consider me your friend."

"You just gave me the 'it's not you, it's me, so can we still be friends' combo speech. It was a kiss, Amara. You don't need to break up with me."

AMARA WAS BACK IN her car after planning some fundraisers and a schedule. Guilt and telling the truth had drained her. She was emotionally spent and wanted nothing more than to lie in bed and pour caramel sauce directly into her mouth. But drowning her woes in ooey, gooey sweetness was no better than numbing them with wine.

She was able to change into faded yoga pants and a threadbare T-shirt before Ryan realized she was home. He knocked on her bedroom door. Something could be said for the fact that he was respecting her boundaries.

She just wasn't sure what that something was. She opened the door about halfway and leaned on the door frame.

Ryan's gaze rolled up and down her body a time or two. "You're not dressed. We'll be late if you don't hurry and get dressed."

"I apologize. I don't feel up to going anywhere tonight."

Ryan shook his head with the disappointment of a parent whose child just got expelled. "You promised to try."

"I promised? I promised?" Her voice went up an octave with each syllable. She jabbed her finger at his chest. "You promised lots of things." She began to count off on her fingers. "You promised to love me. You promised to cherish me. You promised to honor me. You promised to respect me. You promised all those things before God and until death do us part." She put her finger an inch from his face. "You didn't keep a single one of the promises vowed before God to honor until death do us part. So don't try to hold me to a higher standard."

"I want to keep every one of those promises, but I can't if you don't forgive me. Do you think you can manage to forgive me?" His face looked expectant.

His demeanor calmed her. "I'm trying to, I really am, but it's incredibly difficult. I can't just snap my fingers and get over it all. You need to understand that."

"I do. I was just disappointed. I'd been looking forward to spending the evening with you all day."

"I was too. I had a difficult day, and I still have some work to do. I won't be any fun."

"Well, if you take a break or just want some company, you know where to find me."

"What if you give me a couple of hours and then we can order Chinese and watch a movie. I'll even let you pick one of those horrible action movies that are just a series of car chases with dialogue every twenty minutes."

"How about I fix dinner, and you choose the movie."

"Even better."

"You look..." he paused "...cute."

She looked down at herself. "Cute?"

"I was actually thinking sexy, with the way those pants fit and your lack of undergarments, but I'm already on thin ice, so I thought cute would be better."

"You think I'm sexy in this?"

"I think you are intelligent and caring, which makes you incredibly sexy regardless of your attire."

She smiled. "I'll see you in a couple of hours."

She sat at the refurbished antique desk that sat catty-corner in her room. Her mind and heart were at war over Ryan. Hope that they could have a happily ever after was gaining ground, but reason kept trying to push it back and force a retreat. She became frustrated as she looked at the accounts for the campaign. Things weren't adding up to match what she'd believed they'd raised, but she couldn't figure out what was going on. While she was good at many things, accounting wasn't her thing, not at all. It was a good thing she knew someone who lived and breathed for it.

"Hey, Amara. What's up?" Serenity answered her phone.

"Hey. I need a favor from my favorite cousin. I know you're in the height of tax season, but I was wondering if you could help me with something."

"I always have time for my favorite cousin."

"I'm struggling to figure out these campaign funds. Can you take a look?"

"Campaign funds. That sounds fun. I've never had a chance to get into political money. Just send me everything, and I'll give it a look over the weekend and get back to you."

Amara knew her cousin wasn't being sarcastic and did actually think this would be fun. Numbers were her passion, they always had been. "It's taken me forever to get nowhere, but it will probably only take you a few minutes."

"I don't know if I'm that good, but thank you. How are things?"

"They are."

"That doesn't sound good."

"Ryan bought the house from Noli. So now we're housemates."

"Seriously? Do you need help burying the body? Or need an alibi? You know I'll help or lie, whichever you need."

Serenity hated Ryan for outing Senator Layton and getting Amara fired. If she had known that he had done that just days after their wedding, she would have put on chain mail, unsheathed her sword, and mounted her fire-breathing dragon. Her cousin lived in a black and white world. There were no shades of gray and no second chances.

chapter 5

NOW THAT SERENITY WAS ON the case of the funds, Amara decided to concentrate on other tasks. She sent a few emails confirming some dates and responded to some others. All of this was stuff that could have waited for Monday, but she had told Ryan she had work to do, so she wanted to turn the lie into the truth. The aromas of whatever Ryan was cooking kept distracting her from the menial tasks at hand.

She closed her laptop, sending it into sleep mode, then locked the few paper files she had in the desk drawer. Her bare arms were covered with goosebumps, so she grabbed a sweatshirt out of the drawer and pulled it on over her head before heading downstairs.

"Is this one of your mother's secret recipes?" There was no mistaking the sarcasm in her voice.

Ryan glanced over his shoulder and smiled. "I'm trying to win you back."

"Then that's a no. I almost stopped being friends with your sister so she'd never invite me over for dinner again."

"My mom's cooking isn't that bad."

"No, it is. You just were so used to it that you stopped being able to taste it."

"I'm still surprised you can cook."

"Can I help?"

"It's almost done. You can start the movie if you want."

"Why don't we eat and talk and then watch the movie? You know how I hate talking during a movie even if it's one I've seen dozens of times."

"Dozens of times? Are you planning on watching *The Proposal* again?"

"I wasn't, but that would be an excellent choice."

"Since we're not eating on the couch, can you set the table?"

The first few minutes at the table were silent, a rarity for the two of them. He was too afraid to say the wrong thing, so he said nothing at all. There were too many thoughts pinballing around her brain to focus on one that would be a good conversation starter. She'd already complimented him on the food, and he'd graciously accepted the praise. And that was the end of the conversation.

As he cut into his food, she noticed his hand. "You're wearing your wedding band."

He examined his hand as if he hadn't known the ring was there. "I never took it off, except for if I was around family."

"If this somehow works out, how are we going to tell our families that we're married and have been for a while?"

"We just tell them. How they react is up to them."

"Do you think Diane will be mad?"

He shook his head. "Not really. Actually she might be mad that you didn't tell her, but she won't be mad at me."

"Well, I think my dad might try to kill you."

"He already has. I think he may have a hit out on me for hurting his baby."

"I told him to call it off, so you should be safe now." She paused for a moment. "Why didn't you take it off?"

"Because I've held onto the hope that it's exactly where it should be."

"So in the last few years plus, you haven't gone on a date or anything?" she asked the question because she hoped he had. If he had, that would make her minor transgression with Ethan mean nothing. Less than nothing. It would be as if it never happened.

"No, I've not even thought about another woman. I've been a faithful husband. What about you?"

Her cheeks felt warm, and she wondered if he noticed her blush. "No, I've not been a faithful husband," she joked, still feeling guilty and nervous. "Just to clarify, there's been no one since me? Not even a one-night stand? No sex for over a year?"

"I've been celibate. I only want you. But seriously, Amara, do I have some competition for your heart?"

"Yes. You are the Ryan that hurt me, and you're competing against the Ryan I loved." She saw his eyebrow lift and a grimace flash across his face, but then she realized it was probably because she'd used the past tense, *loved*, and not the present tense. She hadn't meant to—or had she?

He didn't verbalize how that had made him feel. "You and Ethan are just coworkers?"

For a moment, guilt had her convinced that he knew, but her rationality won out. There was no way he could know. It was out of character and kind of sweet that he was jealous. "We're friends and coworkers and nothing more. Are you jealous?"

"It's just that I know you're upset with me, and he's totally your type."

"I can't believe this—the great Ryan Clark is lacking confidence. Stop the presses."

"I'm confident, but I'm also smart. I know it's not outside the realm of possibilities for there to be something between you two."

"You have nothing to worry about. My shattered heart is all yours." Silence descended again. She was afraid that if she spoke, she'd not be able to hold in the lie and would tell him about the kiss. It was just a kiss, and there was no need for him to know if they were going to try at their marriage, and especially if nothing else was going to happen between her and Ethan.

"Is that my sweatshirt?"

"No, it's mine. I got it out of my drawer. If I expect you to respect my space, I have to respect yours."

"I meant, is that the one that I gave you?"

She'd known what he meant. It was her favorite sweatshirt, not because it was the first piece of gear from her alma mater, but because it was from him.

Ten Years Earlier

DIANE AND AMARA WERE decorating Christmas cookies at Diane's kitchen table. Most sixteen-year-olds had outgrown baking cookies, especially those with a license. The truth is that they had, too. They'd wanted to go to the Holiday Hoopla tournament in Merrillville like most of their classmates. Since Amara had just gotten her license, they didn't even need to be dropped off and picked up. But Catherine Clark had vetoed the idea because, according to her, "Only Jezebels go to such things so they can parade around with their bodies on display to catch the eye of a ruffian and end up impregnated."

Amara could have gone, but she was the best, best friend a girl could have and stayed with Diane. This wasn't the first time she'd sacrificed a social life for her friend, and it wouldn't be the last. It wasn't all a selfless act, though. She knew there was a good chance Ryan would be home. She'd changed a great deal since the last time he'd seen her this past summer, and she couldn't wait for him to see her.

All the times he had come home before, she'd tried to make him notice her, but he didn't see her as anything other than his baby sister's best friend. This time it didn't matter. Well, it didn't matter as much. Ryan may have been the first boy she'd had a crush on, but she had a boyfriend now. Ryan's chance was gone. Or at least that's what she thought until he walked through the door.

He wore a gray sweatshirt with an embroidered bulldog underneath block letters that spelled out Butler above the graphic and University below it. He had on coordinating sweatpants that fell against his muscle as he walked. She wasn't the only one who had changed since the summer. Her changes were natural, but his were due to a new workout regimen.

"Ryan, you've come to rescue me!" Diane got up to greet him at the door and gave her brother a hug. He kissed her on the top of her head. They kept an arm around each other as they walked to the counter.

"Rescue you from what?" he asked.

"From our mother. She's directing all her parenting on me, and it's driving me crazy. But now you're here to share that burden."

"Sorry, I've got plans to spend as little time here as possible. Why aren't you out?"

"She thinks I'll get impregnated if I go. Why? Did she let you go?"

"Yes, because I can't get pregnant."

"But you can get someone pregnant."

"She knows that won't happen. I'm scared from ever having sex after she demonstrated the proper way to put a condom on a cucumber and a banana because she wasn't sure which was closer to my actual size." Amara giggled. "No hello from you, Amara?"

"Hello Ryan," she said, concentrating on icing a cookie like she was performing brain surgery. He scooped her up into a bear hug. "Put me down," she squealed.

He swung her around. "I'll put you down if you give me a proper greeting."

"Okay, okay. Just put me down. You're making me dizzy."

He returned her to her feet, and she whirled around and hit him in the chest. She bent down into a deep curtsy. "Hello, Mr. Clark, it's lovely to see you again," she said, trying to imitate a British accent and sounding more like Eliza Doolittle meets Jersey Shore.

"You're so hilarious." He pulled her into a hug. It felt different from the many hugs they'd shared in the past. She felt soft and feminine against pressed against her body. She was no longer the scrawny beanpole. The sleek muscles and angles of an adolescent girl had given way to the soft curves of a woman.

He let her go and took a look at her. He wasn't trying to check her out because she was still only sixteen, still just a kid five years his junior. He just wanted to see if he'd imagined the difference from a few months back or if she'd actually changed. She'd definitely changed. Even the way that she looked at him had changed. She used to look at him with puppy dog want. Now she looked at him with the eyes of a girl who had learned she could get any guy she wanted with just a smile—and he was no longer that guy.

He wasn't disappointed in that, but it did bring him down a peg or two. No girl he'd ever dated had ever been as excited to see him as she was—as she used to be. It made him feel special to be able to bring that light to her eyes with his mere presence.

He took a bite out of one of the cookies.

"Hey, those aren't for you!" Amara said, hitting his hand and making him drop the cookie.

"Who are they for?"

"My boyfriend."

"You have a boyfriend now?"

"I do. He gave me this." She pulled a necklace out from underneath her T-shirt.

Jealousy made him wonder if it would make her neck turn green. Now he wished he'd gotten her something too. He'd always thought of her as his. He'd never returned the crush, but it had always made him feel nice to be wanted. He'd even wondered if maybe they could date in the future when the age difference didn't matter and wasn't creepily on the border of wrongness.

"Diane, do we have some wrapping paper?"

"It's in the den in the closet."

He picked the cookie he'd started up off the counter and walked away, avoiding another swipe from Amara. Later that night, he'd returned to the kitchen just after Amara had shut the door behind her. He followed behind her and caught her just as she was about to get into her mom's car and go home.

"This is for you." He handed her something that looked like it had gotten into a fight with wrapping paper and lost.

"Thanks." She opened the car door and threw the package inside.

"Aren't you going to open it?"

"It's not Christmas yet. Santa will think I'm naughty if I open it early."

She looked up at him, the light from the porch illuminating her large and innocent brown eyes.

"You opened this," he said, scooping the thin chain of the necklace away from her neck with his finger.

"My boyfriend gave it to me before he went out of town with his parents. He wanted to see if I liked it before he left."

"What did you give him?"

"A girl never talks about that sort of thing." She fingered the necklace. "Let's just say I was appreciative." She arched an eyebrow suggestively.

"What does that mean?" Had she given her virginity to some little punk just because he bought her a fifty dollar necklace?

She smiled and looked at him through her long dark lashes. "Wouldn't you like to know?"

"I would, that's why I asked."

"That's between me and him."

He put his hands into the pockets of the jeans he'd changed into. "Fine, I'll drop it, but you have to open the gift I gave you."

"I will. On Christmas morning." She got into the car and started the engine.

Defeated, he walked back to the house. He wanted to know if she'd like it, if her face would glow for him like it used to. The way it did now when she mentioned that boyfriend of hers. Amara had always been his, and now he had to share her with a boyfriend and probably a line of other boys waiting to move in when he messed up. He didn't like sharing her.

What he didn't know is that as soon as the door closed behind him, Amara bounced up and down in the seat of the car, excited because he'd gotten her something. That must mean that he was thinking about her too. She shredded the paper of the hastily wrapped present, not caring if it got all over her mom's car. There was a moment of disappointment when she saw the sweatshirt he'd worn home. Then she inhaled his scent, and it didn't matter if it was an afterthought. She clutched it to her and inhaled deeply. She slept in it that night and opened presents in it the next morning. She'd even got put on punishment when she yelled at her mom for washing it.

Present Day

"IT IS THE ONE you gave me."

"I'm surprised you still have it. You acted like you didn't care when I gave it to you."

She blushed. "I was so excited to get it from you, but I couldn't let you know that."

"Why's that?"

"Because I'd learned the rule that if you want to get a guy, you have to act like you don't care."

"Who taught you that silly rule?"

"I can't remember, probably some magazine article. And it's not a silly rule."

"It is. I thought your crush on me was over."

"So you'd known I had a crush on you?"

"I would have had to be in a vegetative state to miss it, and even then I would have known."

"How silly is the rule if it worked?"

"But it didn't. I really thought you were over me."

"But you thought about me, so much so that you're my husband now."

chapter 6

RYAN SAT WITH HIS ARMS stretched out over the back and arm of the sofa. He glanced over at Amara as she yawned for the third time in the past few minutes. She was making an effort to stay awake to finish their first date. He'd been disappointed when she'd canceled earlier, but this turned out better. Amara was curled up just a few inches from him, fighting sleep so she could be with him. He slid closer to her, and she rested her head on his chest and draped an arm over him. He kissed the soft hair on the top of her head and wrapped his arm around her. She was making an effort, and that gave him hope that this would be the first of many nights in.

"Why don't you go up to bed?"

"Because I want to see the end."

"But you've seen this a million times. Even if you didn't, it ends like all romantic comedies. They end up together, just as the formula says they will."

"It's not about the destination, it's about the journey. And I have to see my favorite part."

"Which is?"

"That part of their journey when they have those moments."

"What moments?"

"The moment they find what everyone is searching for. That first moment they feel love. Then that moment when they get back the love they thought they'd lost forever."

"Will we have that moment? The one when we find what we lost?"

She was silent as she drew circles on his abdomen. "I don't know," she finally admitted. She looked up at him, "But I hope so."

There was still conflict in the brown depths of her eyes as they looked up at him, but he could still see a glimmer of the love that used to be there. He had a moment where he knew that they would be together in the end, but he also knew it would be rough getting there, and they still had a ways to go. He wished he could tell her who his source was to ease her forgiveness of him, but he couldn't. If he did, her already damaged career would be ruined, and he wanted to protect her from that.

"Me too." He bent and kissed her tenderly. He was trying to hold back because he knew she wanted to wait until she was more certain of their love to make love. If he kissed those beautiful lips the way he wanted to, he wouldn't be able to stop.

She had other ideas. Her hands began to explore, moving slowly up and down his arms and chest and back. She cupped his head and pulled his mouth to hers. His control snapped, and he allowed his hands to explore the curves he'd longed to touch again. His fingers traced up and down her back, and she arched into him, her soft breasts pressing against him. He let out a moan and maneuvered their bodies so that he was lying on top of her. His mouth found her neck as his hand moved under her sweatshirt. He loved how she came alive in his arms. He wanted to be the only one to bring her pleasure because she was the only one who could make him feel this way. His hand found her breast, and she sighed his name and wrapped a leg over his. He replaced his hand with his mouth, freeing his hand to reacquaint itself with the curve of her butt. Her body writhed beneath him, pressing against his growing desire.

His pocket began to vibrate, followed a split second later by his ringtone. He pulled the phone out of his pocket, hit ignore, and threw it to the floor. He attempted to resume where they had been before the phone rang, but the spell was broken. She pulled her sweatshirt down. The moment was definitely over. He wanted to kill whoever had called.

He didn't know what to say but knew he had to say something. "Amara," he started, and then the phone began to ring again, interrupting him.

"You should get that."

"We should talk." He hit ignore again without looking at who the caller was and turned his phone off.

"There's nothing to talk about. What just happened didn't happen."

"You know that makes no sense, right?"

"It shouldn't have happened."

"Why not? We love each other. There's no reason for us not to express it in every way possible."

"There *is* a reason, a very good one. Sex would be putting caramel whipped icing on the crap cake that is our marriage. At first, it'll taste sweet, but we'll be left with a bad aftertaste."

"You're right. It probably wouldn't be best right now. But you're going to have to stop looking so sexy."

"I have on old yoga pants and a too big sweatshirt."

"But those old yoga pants show how perfect your butt is, making them sexy. And that's my sweatshirt you've held onto for a decade, which makes it sexy."

"What do you want me to do? Wear a muumuu?"

He squinted, looking off into the distance to conjure up the picture in his head. "Nope, still sexy."

"Then what?"

"Sports bra? Baggy sweatpants? Five-day old makeup?"

"That's not going to happen, ever. Well, except for the sports bra."

"I hate those things. They make women look like ten-year-old boys."

"But they make running less painful. No super-sized sweatpants or runny makeup, though."

"You promise?"

Her phone began to ring on the kitchen counter. She looked at the display, surprised at the caller.

"Hello, Mrs. Clark," she answered, looking to Ryan for an explanation for the inexplicable call. She didn't even know his mother had her number. Ryan waved his hands to signal he didn't want his mother to know he was there.

"Hello, Amara. It is my understanding that my son now lives in the house with you."

Amara hated the way the woman would follow a statement with silence as if she was waiting on someone to answer a question. "That is correct," she finally said, hoping that would answer the unasked question.

"I have tried to contact him by cell phone, and he did not answer. I called your mother to get your number."

Again there was silence. Catherine had become a bit softer since her daughter's marriage, but she still had some rigid habits that could be quite annoying. Like now. What was Amara supposed to say to that? She didn't know, so she said nothing. Silence worked both ways.

"Do you know where he is now?"

Finally, a question. "Yes, he's right here. I'll get him for you."

"One moment before you do. I will ask you because I trust you to give me an honest answer. Are you and my son living in sin?"

"Excuse me?" Amara asked, thrown by the question.

"Are you and my son having sexual relations outside of wedlock while cohabitating?"

"No, we are not."

"Very well. I would hate for you to ruin your career further with an unplanned pregnancy, though I am certain my son would do the honorable thing."

"Here's Ryan."

She thrust the phone into his hand and left the room before he could give it back.

"Hello, Mother."

"Hello, Ryan. I called."

"You did?"

"Did you ignore my calls?"

"What's up, Mother?" Ryan asked, ignoring her question.

"Don't use that kind of crude language with me."

"What is the reason for your call?" he asked, mimicking her rigid tone.

"Your father and I will be down there next weekend, and we will be taking you, Diane, and Jack to dinner."

"What if I have plans?"

"You can change them, unless they are career related."

"Why didn't you just text me to let me know."

"I will not communicate with my son using broken English and symbols where letters should be."

"Is there anything else, Mother?"

"Yes, there is another reason for my phone call. I am sure you know that Amara has been in love with you for a very long time. Do not use the current situation to take advantage of her misguided affections."

"Why would loving me be misguided?"

"There is nothing misguided in loving you. You are a handsome and intelligent man, and if she were to fall in love with you, that would be understandable. However, she became infatuated with an older boy who was nice to her because she was his younger sister's best friend, and she confused it with love."

"I hope you know that I wouldn't take advantage of Amara—or any woman. You and dad did raise me to be that kind of man."

"Very well. I will see you next weekend."

He exhaled loudly and leaned against the kitchen island, his head resting in his hands. He relaxed when he felt Amara's hands rubbing his back.

"You okay?"

"It's just talking to her," he trailed off, shaking his head to get the thoughts out. "She gets to me every time." He turned to face Amara, and she took him into her arms and rested her head on his chest. The gesture comforted him, and he instinctively returned the embrace.

This was one of the many reasons he loved her. She may put on the guise of a take no prisoners, no-nonsense woman, but she was really the sweet girl who waited for magic moments in movies and comforted people when they needed it.

"I wish I had a mother like yours. One who loves me."

"Your mother loves you. You have to know that. It's not conventional or affectionate, but it's love," Amara said.

"You keep saying that, but I don't see it, and I definitely don't feel it."

"Diane said things were getting better."

"They are—for the two of them. I've glimpsed some changes, but she's still so hard on me."

"That's just part of the way she loves you."

"Amara, I need you."

"You have me."

"Not just now. I need you always. These last months without you have been unbearable. You make my life better. Promise me that even if you decide you don't want to be my wife, you'll still be my friend like you always have been."

Her eyes glistened with tears. "Yes," she said. The one syllable came out soft and broken by her shaky voice, so she nodded her answer.

"You may not know this, but you're my best friend."

"Oh Ryan, why did you have to do that story and ruin everything," she said with her face buried in his shirt collar.

"I don't know, but I wish I hadn't."

"Really?"

"Really. I tried to have everything I thought I wanted, and I messed up the one thing I needed." She looked up at him and kissed him. The kiss deepened, and he pulled away. "I really want to lose myself in you right now, and since that can't happen, I'm not strong enough to continue. My mother doesn't want me to take advantage of you and steal your virtue, either."

"Did you tell her she's too late for that? She asked me if we were living in sin."

"I'm sorry."

"No need to be. Speaking of living in sin, I don't want them to know that we're married, at least not until after we know we're going to stay that way. Okay?"

"Okay. How about we tell them around our fortieth anniversary?"

chapter 7

"TELL ME ABOUT YOUR SHOW," Amara said, unable to endure the silence at the dinner table any longer.

"You truly want to know about my show?" Ryan asked.

"I wasn't asking to be nice." Amara stabbed a cherry tomato with her fork and put it in her mouth.

Ryan sighed. "I was just surprised that you would ask."

"Why are you surprised? I have a vested interest in your show. It cost me my career after all." She didn't try to spare him any of her negative emotions.

"Amara, is this how you're going to try to make it work? By picking a fight with me at every opportunity? You're mad, and I get that. Just get it out of your system now so this isn't us for the next six months. Yell at me, hit me, do whatever it takes. Just get it out so we can move on."

Amara grunted a laugh. "What is this? That Prince song?"

"Which Prince song?"

"That girlfriend song."

"Which girlfriend song? I don't know which one you're talking about. How does it go?"

Amara began to sing, *"Would you run to me if somebody hurt you, even if that somebody was me?"*

"Ahh, that song." Ryan had a smile on his face.

"Are you laughing at my singing?" Amara said, fighting the urge to smile.

"Oh, that was singing?"

"I might not be able to hit a note, but neither can you."

"Oh, you hit those notes. Beat them even. Beat the life right out of them."

Amara laughed and threw her napkin at him. "This is what I'm talking about. You've always been able to make me laugh no matter how upset I was. You've been my go-to more than Diane, and right now I can't go to either of you. I want to cry on your shoulder and tell you how my idiot husband betrayed me and ripped my heart out, but I can't do that because you're that idiot."

"My shoulder is still here for you to cry on. Complain all about your idiot husband. I won't try to defend myself, and I won't make a single excuse for myself. I deserve to hurt as much as I hurt you."

"You couldn't possibly hurt as much as I hurt. Well, maybe if I kicked you in the balls. Can I kick you in the balls?"

"Let me go get my cup, and then you can kick me with your highest heel."

Amara began to laugh then bit her lips to stop it. "Don't make me laugh anymore. You are no longer allowed to make me laugh."

"I don't want to not make you laugh. I love to hear you laugh. I love to see you smile. I want you to be happy. I want to be a part of what makes you happy. Seeing you angry and hurting with tears in your eyes, and knowing that I'm the cause of it hurts my soul. If using me as your verbal punching bag makes you feel better, I'm willing to take the blows—as long as I'm wearing my cup."

Amara raised her eyes toward the ceiling as she always did when she was thinking through something.

"If you tell me how you feel, I'll listen and agree with everything you say. I'm sure nothing you say about me will be worse than anything I've thought about myself."

Amara looked at him, her eyes narrow as she continued to think. Ryan wanted to know how she felt so he could determine if they had a chance and figure out how to repair the damage if there was hope. Even though she had agreed to try, she was doing little more than tolerating him. He understood her unwillingness to fight for their marriage, which made him want to fight that much harder to save it.

"Fine. I'll bare my soul to you, but if you utter one word in your defense, I'm kicking low and hard. First, though, I want to hear about your show. I'm actually interested. Some masochistic part of me is even happy for you." Amara stood up from the table. "I need coffee. Do you want coffee?"

"It's too late. Won't it keep you up?"

"I'm not an amateur like you. My caffeine addiction goes way back—I'm a professional. If I don't have some, I probably won't be able to sleep."

Ryan studied her as she made her coffee. He needed this to work. He missed her smiling up at him just before he would kiss her. During that brief time that everything was right with them, he would have nuzzled her neck while she waited on the Keurig to finish brewing her cup of coffee. He knew if he did that, she would have done him some major bodily harm, so instead, he cleared the table, walking close enough to smell her scent when he moved to the sink.

"About my show, it's still about politics but with a more local focus."

"Local like just Indiana, or..."

"Local like everything in the lower forty-eight. If I'm lucky, maybe even Hawaii."

Amara looked at him with a raised eyebrow. "And you convinced the network to go for this?" she asked skeptically.

"Of course. I had lots to motivate me. Plus the network's national show is already doing well, and they didn't want to lose me to another network. I pitched the idea to them to cover national political issues on a local level as well as cover some of the larger local elections like gubernatorial and congressional races that impact the entire nation."

"That would include Ethan Bedloe." Her arms were folded across her chest, and he could see her jaw lock into place. "I'm not trying to air any politician's dirty laundry, so you don't have to worry about me breaching the Chinese wall. When I want to interview him, I'll go through the normal channels—I'll contact you at work. My focus for the primaries is more the voters and their perception of the candidates and less about giving politicians another outlet to spin their platform."

Amara rolled her eyes and shrugged. "How did you convince them to base you in Indianapolis instead of DC?"

"Once I knew the ball was in my court because they wanted me to stay with the network, it was easy to convince them that flying out of Indianapolis is just as easy as flying out of DC. I'll also be covering some nonpolitical news stories in parts of the Midwest."

"Sounds like you'll be traveling a lot."

"Don't get your hopes up. I'll be here more than I'll be away."

Amara snapped her fingers in an exaggerated motion as if she was disappointed. Then she said, "I said that because I thought I would miss you while you're gone."

"Really?" Ryan said smiling.

"Don't get *your* hopes up. I'm sure you'll be here more than I want you to be. That's the catch-22 that is my feelings for you. I miss you, and I want you here. But then you're here, and I just want you gone because seeing you takes me right back to that day and those feelings, and I realize I'm not over the pain at all." She finished stirring sugar into her black coffee and then went and sat in the oversized chair, tucking her feet up under her.

As promised, Ryan said nothing. He silently followed her into the family room and sat on the couch, his hands clasped together on his lap as he watched her intently and waited for her to continue. Amara stared into her coffee for a few minutes. He could see her facial expression shift several times, but she didn't articulate any of her thoughts. She took another sip of her coffee and then began to speak.

"When I first saw you reporting on Sen. Layton, but maybe you're just doing your job. But I switched to other stations," she shook her head, "and no one else was reporting on it. It wasn't just you following a story, it was you *breaking* the story. I tried to think up some way you had gotten that information from someplace other than me, but I came up with nothing. I knew I hadn't told you, but I also knew that I had the proof and that somehow you must have found it. The picture of the senator and his boyfriend broadcast on the TV screen as your voice discussed the hypocrisy of his stands against gay marriage was the same photo I had on my phone."

She stopped again, this time staring at some point on the wall. He didn't know if she was trying to organize her thoughts or hold back tears. Possibly both, but he remained silent. He wanted to defend himself and say that he hadn't gotten that photo from her, but he couldn't. He'd promised he wouldn't, so he was going to keep his mouth closed. He also knew that if he did defend himself, she would ask him where he'd gotten the picture, and that was something that, in her best interest, he couldn't disclose.

"Nothing made sense. What I saw on the TV...that man was not the man I married. He wasn't the man I'd loved since before I even really knew what love was." A tear rolled down her face and landed in her coffee. If she noticed, she didn't care because she took another sip. "I figured the man I married was a figment of my imagination—that I had idealized you and made you what I wanted you to be, not what you really were. I figured I had been the only one in love, and that you had seen an opportunity to get ahead and had taken it, even if that meant marrying me. I thought me moving out was what you wanted me to do because you wouldn't have to continue to pretend to care about me. You'd finally be rid of your lifelong nuisance. I was shocked to hear you at my parents' door."

Ryan almost said something. He hadn't thought Mrs. Adams would be that convincing of a liar. When she'd said Amara wasn't there, he'd believed her—right up until this very moment.

"Mother didn't know exactly what was going on, but she knew I was supposed to be moving in with you that day. And that I was bawling my eyes out and inhaling caramel like it was going out of style in my old bedroom. I was surprised—and grateful—to hear her tell you I wasn't there.

"Ever since that day, I've felt empty. I lost a big part of me. It was like you had reached through the TV screen and ripped out my heart. For a couple weeks, I could barely function. I could barely muster up enough energy to brush my teeth and take a shower. My father, in his infinite wisdom, told me to pull it together because no man was worth being stinky over. He also said I needed to get my act together and get out of his house because he in his wife had looked forward to being empty-nesters, and I was ruining it for them." Amara managed to smile at the memory.

"I became a pariah. No one would hire me. But even their rejection didn't hurt as much as your rejection of me did. Somehow I managed, and by the grace of God, I even got through the first time seeing you again. Each day the pain became less palpable. Then Ethan hired me, and I had something to focus on and not as much time for self-pity. And that brings us to now. I still hurt, but I've learned how to manage it so that I can function."

She raised her mug to her lips then pulled it back down and looked into it. "Well, my coffee is drained, and so am I." With that, she stood and went upstairs after placing her mug in the sink.

chapter 8

"**N**OW THAT YOU'RE A MARRIED woman will you still be coming to all the fundraisers with me, or do I need to find a new plus one?"

"I've been a married woman. It's my job to be there. A plus one will be more appealing to voters though. Most people don't trust a man your age who's not married or at least in a serious relationship."

"I can never tell if you're making it up or if it's an actual fact. You really should be the candidate."

"I would never get elected. My policy beliefs don't fall in line with any one party, and independents don't win."

His brow furrowed. "So do you agree with my policies?"

She smacked his hand.

"Oww! Why'd you do that?"

"I'm going to do that every time you start a sentence with *so*."

He rubbed his hand as if it were still hurting. "Do you agree with my policies?"

"Some yes, some no. But it doesn't matter."

"It does matter. Do you agree with my economic plans?"

"For the most part, but I don't think they're any better than your opponent's in this primary, or the guy that you'll be up against in the general."

"If you think I'm full of crap, why would you want me to be in office?"

"I didn't say you were full of crap. If you were, it wouldn't matter. There's crap to the left, and crap to the right," she said, extending each corresponding hand. "It's my job to convince the good citizens of Indiana that your crap is exactly the fertilizer that's needed to make everything come up roses."

"So you—" he pulled his hand out of her reach when he saw her raising hers to hit him again "—you don't even think I'm the best man for the job?"

"I most certainly do think you're the best man for the job. I know that you'll do what's best for your constituents regardless of whether it's your idea or an idea from across the aisle. You're a good man."

"Well, that's something at least. Is your husband a good man?"

"At home, we have a Chinese wall prohibiting the discussion of work. Do we need to erect one at work prohibiting the discussion of home?"

"I'm just curious about the guy who managed to land the most amazing woman I know."

"You are one of only a couple people who know we're married. Actually, you're the one person besides him and me who knows. It's been really difficult not to discuss this huge part of my life with anybody."

"We're friends, and I'm here to listen, even if it's about him."

"We did have a good weekend, for the most part. Friday and Saturday, I was reminded of all the reasons we work."

"But something happened Sunday?"

"The fact that I don't trust him happened. I can't let go of all the pain his betrayal caused. I want to, and I tried for months to make it disappear, but I can't when there are so many unanswered questions for me.

"Like?"

"If I wasn't his unknowing inside source, then who was? It had to have come from inside."

"Who besides you knew that Senator Layton was gay?" Ethan asked.

"I'm only certain his wife knew and, of course, his boyfriend."

"Would either of them leak that info?"

"She was too in love with them being a political power couple to let anything jeopardize it. His boyfriend loves him too much to jeopardize the relationship."

"What about former lovers?"

"He's been with his current boyfriend for quite some time, like eight years. Prior to that, I guess he was straight because no others have come out of the woodwork. If they outed him, I'm sure they'd want their fifteen minutes of fame."

"You just need to think about who knew and what they've gained from him being outed. Work backward. There are many people who benefited from him not pursuing that presidential run. Even my father is thinking about running now that he's out. Cast a wider net, and I'm sure you'll figure it out."

"Speaking of figuring things out, I couldn't figure out some of the campaign funds. I asked my accountant extraordinaire cousin to look things over. She said there were some weird-looking transfers between accounts that were throwing the totals off. Do you know anything about that?"

He grimaced and his eyebrows came together, causing lines to appear. "I didn't want to waste my limited funds on an accounting firm, so my father's people are managing my funds."

"Then it's probably nothing. I'm sure they know more about it. She's an admitted novice in the murky waters of political finances." But she knew her cousin—if she said something smelled fishy, then something was fishy. She liked Ethan and hoped he wasn't doing anything he shouldn't be. She hoped she hadn't misjudged another man and believed him to be better than he was.

"I HAVE GOOD NEWS and bad news. Which do you want first?"

"The good news."

"I shouldn't have asked because I'm giving you the bad news first. It appears the series of transfers were made to disguise the trail of money being moved to a personal account."

"I asked for the good news first because that's what I was afraid you'd say. Looks like another campaign bites the dust."

"Not exactly. The good news is, from what I can tell, it's not your Ethan behind it."

"He has his father's people managing the finances. One of them is likely skimming."

"Or the father is. I've never voted for him. I don't trust his eyes or the way his lip curls up on just one side."

Amara laughed silently. "Speaking ill of your governor is treason."

"Then they'll have to lock me up because when he talks, it looks like he's showering the front few rows with saliva."

"That's just nasty, Serenity."

"Sorry, but sometimes the truth is nasty."

"Is there someone at your accounting firm that would be able to take over from Governor Bedloe's firm?"

"Yes, I'll give her your contact info."

"Thank you for looking into this. Be sure to send us an invoice."

"No need, I gave you the friends and family freebie on this one."

"Then I'll have to take you out for dinner to say thank you. Or maybe Ethan could. His lip doesn't curl when he talks, and he's yet to spray me." Amara would share that he was a good kisser, but she wouldn't want to admit she had firsthand knowledge of that.

Amara walked over to Ethan's office as she said her goodbyes to her cousin. He was on the phone when she got there. She sat in one of the chairs across from his desk and crossed her legs at the ankle. She didn't want to cross them as she usually did because it would expose too much thigh, and she didn't want him or herself remembering how it felt for him to touch her there.

He pointed to the phone then touched his fingers to his thumbs, repeatedly opening and closing them to mimic someone talking. She began to check her emails as she waited for the talkative person on the phone to let Ethan go. She smiled each time he attempted to excuse himself and end the call. He must be on the phone with another politician. They loved to hear themselves talk and hated to listen. Almost a half hour later, he was finally able to toss his phone on the desk.

"You want to grab lunch and go over a few things?"

"I'd love to, but I have lunch plans with my mother."

"That's right, it's Tuesday." Ethan was a good son and had a standing lunch date with his mother every Tuesday.

"What is it you wanted to go over? I thought we'd finalized all my appearances for the next couple of weeks."

"We did. I wanted to discuss some financial things with you."

"Those transfers you mentioned? Did your cousin figure them out?"

"She did." Amara relayed to him everything which had been explained to her, leaving out the possibility that his father was the perpetrator. "That's why I want to move the management over to our own people. I have a contact at her firm, but we don't have to go with them. We can find someone else if you like."

"I trust your judgment." He looked at his watch. "I'd better go, or I'll be late."

ETHAN LET HIMSELF INTO the Tudor style governor's mansion which had served as his parents' home for the past few years. He hadn't grown up in this house because his father hadn't been elected until after he'd graduated college and was out on his own. He had grown up with his father plotting and planning to get here and then move on to a government-subsidized house in Washington DC. That may be coming sooner with Senator Layton no longer in the running.

Party politics had a slightly less vicious hierarchy than high school. The popular kids had the full backing of the party, and everyone else had to settle for scraps. The party darlings got selected for national shows, both to be the face of the party and to discuss the hotbed topic of the week. They also got the money to run their campaigns. Even with the name recognition he'd inherited from his father, he was fighting an uphill battle, running against one of the most popular guys in the party. His father had faced the same thing with Senator Layton as the most popular, but with him out, it left a vacancy for a second-tier popular to move up.

"Sorry, I'm late, Mom." He hugged his mother, pleased to not smell a pre-lunch drink or three on her.

"You're here now, that's all that matters. What kept you?"

"Amara needed my okay to change accounting firms."

"What's wrong with your father's?" Her tone was casual, but her face showed deep interest in the answer.

"There was some creative accounting going on, and Amara thinks someone at the firm has been embezzling." He didn't add that he suspected the culprit was his father. Nothing happened right under his nose without him knowing. "She wants to move the funds somewhere where she can keep a better eye on them. Getting account information has been difficult at best. She had to make several requests, and there was always a reason they weren't available."

"That's probably for the best. Let's go to lunch."

ETHAN HELPED HIS MOTHER into her coat. As they left, neither noticed that Governor Will E. Bedloe was just outside the doors on the opposite side of the room and had overheard their entire conversation. He sent a text letting the recipient know he'd be there in an hour. He waited until his wife and son had pulled out of the long driveway before getting in his car.

He drove forty-five minutes to a small town in Southern Indiana, making a pit stop at the bank. He used his key to let himself into the apartment. Misti Sloan was laid out on the couch in what amounted to lace swatches trying their best to cover her young full, augmented breasts. He had intended to come here to discard a mistress who had outgrown her practicality, but there was no reason not to bend her over one last time.

It was just a matter of time before his son and his nosy campaign manager figured out he'd been siphoning funds from Ethan's campaign to support his mistress and bastard child. Then he'd have to lay low for a while before he could afford to keep another sweet, young thing on reserve for whenever he needed. He wouldn't have to use campaign funds for this purpose if his wife hadn't become so stingy with her money.

When her father died, she'd become bold and had taken over her trust and the inheritance. When his father-in-law had been alive, he'd had free reign. The man had known there had not been a day when Will had been faithful to his daughter, but it didn't matter to him because he didn't want to lose a politician in his pocket.

It wasn't like that old man didn't understand the occasional need to step outside of the marriage—he'd had his fair share of mistresses before he died. The man was a master and had taught Will everything he knew. There were some lessons that Will had ignored, though. Like always use protection so there were no bastards running around.

But for Will, nothing felt better than being with a young nubile woman with nothing between them. He was glad that the anti-abortion movement had not prevailed as he'd had to pay off a woman or two on the condition that they got rid of their spawn. This one had been crafty and hadn't told him until after it was too late for anything to be done. She had him paying for her and his bastard son. He didn't mind, though. She was by far the best piece of tail he'd ever had. She was willing to do almost anything as long as her bills were paid.

He'd even risked being caught in a grand fashion last Halloween. He'd invited her to the Governor's mansion for a masquerade fundraiser. She'd showed up in a dress that left little to the imagination and no visible panty line. She was the hottest thing in the room, and his wife was the dowdiest. His wife had a decent body for a woman her age, but propriety kept her from displaying it. Misti had been begging for months for him to have sex with him in the master suite of the mansion one of the times his wife was away. She said it would make her hot doing it in the bed he shared with his wife. That particular night, she said it would be even hotter to be upstairs being naughty while his wife passed out candy to trick-or-treaters and entertained the bigwigs downstairs. She promised to do that thing he'd been begging for if he'd take her up to the master suite for a quickie. He had to admit, the thrill of getting caught had turned him on too. Not enough to last longer than a few minutes, but enough that they were able to do it twice in a row. He wished now that he'd said no because that was the night they'd conceived.

Between the little blue pill he'd popped that night and her talented mouth, he was up and ready in no time. It had taken even less time than usual for him to finish. He didn't have the stamina to go for long, but stamina was overrated. The best part was the end, and he found it as quickly as he could. Sure a good lover would try and make sure his partner was satisfied, too, but he had visions of grandeur and thought he was a good lover. But he never had been.

She lay on the bed, faking an afterglow as he fastened the pants that he'd not even bothered to take off, and he pulled out the bomb he'd come here to drop in the first place. "Misti, we're done. I can't do this anymore. This will be our last time together."

He thought he saw a moment of relief in her eyes before her fake adoration covered it. "You'll still take care of me and our baby, though, right?"

"The only reason I've been taking care of him was so I could continue to screw you."

She gasped and jumped up from the couch. Her fake breasts didn't move. "Do I at least get to keep the apartment?"

"Yes." Relief washed over her angry face. "Until the end of the month—unless you can afford it on your own."

Her anger returned. She stood completely naked with her hands on her hips. He was fully dressed, even his coat was on. He studied her body so he could memorize it for later fantasies when he was taking care of things on his own, or in the unfortunate circumstances he became desperate enough to lie with his wife.

"I'm glad I was smart enough to save most of the money you've given me."

"Yes, thank you for that. I cleared it out of that account so I could put the money back where it came from."

"How could you do that?"

"You kept me on the account as a signer. You should have been smart enough to move it to an account I didn't have access to."

"I meant how could you be so cruel? You can't just abandon your child. There are laws! I'll take you to court."

He threw his head back in a laugh that originated in his rounded gut. "Do you know how many judges owe me favors? About half. The other half are too deep in my pockets. You wouldn't see the inside of a courtroom unless I filed attempted extortion charges against you."

"But that's your child," she said, pointing down the hall.

"Prove it. I have one child, and it is not that little bastard sleeping in the other room. Go on welfare. That would almost be like me paying child support since I'm the governor."

"Don't you care about your child?"

"No, I don't. The only reason that child exists is because you waited to tell me until it was too late to get rid of it."

She brought her hand back to slap him, but he caught it before it could make contact. "Don't you have a heart?"

He laughed again. "I gave it to someone who gave a crap a long time ago." With that, he pushed her backward with enough force that she landed on the couch. Her glorious synthetic orbs still did not move.

chapter 9

AMARA HAD MADE IT HOME before Ryan got there and decided a long soak in the tub would relax her muscles. She lay surrounded by warm water, her head resting on a pillow made especially for the purpose, the jets massaging her tired body with bubbles. The only light in the room was that coming through the sliver of the door from the bedroom and the couple of candles she'd lit.

She was trying to relax, but Ethan's questions had spurred a million questions of her own. She'd been so blinded by anger that she'd convinced herself the only way Ryan could have gotten the information was by taking it from her. He'd always maintained that he'd gotten it from someone else. Maybe he was telling the truth. The last time, he'd told her he couldn't tell her. What if he didn't know? What if the source was anonymous?

Which lead her back to the original questions. Whether or not the source was anonymous, who had the most to gain—or anything to gain for that matter? Who knew his secret besides her? The list of suspects seemed to be small. Obviously his lover knew. Had love driven him to outing his boyfriend? If he was tired of being a part-time lover and keeping their relationship in the closet, he had become a full-time one once Layton was out. They were still together.

If that wasn't his first male lover, others in the gay community had to know that he was one of their own. If someone with loose lips let something slip, down would fall one of the most outspoken opponents of gay rights. Many saw his opposition as ironic. Others thought it hypocritical that he would say he believed homosexuality was a sin while at the same time practicing it. Amara saw it as politics as usual. There were no true beliefs. The only beliefs in politics were those that would get you elected.

Layton's wife had known for quite some time. Amara had always found that strange. Many politicians' wives would stand by their philandering husbands because they enjoyed sharing the spotlight. That wasn't the case with Mrs. Layton. She had her own spotlight as the regional head of the party and didn't need to share his. When the news came out, she did play innocent as if she hadn't known. And suddenly her spotlight began to shine brighter, and she had helped her estranged husband's spotlight quickly shift to Governor Bedloe, who picked up the anti-gay rights ball and ran with it.

The buzz of him leaving Indiana for DC was growing ever louder.

A thought was forming on the outskirts of her mind but was just out of reach. She closed her eyes and sank deeper into the tub. Still, she couldn't concentrate enough to reach the thought. She turned the jets off, plunging the room into silence. The only sound was her mind sifting through her thoughts. She was almost there—it had something to do with...her phone began to vibrate and send her ringtone wafting through the air. Just like that, she lost the thought. It was out of reach and out of sight. Her eyes flew open, and she grabbed the phone just shimmied itself off the tile and into the water.

She was frustrated that she couldn't figure out the leak, and she had almost grasped the key to it all, but she couldn't focus with the stupid ringing phone. "Hello," she bit out.

"Amara, that is not a proper way to answer the phone."

She held back a groan for fear of being reprimanded again. "Sorry, Mrs. Clark, I was in the middle of something when the phone rang. How may I help you?"

"I have been trying to contact Ryan all afternoon, but I have been unable to. Do you know where he is?"

Seriously? Did this woman think she kept him in her pocket? "I know he had to go to the station today for some meetings. He should be home at any time according to what he told me this morning."

"Very well. Will you tell him to call me when he gets in?"

"I certainly will."

"Thank you, Amara. Besides being stressed, how are you?"

Besides stressed? Right now Amara didn't know any other feeling existed at the moment. There was a mystery leak that had given Ryan information very few people knew. There was missing money that she was fairly certain the governor had taken, but she couldn't take that accusation to his son without proof. Will Bedloe was a known philanderer, but was he an embezzler too? After talking with Ryan, she'd spent time trying to answer that question. She had done dozens of searches on the man. Then she remembered that one of the things she'd learned would make this peace-interrupting phone call not a total waste.

"I'm doing great. The new campaign is going well. I was doing some research today on Ethan's father, Governor Will Bedloe, and noticed that you and Robert were at the university at the same time he was in law school there. Did either of you happen to know him?" Amara thought his pre-college narrative of his life seemed too polished, which meant it was most likely manufactured. Perhaps her in-laws could remember a crumb of information that would give her some leverage when she confronted the Governor.

There was silence. Amara assumed Catherine was trying to access old memories. Or was she waiting for her to reform her question into a statement?

"I did not know him. I was not even aware that we attended the same university."

It was plausible she didn't know much about her governor. Though Gary was technically in Indiana, it was practically part of Chicago. Catherine could probably tell you everything you wanted to know about the Governor of Illinois.

"It was a long shot, but I thought I'd ask."

"Please be sure to give my son the message to call me."

"I will, as soon as he gets in."

Amara returned to her pre-call position, but her mind was blank. There was nothing left to remember. She wished Ryan would just tell her. She took a deep breath, sinking down further in the tub until her entire head was submerged. She was just about to come up for air when she felt hands grab her arms and jerk her out of the water. Being taken suddenly from the warm water to the cold air caused her skin to break out in goose bumps from head to toe. Her nipples also hardened into pebbles at the tip of her breasts. She tried to cover herself, but the grip on her arms wouldn't allow it.

"What on earth are you doing, Ryan?"

"Thank God you're okay." He pulled her close to him, holding her tight. Suds and water soaked his shirt. "You scared me."

"I scared *you?* I'm the one who was scared out of her mind. I don't see how I could have scared you."

"I called out, 'Honey I'm home' when I got in, and when there was no wisecrack response, I thought something was wrong. Then I found you under water. I thought you'd slipped and were drowning."

"Who slips and has both knees side by side above the water?"

"I acted on instinct, okay?"

"I think you just wanted to see me naked." She stepped out of the tub the rest of the way and put on her robe.

"Always, but this time I thought you were drowning. Why were you under the water?"

"I was trying to wash away the frustration of the day?" She left the bathroom and grabbed the lotion before sitting on her bed.

"Want to tell me about it?"

"Can't. Chinese wall and all."

She wished she could be open with him, share her entire life with him. She could if she trusted him. She needed to prove he had another source or that he'd stolen the info from her. That would determine if she could call off the divorce.

"I can tell you one part of it, though—I got to speak with Catherine the Great. She wants to talk to you. She wants you to call her."

He grimaced. "I don't feel like it."

"You will call her because if you don't, she'll accuse me of not giving you the message."

"I'll call her back if you agree to join me for dinner with her and the rest of my family on Saturday."

"Is this *Let's Make A Deal?* Why is everything I'll-if with you?" She began to apply lotion to her legs. When she saw him looking, her strokes began to linger and knead her flesh more than necessary for the task. She smiled when she noticed it had distracted him.

"What are you talking about?"

She deepened her voice to sound more masculine. "I'll sign the divorce papers if you...I'll call my mother if you..."

"Why are you talking like that?"

She ignored his question just as he ignored hers. "Don't call her, or call her. I don't really care."

"Does that mean you're not going to dinner?"

"It means I'm not playing this game with you anymore."

"I need you to come. You being there will make it bearable."

"If you leave so I can get dressed, I'll think about it."

"I thought you weren't playing let's make a deal with me anymore."

"This time I'm not playing with you, you're playing with me."

"I like playing with you."

Her hand flew up, and she extended a finger to point at the door. "Out."

chapter 10

SINCE AMARA AND RYAN WERE the only two living in Indianapolis, they arrived at the restaurant first. They were about a half hour early, so they enjoyed a drink together at the bar. Amara sipped her glass of wine instead of guzzling it like that first night.

"Thank you for coming."

"I didn't come for you. I came because I haven't seen Diane in a while." She sipped her wine to hide her smile.

"That's probably true, but I'm still glad you came." He leaned in for a kiss.

She leaned back and away from him. "Your parents and sister are due any minute. How would we explain us kissing?"

"With the truth?" He settled for taking her hand and was happy when she didn't pull it away.

"The truth is in the eye of the beholder."

"That's beauty. Beauty is in the eye of the beholder."

"You say tomato, I say potato."

"It's you say tomato, I say tomato."

"I know, I just love seeing you get frustrated when a phrase gets messed up."

"So you do that on purpose?"

"Yes. I also mess up song lyrics on purpose. I like to get under your skin."

"Believe me, you've been under my skin." He began to caress circles on her palm.

She looked down at where their hands were joined. "You need to take that off," she said, indicating his wedding band.

"This way people know I'm off the market. I wish you wore yours so people knew you were off the market."

"People or person?"

"People. I want everyone to know that we're together. There's one person in particular that needs to know you are mine."

"You own me now?"

"Just your heart."

She pulled her hand away. "That's nothing to be proud of. It's not worth much. It's broken and shattered into a ton of tiny pieces."

Two steps forward, one step back. That was his life with Amara right now. Actually, it was more like hot and cold. One moment she was flirty and warm, the next she was distant and cool. Even when he was carefully walking on eggshells, every now and then he'd say something that would poke at the pain he'd caused. She hadn't asked about his source in a week, but he hadn't deluded himself into believing she'd forgotten.

Amara chuckled as she took a sip of her drink.

"What's funny?" Ryan asked. Amara was looking directly at Ryan, but he could tell her thoughts were a million miles away. He wished he knew what was going on in her mind, but she'd become very protective of her thoughts, and not even her usually expressive eyes gave him a hint as to what she was thinking.

"I just found this song playing while I'm sitting here with you a bit amusing."

He listened for a moment. He recognized that the song was Norah Jones' rendition of "The Nearness of You". That song had no special meaning to them as a couple. He listened to the lyrics but did not see humor or irony. He looked at her with a raised eyebrow.

She rested her hand on his thigh. "When we're apart, it's easy for me to remember you're not trustworthy and I shouldn't love you. When you're near me," she paused for a moment and took a deep breath before continuing, "I want to spend the rest of my life loving you and can't seem to remember a reason why not."

He traced his finger down the smooth skin of her arm. "That means we should spend more time together."

She looked at him, pain piercing through the desire in her eyes. "I thought we should spend more time apart."

He was about to respond when a hostess approached and told them the other members of their party had arrived and they could join them at the table. He stood and slipped his hand into his pocket where he removed his ring. One of his buddies who was married but still looking had taught him the fine art of removing a ring without being seen. He'd never been one to cheat, so he never thought he'd need to use that skill. It was ironic that he was using it now only because if he kept it on, he might lose his wife.

He'd hoped it was his sister and brother-in-law who had arrived first, but as the hostess led them around the corner, he saw it was his parents. A look he couldn't understand crossed his mother's face, and he wondered if he'd frowned his disappointment when he saw her, but the look vanished as quickly as it had appeared.

His father stood and hugged him before greeting Amara with a kiss on the cheek. They spoke greetings to Catherine Clark as they had grown accustomed to over the decades.

"Ryan, I did not know Amara was coming," Catherine Clark said, not even bothering with a polite smile.

"I invited her. I thought it would be rude to leave her home alone," Ryan responded. He wondered why she'd addressed him as if Amara wasn't standing right there beside him. He pulled his wife's chair out, discreetly running his thumb across the top of her back as he helped to push it in.

"I suppose you are correct. Inviting her was the polite thing to do."

His mother was normally standoffish, but she was unusually cold to Amara that evening. He noticed that Amara had taken notice of the fact too. Her body language was stiff, like she was facing an opponent. He didn't bother pointing out his mother's behavior because she would never see that she was being uncivil. She never admitted to anything less than perfection, and her family had learned that it was futile to argue otherwise.

Robert Clark struck up a conversation with his son, leaving the females at the table in silence. Amara was one of the biggest proponents of Catherine, and Ryan could see that she was caught off guard by the woman's hostility. He wanted to reach out to her, but knew that would upset her more. Roommates didn't comfort each other that way. Amara's phone vibrated, and he noticed the incoming message was from Ethan. He couldn't read it without being obvious, but it annoyed him when she smiled and let out a clipped chuckle.

"How is it as my son's roommate?" Robert asked then continued on without an answer. "I know I was pretty happy when he went off to college. Within a week, the smell of stale, dirty laundry was gone from the house." Everyone but Catherine laughed.

"Dad, you're exaggerating. Even if it were true, that was a long time ago. I've matured since then."

"He still doesn't do laundry. He matured right to taking everything to the dry cleaner. If only the dry cleaner did dishes too," Robert said.

"The chef doesn't have to do the dishes," Ryan said.

"While you are a surprisingly good cook, I don't know if your culinary skills are great enough to earn the title chef," Amara said.

"There is no need for him to do dishes or laundry. Someday he will have a wife that will take care of those things, as well as the cooking. A man's place is not in the kitchen," Catherine stated.

"Perhaps not in 1952. We're in the twenty-first century now, and no room or chore is designated to one gender. Every member of a family pitches in to make a house a home," Amara said, not able to bite her tongue any longer.

"Perhaps the problem with the twenty-first century is that women are more focused on climbing the career ladder than being halfway decent at being a wife and raising a family. That is neither here nor there because you and Ryan are not a family. He should be taking young ladies out to eat and finding a wife with the proper priorities instead of cooking for his roommate."

"Amara, I didn't know you were coming," his sister Diane said as she waddled up to the table. Amara stood, and the two lifelong friends embraced. "I'm so happy you're here. This will make dinner so much better," Diane whispered in her ear.

Ryan and Robert shook Jack's hand. They waited until Amara stopped feeling Diane's ever growing belly to give her a hug. Jack spoke his greetings to Catherine from across the table, and pulled a chair out for Diane. Ryan had been skeptical when his sister had announced her engagement to a man she'd met only a few weeks before, but it was obvious that Jack Sloan was in love with her. On the few occasions he'd had a chance to spend time with him, he learned that he was an all-around good guy.

"Sorry, we're late. My wife didn't believe me when I said she was beautiful and didn't look fat in the first five outfits she tried on," Jack said, kissing Diane on the cheek and touching her belly.

"We're late because Jack drove the entire way here at least five miles under the speed limit because he had 'precious cargo' on board. I'm driving home." Jack shook his head in disagreement but halted when she turned toward him.

The waitress came and took everyone's drink orders. Robert also placed an order of appetizers for the table. The first half hour went by pleasantly enough. There were no more discussions on the roles of women. Instead, they caught up with each other. Diane and Jack displayed ultrasound pictures and explained that they were waiting until the birth to learn the baby's gender. They also filled them in on the goings on of Ryan and Diane's cousin Magnolia with Jack's best friend, Cooper.

Ryan and Amara weren't the only ones with secret relationships. Some time ago, while Magnolia was planning Diane's wedding, she'd fallen for the tall and muscular lumberjack look alike. On New Year's Eve, she surprised everyone when she showed up pregnant and on the verge of delivering. In another similarity to his relationship with Amara, the couple was trying to work through their differences and make things work.

Occasionally Ryan caught his mother throwing his secret wife a look that he couldn't decipher. Amara avoided looking or talking to his mother altogether. He didn't know what the issue was but suspected his mother was the cause. Amara would have never agreed to come if she were upset with his mother, and she seemed genuinely thrown off guard by the woman's demeanor.

"How's the roommate thing working out?" Diane asked innocently. "Noli told me you were surprised when Ryan moved in because she'd forgotten to tell you. I've been waiting for the call that the police found a body. I'm surprised there hasn't been one yet."

"Diane, that is a crude thing to say," Catherine said, looking at Jack as if he had somehow negatively influenced her daughter. "Why would there be any disagreement about him living there too."

"Perhaps because your son was to blame for me losing my job?"

"You should take responsibility for yourself instead of blaming others. Have you thought that you lost your job because you were underqualified and shouldn't have had the job in the first place?"

It's been said that animals have a heightened sense that sends dogs barking or birds flying moments before disaster strikes. Ryan wasn't a dog or a bird, but he knew a major disaster was seconds away, and he truly wished he could flee. Amara had a pleasant smile affixed to her face as she sized up his mother. He could tell she was calculating which blow would hurt the most.

Not caring if everyone saw, he put his hand over hers to caution her. She slid her hand out, not looking his way to see the subtle shake of his head. He wasn't trying to stop her because he didn't believe she was just in whatever she was about to say, but because he just didn't want to see the bloodshed. Catherine was used to having the sharpest tongue in the room, but that was because Amara usually held hers.

Amara sipped her water, all the while not taking her eyes off the other woman. A split second passed, but it seemed like this had been a standoff for so long that negotiators may need to be called in.

"If, by some stretch of the imagination, I was underqualified, I don't see why that should stop me. Being underqualified has never stopped you from attempting to cook. And if you were qualified as a parent, I wouldn't have to constantly reassure your son that you love him."

Diane's hand flew to her mouth. Jack sat back in his chair to stay out of the line of fire. Robert continued to eat because he'd learned a long time ago to let his wife fight her own battles, especially when she started them. Ryan just sat there, looking from his mother to his wife, unsure what to do, or if he should do anything.

"I did not arrange this family dinner to sit here and be insulted, especially by someone who is not family."

Amara smiled, and Ryan was the only one at the table who knew why. He knew that Amara contemplated throwing the dagger that she was his wife and had been for quite some time. But she didn't. Maybe it was because she didn't want it thrown back in her face later if things didn't work out, or maybe it was because she didn't want her best friend to find out that way. More likely, it was because she knew it was sometimes best to save some ammunition for a sneak attack down the road.

"I wasn't insulting, I was merely stating a fact. I am not family, but fortunately, I'm a friend, which means they *choose* to spend time with me and don't feel obligated to like they do with some members of their family." With that, Amara pushed her chair back and walked away from the table.

chapter 11

THERE WAS STUNNED SILENCE AT the table until Ryan spoke. "Mother, none of what you said to her was called for."

"None of what she said to me should have been said."

"You provoked her, Mother."

Diane began to stand.

"Where are you going?" Catherine asked her daughter.

"I'll go," Ryan said, rendering a response to their mother from Diane unnecessary. Not having the excess weight of a baby to maneuver with, he was up and gone from the table before Diane could argue.

Amara was just getting her coat from the coat check when Ryan entered the area.

"You have the keys," she said, acknowledging his presence but not looking directly at him. She was struggling to get her coat on.

He stepped behind her to help her with the task. "I'm sorry, Amara. I don't know why—"

"Keys," she interrupted. With her coat now on, she held her hand out. Her chest rose and fell rapidly from the adrenaline still coursing through her body.

He took her hand and pulled her to him, kissing the top of her head and rubbing her back. "I'll drive us home."

She nodded into his chest. "I'm sorry. I shouldn't have said those things."

"I'm surprised you were so nice."

"I'm sorry I said that thing about her parenting."

"It was the truth."

"I know. I'm just sorry because I'm sure she'll guilt trip you now."

"Maybe I'll follow your lead and stand up for myself." He tilted her head up and brushed a kiss on her lips. "You were pretty amazing in there."

"You should go back. Visit with your dad and sister."

"I'd rather spend time with my wife."

"Your what?"

They both turned to see Diane standing only about two feet away. They broke apart like they'd been caught by the police ripping tags off of mattresses.

"It's too late to stop your canoodling. I've been standing here for a few minutes, so the shock of it has worn off. Did I hear you call her your wife?"

"Listen," Ryan started.

"I can explain," Amara began at the same time. "You tell her."

Diane just stood there with her arms folded. Amara bit her bottom lip. Ryan's hands were in his pockets. He started several sentences but couldn't finish a single one. He stopped trying when he saw the smile on his sister's face. She tried to pull them both into an embrace, but her stomach made it awkward.

"Just because I'm happy doesn't mean you're off the hook with an explanation. Jack and I will be at your house in an hour. Maybe by then you can find the words to explain."

Amara hugged her. "I'm so happy you're not mad at me. For this," she said pointing between herself and Ryan, "or for what happened in there."

"What was wrong with your mother? I thought you'd said she'd changed," Ryan said, continuing the siblings' tradition of assigning ownership of their mother to the other.

Diane threw her hands out and hunched her shoulders. "She had. She was Catherine Clark 2.0. You saw her at Noli's shower. Then something must have happened because she reverted back to classic Catherine with a vengeance mid-week. I almost lied and said I didn't feel up to the drive up here."

"But I was afraid she'd come to check on her," Jack said, instinctively placing a hand on his wife's back. "Are any of you coming back? You're dad's eating like nothing happened, and your mom is...I just don't want her to start talking to me."

$\heartsuit$

"HOW WAS THE REST of dinner?" Ryan asked, taking his sister's coat.

"It was much quieter," Jack said. "Is your father deaf?"

"No. Why?"

"Because he just kept eating like he hadn't heard any of that politely vicious exchange occur."

"Enough about that. Tell me about secret marriage."

They went into the family room. Jack and Diane sat on the loveseat. She was snuggled close to him, and his arm was draped over her shoulder. Ryan sat on the couch, but when Amara joined them, she walked past him and sat in the oversized chair with her feet curled underneath her.

Amara began, "Back in September, we were at a national political fundraiser in Las Vegas. On a spur of the moment, he asked me to marry him. On a whim, I said yes. Given the sudden nature of our nuptials, we decided it would be best to wait and plan an actual wedding for the entire family." Amara rolled her eyes at the word that had been inaccurately thrown in her face earlier that evening. "The Vegas wedding was going to be just ours. That way, everyone—well mainly just you Diane—wouldn't be caught off guard by our relationship."

Ryan jumped in, seeing an opportunity to explain things to Amara that she had been unwilling to hear. "When we got back to Chicago, a source gave me the information about Senator Layton. I knew what doing the story would do to his presidential hopes, and I wanted to verify it before I went to Amara. I kept my investigation as far away from her as I could. I didn't want it to come back that she was somehow my source. I'd planned on talking to her the night before it aired, the same night she moved into my apartment. Then the network decided to air it a day early. I couldn't get in touch with her before the news, and afterward, she was gone."

"I can't believe you're still trying to sell this mystery source bit."

"Amara, how could I have stolen the information from you when I didn't even know you knew?"

"If you didn't get the info from me, why were the photos you used the same as the ones I had?"

"My source must have had the same photos. I honestly didn't know you knew."

"Fine, I don't want to discuss this anymore. Not tonight."

"You never want to discuss it. And on the rare occasion we do, you don't listen to anything I have to say."

"I listen to everything you say. I just don't believe it. Would you listen to me? I don't want to discuss this now."

"If we don't talk about it, how are we ever going to start to get past it?"

"Tell me who this mythological source was. That's how we start to get past it."

"My source isn't mythological. I told you that I can't tell you."

"Can't or won't?"

"Trust me, it's better you don't know."

"How am I supposed to trust the man who stole information from me and ruined my career while boosting his?"

"I told you I didn't get the information from you!" Ryan shouted, raising his voice at Amara for the first time ever.

"Hold on," Diane said before things escalated any more. "Ryan, can I talk to you for a moment?"

He answered by getting up, and he led her to the den.

"She is driving me crazy. That woman is either hot or cold, and the switch from one to the other comes from out of left field every time."

"Amara is always hot. It's just a matter of if she's on the love side or the anger side. You've done things on both sides. Sometimes you say or do things that make her flip that coin."

"I walk on eggshells around her, and I'm careful not to say the wrong thing. What else can I do?"

"Tell her your source. Why won't you just tell her?"

"I can't."

"Why not?"

He went to the door to make sure neither Jack or, more importantly, Amara had followed and then shut the door. "Right now, her career is just tarnished. She can recover from this. She's already started to polish herself off. This pretty boy that she's working way too closely with has potential. But if I tell her my source, her career is ruined, and there will be no coming back."

"I don't understand. How could telling hurt her?"

"If I tell her who it was, she'll want to know why the person did it, and she'll start digging. She would make an excellent journalist or detective because she doesn't stop until she gets answers. My source has power, and if she starts digging, all that power will be wielded to make sure Amara couldn't even be hired to help a kindergartner be elected door holder."

"Then tell her that. Tell her why you can't tell her."

"Do you not know her? Have you never met your best friend?"

"Yes, I've met her. She's going to dig whether you tell her or not. Don't you think that a part of her believes you, or at the very least wants to prove you're lying? She's *already* digging. If she figures it out on her own, don't you think it'll be worse? She'll probably confront the person directly."

"I don't know what to do."

"What if you lie? Tell her you took it and fall to your knees and beg for forgiveness."

"That would end our marriage. She'd never get over that. Look at how often she brings it up now."

"Do you remember Rochelle Smith?"

"No."

"They were friends in sixth grade. Amara accused her of breaking her Furby. Rochelle refused to admit that she had. Amara stopped speaking to her. She didn't even go to her going away party a few months later. I asked her if she was really that upset about her breaking the toy and if she could forgive her because it was replaced. She said she didn't care that it was broken—she was upset Rochelle never accepted responsibility and admitted the truth because you can't forgive someone who doesn't acknowledge their wrongdoing."

"I've admitted I was wrong."

"Have you? You've admitted that you got that information from someone else but you told her you can't tell her who it was. I believe you, but I still think it smells fishier than *The Deadliest Catch*. Since you can't tell her the truth, just tell her the truth she wants to hear. Then maybe she'll start to move on."

"Maybe you're right. Maybe she's not been able to forgive me because I haven't admitted culpability to her satisfaction."

"I can't believe I just gave my brother advice to lie to my best friend."

"How do you feel about us being married?"

"I'm a little shocked. I thought maybe you two were dating, but married? Seems kind of sudden. But who am I to talk? It took all of thirty days for me to get engaged."

"We've been kind of seeing each other for years."

"What? Don't say anything else. Both of you need to explain." Diane placed a hand on Ryan's arm as he began to open the door. "Don't go confess right now. Wait and do it in private. But *do* go in there and apologize for starting an argument in front of me and Jack."

"But I didn't start it."

"Do you want her back or not?"

"When did my baby sister get so smart?

"I always have been, you're just too dumb to see it."

He followed her instructions. Amara was standing at the kitchen counter, squeezing caramel sauce into a spoon and eating it. He went over and put his hands on her waist and bent to whisper in her ear. He paused for a moment, letting her feel his heat so near to him. His thumbs stroked back and forth against the soft fabric of her dress.

"I'm sorry I started that. Add it to the list of stupid things I've done. You forgive me?" She didn't respond. He nuzzled her neck. She moved her neck away, breaking contact. "Please," he pleaded, nuzzling her neck again. This time she leaned into it and closed her eyes.

Diane was sure to remind them they weren't alone. "Please stop making out in front of me. Don't ever do it again."

"If you thought that was making out, then you're not doing it right," Ryan joked.

"Oh, believe me, she does it right," Jack said. He rubbed her stomach. "How do you think she got this way?"

"We should leave soon so I can demonstrate how right I do it," Diane said, placing her hand on her husband's thigh.

"We can leave right now," he responded.

"Oh, for all that is holy, please don't say another word. I didn't want to know my pregnant sister has sex."

"And I don't want to see my brother and my best friend getting it on. That might be worse than Mom and Dad." Everyone shuddered at that thought.

"It is getting late, and I'm sure you need your rest," Amara said.

"You're not getting out of telling me about you two."

"It was worth a try."

Ryan sat in the chair that Amara had previously been in, so she sat on the couch. He then moved to the couch to sit next to her.

"You always have to get your way, don't you?"

He hunched his shoulders. "I'll move if you really want me to."

She shook her head, and he took her hand into his.

"When did you two start dating?" Diane asked since neither of them seemed to know where to start.

"I wouldn't really call it dating," Amara said.

Diane exhaled deeply. "Let's not play the semantics game tonight. When did you two start seeing each other, hanging out, sleeping together, whatever you want to call it? When did it start?"

"Kind of back in college, during my freshman year," Amara said. "But not really until a couple of years ago when we were both in Chicago."

"Why was it such a big secret?" Diane asked.

"It wasn't a secret. We were friends, everybody knew that," Ryan said.

"We were both dating other people then. One of us more than the other," Amara said.

"I dated a lot because none of them compared to you," he said.

She raised an eyebrow in disbelief.

"What? I'm serious," Ryan protested. "None of them made me feel even close to as happy as I am when I'm with you. Not a single one was as beautiful as you—and I've seen you first thing in the morning."

"Why do you always follow a compliment up with a slap in the face?" Amara said.

"I don't want you to get a big head."

"Why? Because two big heads won't fit in the house?"

"This is going to take forever, and I'm sure Jack could care less," Diane said. "How about the cheat sheet version now, and Amara can give me the full version later."

"Why her?"

"Because you're a boy, and you don't tell a love story well. You would totally miss the moment and all the other good parts."

"She just taught me about 'the moment' the other day, and I thought it was just a movie thing," Ryan said.

"What moment?" Jack asked.

"See?" Diane said, pointing at both of them then flipping her hand up as if to dismiss them both. "If you were to ask Jack about our story, he'd say something like I helped her when her car was broken down. I fed her. We got married, and now we're having a baby."

"That's exactly how it happened," Jack joked.

"Then let me do the summary, since that's all I'm good for. You two were friends. Then she and I became friends. Then we became a little more than friends. We got married in Vegas. I messed up, and she left, not speaking to or seeing me for months. The first time I saw her again was at your wedding, and the next time after that was when we were visiting Noli in the hospital after she delivered."

"That's when you two made up and decided to move in together?" Diane asked.

"No, we've never really made up. I'm just living with him because he wants us to fight for our marriage before he'll give me the divorce I want," Amara said.

"We're trying to make up so that divorce isn't necessary," Ryan countered.

"I think you two will stay married. You're really good together," Jack said. Everyone looked at him as though he were crazy. "I mean, other than that thing earlier. It's obvious that he loves her."

"We're on *her* side. If they divorce, we get her. Mother and Dad get him," Diane said to Jack.

"No more Catherine?" Jack asked hopefully. "Then I'm sorry, Ryan. You should just call it quits now."

Everyone laughed at that. No one could blame him for wanting to be rid of his mother-in-law. "Seriously, even though Amara is mad, you can still see how much she still loves you. I have faith you two will work it out."

"You're smart *and* handsome. I'm so lucky," Diane said, kissing him on the cheek.

"You ready to get home and get to bed?" Jack asked.

Ryan shook his head, sure a double entendre was meant. They talked and laughed for a little bit longer, and Ryan got to see some of what had his sister falling in love so quickly. His brother-in-law was a good guy, and pretty funny too. They said their goodbyes before it got too late. Ryan and Amara headed upstairs together to go to their separate rooms.

"Amara," Ryan called before she entered her room.

"We're not sleeping together tonight, Ryan."

"I wish we were, but I knew that wasn't going to happen. I wanted to know if Jack was right. Do you love me? You've said it to you, but you've not said it to me."

She just stood there looking at him, scared. Finally, she nodded.

He shook his head. "I need to hear it. Please."

She looked at their feet mere inches apart. "I love you, Ryan."

He took her chin between his thumb and index finger and tilted her head up until she was looking at him. "I love you, Amara." He claimed her mouth, kissing her with not just the physical passion he felt, but with the depth of the love he had for her.

chapter 12

THE NEXT MORNING, AMARA WOKE up to the smell of coffee brewing. It was the only reason she was willing to face the day. Her dreams were far better than her reality. She opened her eyes to a cup of coffee sitting on the nightstand and the man she dreamt about sitting at the foot of the bed.

"What are you doing in my room?"

"I wanted to talk to you."

"So you brought a bribe to keep me from kicking you out?" She took a sip of the coffee. It was exactly the way she liked it. "This has bought you some time."

"You're right."

"I'm going to need you to be more specific. I'm right about so many things. I need you to narrow down the list."

He smiled and enough heat to make the coffee boil rushed through her. He stood and started pacing at the end of the bed. Then he walked over to her dresser and started tinkering with some of the items there. When he turned back around, the serious look on his face sent a chill through her that made her shiver.

"This is more difficult than I thought it would be."

"Just say it."

"There is no source. I got the information from you. Can you forgive me?"

Of all the things she was expecting him to say, that had never crossed her mind. She didn't know what to say. For months, she'd wanted a sincere apology from him. Now she had one, but it still hadn't squelched the hurt and anger that lingered at the back of her mind and kept her from forgiving him. Maybe she hadn't forgiven him because she didn't want to. If she did, that would mean leaving her heart vulnerable to him again.

"Why did you lie about having a source?"

"Because I thought it would make you hate me less. I know this doesn't fix things, but maybe it can help us start to repair our marriage."

"Thank you for finally being honest with me. You continuously sticking to that lie enraged me."

"I know. I'm a bit stubborn too. Once I lied, I had to stick with it. Like high school debate. I was going to stick with my argument, whether it was the truth or a lie, whether I believed it or not."

"Mr. Wells," she said, shaking her head at the memory of the high school debate teacher. "He did teach us to argue any side of anything."

"You had him too? I thought after the hooligans in my class, he'd retired," Ryan said.

"No, he was still there, expanding young minds. He always knew which side of an argument I wanted but would give me the opposite."

"He did that to everybody. He always said it's easy to argue for something you believe in, but it takes true talent to convince others of something you think is a crock."

"And that's how my career in politics was born. Even if I don't believe what my candidate is saying, I can convince others he's the answer to all their woes if they would just elect him."

"You think you're that good?"

"I know I'm that good. I'm a very talented woman."

"I'm well aware that you're a woman of many talents," he said, his eyes stroking her body.

Her breath caught as memories of him making love to her flooded her mind. She would invite him to join her to create new memories. She wanted to repeat the kiss from last night, and she would have if her mouth didn't taste like morning breath and coffee. Her breath wasn't the only reason she didn't act on her physical desire. Something about his confession was wrong.

"Why now?"

His eyes returned to hers at the question. "Because last night you told me you loved me. I had wondered if you still did. I knew you were still attracted to me, but that wouldn't be enough."

"Who says I'm attracted to you?"

"You do."

"I've said no such thing."

"Not with words. But your eyes have said it when they look at me and make me feel naked. And your lips have said it, too, the way you eagerly part them when I kiss you. Or the way I feel your nipples harden against my chest when I hold you close. Right now, your cheeks are saying it with all that blush. You know you're too light to hide that."

"Get out." She picked up a pillow and flung it at him, and he bobbed out of the way so it landed on the floor."

"You don't want me to go. You want me to come over there and prove my point."

He was right, but she wasn't going to admit it. She picked up another pillow. He was out the door with it shut behind him before she could toss it. Then the door opened a crack, and he peeked his head in.

"If moaning and sighing is a language, you've definitely told me how attracted you are to me."

She threw the pillow like it was a ninety-mile-an-hour fastball. He was still quicker, shutting the door and laughing at the soft thud the pillow made.

"ROBERT, WE ARE NOT heading home," Catherine said.

"No, we're not."

Lena Hampton

"Where are we going?"

"You are going to apologize to Amara," Robert said, emphasizing the first word.

"Why do you think I am going to apologize to her?"

"Because your behavior toward her was uncalled for." It was the first time since last night that Robert had even acknowledged what had taken place at dinner. He rarely put his foot down with his wife because he knew she'd already chastised herself far worse than anything he could say. His wife may seem cool and commanding to everyone else, but he knew that was just the facade she put up to protect the fragile woman she actually was from the rest of the world. He never corrected her behavior in public. He'd done it once very early on in their relationship, and she'd cried until she hyperventilated. That pain he had felt that day was still palpable.

"Are you going to make her apologize to me?"

"No." While Amara's words probably hurt, he knew the girl had only slung them because she was wounded. He didn't understand why his wife had censured Amara's every word, but he knew she hadn't deserved it. Whatever had her in a mood for the latter half of the week was likely to blame. He'd asked a couple of times what was wrong or what had happened, but she insisted that absolutely nothing was wrong. Which meant something was very wrong.

The car remained quiet for the rest of the ride. When they pulled into the driveway, Robert kept the car

130

THE NEARNESS OF YOU

running for the heat and reclined his seat to indicate this car wasn't moving until after she'd apologized. Catherine sat with her hands folded on her lap, staring out the window. They never butted heads. That was too aggressive for either of them. When they disagreed, they each dug their heels in and waited. Robert knew that Catherine was more afraid the garage door would go up and they'd be spotted, forcing a confrontation or at least an explanation for the unexpected visit. He just needed to be patient until she caved.

It took twenty minutes, but she finally did.

"Robert?"

He pulled the back of his seat back up and lowered the volume of the radio. "Yes, dear?"

"Perhaps you are correct. My hostility was slightly less than cordial. For the record, I had reason to be."

"I'm listening," he said when she didn't continue.

"I called Amara, trying to ensure Ryan got the details for tonight. During the call, she inquired if I was acquainted with William Bedloe during college."

Robert nodded his head in understanding. The mention of Will Bedloe's name always made her anxious. He had to admit, knowing that Amara had reason to ask if they knew the man had him on edge as well.

"What did you tell her?"

"I told her I was not even aware that we had attended the same university."

"Did she believe you?"

"Why would she not? I am a very honest person."

She was a very honest person, except when she lied. "Though I understand the reason you may have been hostile, I still believe you owe her an apology."

"Very well."

AMARA CAME OUT FROM her closet at the sound of her bedroom door being opened. Ryan had a simple breakfast on a tray. Now that she was standing with no cover to conceal her lower half, he saw that she wasn't wearing any shorts with her T-shirt. The oversized tee touched the top of her thighs, barely covering her panties. If she was wearing any. He really wanted to find out.

"Good, you're not dressed yet. I made us some breakfast."

"I was on my way downstairs. Wait, what do you mean 'good I'm not dressed'?"

"Breakfast in bed kind of breakfast."

"Oh really?"

"Really," he said.

He placed the tray on one of the nightstands and took his T-shirt off. His sweatpants were slung dangerously low on his hips. He smiled when she saw it caught her attention, and she bit her bottom lip. He stretched out on the bed with one arm under his head. He picked up one of the strawberries, dipped it in

THE NEARNESS OF YOU

caramel, and extended it out toward her. She sat on the bed, her legs still dangling toward the floor. He pulled the strawberry back when she reached for it.

"It's breakfast in bed, and you're not in bed yet."

"Fine, but I'm only getting back in the bed because I'm tempted by the caramel and strawberries, not you."

"I bought the caramel to tempt you because you tempt me."

He handed her a flute of mimosa. She took a sip. "Are you trying to get me drunk?"

"We both know it would take a lot more to get you drunk." He took a strawberry and dipped it in the bowl of whipped cream. He licked the cream off the tip. She moaned. "That moan translates, 'I wish he would do that to me.'"

He took her glass from her and returned it to the tray. He dipped another strawberry into the whipped cream and traced her lips with it. He looked her in the eyes as he slowly lowered his mouth to hers, giving her an opportunity to stop him. When she didn't, he tasted the cream on her lips and then dipped in to taste mimosa mixed with a flavor that was purely Amara.

His hand started in her hair and began a gradual descent down her body. He ran it along her arm, grazing the outside curve of her breast and continuing downward. He had already glimpsed the black satin confirming, to his disappointment, that she was wearing underwear, but he put his hand under the hem of her T-shirt to verify. Then he ran it up her flat abdomen, lifting the shirt as he went.

He pulled his mouth from hers so that he could reach and dip a strawberry into the whipped cream. He'd brought the caramel for her sweet tooth, but the whipped cream was for him to enjoy. He moved the cream-covered strawberry across her exposed stomach, spelling out the word love and then used his mouth to lick and kiss it until it was gone.

Her body moved beneath him. Her hands gripped the sheets. He fed her the strawberry then continued the tour of her body with his mouth and hands. He missed the feel of her. The way she moved under his touch made him feel alive. He wanted to bring her pleasure to erase some of the hurt and pain he'd caused. He dipped a finger underneath her panty. Both moaned in unison at the feel of it.

Her voice cracked as she called his name. He knew he had to bring her to climax before feeling himself inside her. She felt too good, and it had been too long. There was no way he'd be able to make it last. He was ready to explode just hearing her breathless voice call his name. The same must have been true for her because within moments, she was shuddering at his touch as she sang out his name and her nails dug into his back.

He reclaimed her mouth and settled his body between her legs so that she could feel his need for her. She wrapped her legs around his waist, pulling him closer. He needed to have her, make her his again. He needed to claim her to feel whole again. His only thought was to make them one.

The passion-induced trance Amara was under was broken by the sound of the doorbell chiming. She reached between them to pull at her T-shirt, trying to cover herself. "The door. Someone's at the door."

"Just ignore it," he said. He began to kiss her neck slowly while his quick fingers lifted her shirt again. There was a second in which she didn't resist him, but only a second.

The doorbell rang again. "You should get that," she said, pushing softly at his chest for him to get off her.

He groaned but rolled to the other side of the bed. As she pulled the shirt down to cover herself, he saw in her eyes the wall that had kept them apart go back up. The moment was over, and the chances of another opportunity like that coming any time soon was unlikely. He closed his eyes and shook his head. He wanted to hit something. He wanted to hit the person who had rung that doorbell.

He got off the bed and walked over to the window. In the driveway was his father's car. His father was still inside, which meant his mother was at the door. "My parents are here."

"I'm not here," Amara said.

chapter 13

RYAN YANKED THE DOOR OPEN and leaned against the doorjamb. If his posture didn't give the message that she wasn't welcome, his words surely did. "What do you want, Mother?"

"Good morning, Ryan." She waited on a polite response but got none. "I would like to speak to Amara."

Ryan only arched his eyebrow. He didn't move, and he didn't say anything. As a son, he was usually respectful and accommodating to her regardless of the situation. Today, she saw a different side of him, and she found it intimidating. She wasn't afraid that he would hurt her physically, but she could see in his eyes that he might hurt her emotionally. He had already ignored her phone calls, which is why she'd started calling Amara. If what Amara said was true, her son didn't understand how much she loved him. She hadn't been raised in an affectionate household and didn't really know how to express her love, other than by protecting them. Evan last night, she had spoken out of a need to protect him, but she hoped he'd never have to know that.

"May I come in?"

"After last night, I don't think Amara wants you in her home."

"It is your home too. I have come to apologize."

"You should have called first. I would have told you there was no need to come."

"If I had called, the likelihood that you would have answered was slim. At any rate, I didn't know I was coming until we were almost here."

Ryan grunted a laugh and shook his head. "You didn't come to apologize. Dad made you come. I can't deal with this. Have a safe trip home. I'm just not in the mood for you today."

He shut the door in her face before he could see the tear roll down her face. She just stood there, frozen by the shock of the pain she felt. She forced her feet to move and went back to the car, wiping away her tears before getting inside. She knew Robert would overreact. She automatically put her seatbelt on, and he followed suit.

"That was quick. I take it she didn't accept your apology."

"I did not get a chance to apologize to her."

"She didn't let you in?"

"I did not see her. Ryan answered the door."

"She didn't come down?"

"He didn't let me in." Robert unsnapped his seatbelt. "Robert!" she called but knew he couldn't have heard her over the sound of his slamming car door. She ran after him, catching up just as he was about to knock.

"Do not. He will think I sent you to fight my battle, and it will only make things worse. He just needs time to cool down." She hoped the words were more convincing to her husband than they were to herself. Ryan did not seem to be in a forgiving mood. She could not understand why he was so upset with her for the things she had said to Amara. His sister, maybe, but not him.

"I don't care what he thinks, he's not allowed to send you to the car crying."

Robert was too angry to bother with the doorbell. He knocked. He knocked so hard that some of the neighbors may have thought someone was at their door. Ryan opened the door, and Robert walked in before his son could even speak.

"You are never to deny your mother entry again," Robert shouted.

"Dad, this is my home. I make the rules." Ryan didn't shout. He spoke firmly and stood his ground.

"This may be your home, but that is your mother. If one of your rules is to be disrespectful to her, I might need to slap some sense into you."

Ryan took a step back. "She didn't even want to come here, so she should be happy she doesn't have to apologize."

Robert took a step forward. "I really think you need to remember we're your parents."

"Robert," Catherine said putting a hand on Robert's arm. "Please, may we just go?"

"See? She doesn't even want to be here."

"But she is here. There has never been a time when she hasn't been here for you."

"She's usually here to tell me what I've done wrong or how I can be better. She's been here to tear me down. Who needs that? Who wants a mother like that?"

"Ryan!" Amara said. She was standing on the stairs, the shouting having brought her out of hiding. "What is wrong with you? You made your mother cry."

The two men looked at Catherine for the first time and saw the tears on her face. Embarrassed that they had all seen her display, she turned and left the house. Ryan stood immobilized from the sight of his mother showing emotion. Even when the woman was angry, her facial expression never seemed to falter. It was as though she had been receiving Botox injections since birth. Robert gave his son a look of disappointment that mirrored Amara's. He turned to go to his wife.

"I'll go, Mr. Clark," Amara said, surprising everyone, including herself.

She didn't even bother to put on a coat or shoes because if she stopped, she might not go out there. The blast of cold air made her regret that decision. Her feet danced across the cold ground like those insects that could skim across water. She sat in the driver's side, too chilled to speak.

Catherine's face was in her hands. "I told you not to press the issue. I told you it would make him hate me more," she said between sobs.

"I'm sure he didn't mean those things."

Catherine jumped and immediately began to wipe her tears. Growing up, tears had led to more chastising and sometimes even whippings. Her father had raised her to suck it up and never show emotion. That's part of the reason why, when she left home, she never really went back. Robert had shown her it was okay to express emotions, and she did with him. But she failed with others. Especially her children. It didn't come naturally to her, or if it had, her father had worn it out of her long before she had memories of it. Memories of a lovely and kind mother danced on the fringes of her mind, but they were faint because she had died when Catherine was so young.

"Thank you. Your kindness is more than I deserve right now. He meant what he said. He wishes I was not his mother."

"I don't think that's true."

"Yes, you do. You said so last night. He just confirmed it." The tears began to flow again. This time they wouldn't stop.

"It's okay. I promise you he didn't mean it. I didn't mean it last night, either. You'd hurt my feelings, so I tried to hurt you back."

"About last night, I apologize. I had a bad week, and I misdirected my frustration at you. You are like family.

My children definitely see you that way, and so do I. I hope you can forgive me."

"Only if you forgive me too."

"There is nothing to forgive you for. You were only telling the truth. My daughter only began to like me a few months ago, and my son has never liked me. He has always kept his distance, and it has only gotten worse. That is why I call you. I know you will pick up my call even when he ignores me." She began to cry, not caring anymore that Amara was seeing her in such a state. It probably didn't matter much anyway since she didn't think they'd see much of each other. Diane rarely came home anymore, and with a baby on the way, it would be even less. Ryan would be happy if he never saw her again. If it weren't for Robert, whose love had always baffled her, she'd be alone.

Amara reached out her hand to comfort the woman then pulled it back. She repeated this move several times then finally began to rub her back. This only increased the crying. She hugged the woman—awkwardly because the gearshift sat between them and because Catherine returned the hug as if it were a foreign practice. They remained in the embrace for several more minutes, the older woman making up for lost time.

"Amara, can we keep this between us?"

"Sure," Amara said. "What exactly are we keeping between us?"

"My utter lack of decorum."

"Mrs. Clark, you cried. Humans do that, and you're human."

"Of course, I am human."

"I meant it's normal. I actually think it would be good for Ryan to know. As children, we tend to forget our parents are people too. Especially so when they are good at," she thought carefully about her next words, "masking their emotions. If Ryan saw this side of you, it would make a big difference."

"I do not want him to see me like this."

"Okay, start a little smaller. Give him a hug. It's been a while." Amara rubbed her hands together for warmth.

"You do not have any clothes. You must be freezing."

"I'm a little chilly, but I won't go into that warm, cozy house until you're ready."

"Thank you. I am glad you are Diane's best friend. I hope I am right that there is more than just a friendship between you and Ryan. I think he would not be this upset with me if you were not important to him. Are the two of you in a relationship?"

"I, um, it's really cold. We should get back in." She opened the door and ran to the house the same way she had run to the car earlier. She was going to start keeping a pair of shoes by the front door.

She opened the door to find the two men standing with their arms folded, glaring at each other. Like father, like son.

"Is she okay?" the father asked Amara.

"She's on her way in. You're going to apologize to her when she gets here," she said, pointing a finger at Ryan.

"He does not have to," Catherine said, shutting the door behind her. "He was upset, and we all say things when we are upset." She slipped her cold hand into her husband's warm one. "Amara has accepted my apology. Will you?" she asked her son.

"Why are you apologizing to him?" Robert asked, still upset with his son's sudden lack of respect.

"Robert, you are not helping," Catherine said with a gentle squeeze of her husband's hand.

"He's right, Mother. I'm sorry. You shouldn't be apologizing to me. I was in the wrong."

"I think we were both in the wrong. Let us just accept each other's apology and move forward."

Ryan's eyebrows furrowed, but he nodded. Catherine took a step toward him and encircled him with her arms, just barely making enough contact for it to be considered a hug. Having never received a hug from his mother that she initiated, he stood in shock before returning the embrace. Catherine smiled when he pulled her to him. Amara thought Ryan was the one who needed this, but it was his mother who needed it. Perhaps it was time to share her emotional side with more people than just her husband.

She adjusted her coat and brushed off invisible lint. "We should be going now so you can get on with your day. Amara, thank you."

Amara smiled. "You're welcome. Have a safe trip."

Robert hugged his son. "You need to fix this. Your wife's a keeper," he whispered.

"What?" Ryan asked, surprised, taking a step back. He glanced over and saw his mother was talking to Amara at the front door.

"You were playing with that band on your hand the entire time they were in the car," Robert said.

Ryan slipped his hand in his pocket at the reminder that he was wearing it. "How do you know she's my wife?"

"You followed her here instead of going to Washington. Indianapolis isn't a political hotbed. You're wearing a band, and she's not. You wouldn't be staying with her if she weren't your wife, at least not if you were trying to get your wife back."

"Don't tell Mother."

"Don't worry, I don't want to deal with being the one to tell her you got married and kept it a secret."

"Robert, are you ready?" Catherine called from the door. Robert smiled and went to hold the door for his wife. "We will call to let you know we arrived safely. I love you. Ryan."

"I love you too," Ryan said. After the door had closed, he turned to Amara. "What did you say to her?"

"That's between me and her."

chapter 14

"**WHAT'S WRONG, AMARA?** You've been distracted the last couple of days," Ethan said as they drove back to Indy from a couple of campaign stops in the southern third of the state.

"It was a very distracting weekend." She was functioning at ninety-nine percent, so if he noticed something was off, he must know her pretty well and be quite observant.

"Tell me about it."

"You don't want to listen to my problems."

"I wouldn't have asked if I didn't want to know. Is it your husband?"

The last word came out strained as if he had a hard time saying it. "It is," she admitted. "He confessed that he stole the info for his story from me."

"How does that make you feel?"

"More determined than ever to find out who his source was."

He looked at her like she'd just said the sky was green and grass was blue. "I was feeling a little envious of the guy because you married him. Now I want to know how to contribute to his therapy bill. He finally confesses to the exact thing you've been saying he'd done, which made you believe that what you insisted was a lie is the truth. That is insanely illogical logic."

"My logic is perfectly logical. For months he's been saying he had a source, then he does a one-eighty, and now he doesn't have a source? That is what's illogical."

"Maybe he didn't feel like lying to you anymore."

"Or maybe he had reason to *start* lying to me."

"That makes no sense."

"What makes no sense is his confession. He's been saying he couldn't tell me. Not that he didn't want to or that he wouldn't, but that he couldn't. Just hours before he admitted culpability, he said that it was best that I didn't know who his source was. That made his confession extremely suspicious. Especially since you've had me wondering who had something to gain from the truth about Senator Layton's sexual preference coming out."

"Was my father on that list? There's been more and more talk about him running for president since Layton is no longer a potential candidate."

There was no connection between Governor Bedloe and Senator Layton, but there was a link between him and the missing campaign funds. She didn't want to bring that up because she didn't want to put him in the position of confronting his father. "Though he's benefited, he didn't know, so he couldn't be the leak."

"So—I know I just said the forbidden word but don't hit me. I meant to say, who are your front runners for a source?"

"Same as before—the boyfriend, the wife, and the approximately ten percent of the population that share his sexual preference."

"I don't think the entire gay population knew he was gay."

"It would only take one. Maybe a jilted ex."

"But I thought he'd been with his boyfriend for a while."

"He had. He'd been with him almost as long as he'd been married."

"How did you know? Did he disclose it to you as something that might come up?"

"No, he didn't tell me. I found out by accident," she said, stretching out each syllable of the last word as those thoughts on the outskirts of her mind grew closer. She closed her eyes to think. She could see bits and pieces, but not enough to get the whole picture. It was kind of like those games when different features of a celebrity's face are revealed one at a time until you guess who it is.

"You don't think it was an accident that you found out?"

His question revealed the rest of the pieces for her. "You know what? I don't." "What if it wasn't an accident that I found out? What if Ryan's source wanted me to know so I could be the scapegoat? Everyone has just assumed I was the source and no one has dug beyond me."

"So that cuts out some jilted ex. They'd want the world to know."

"True, but his boyfriend wouldn't want the attention and neither would his wife."

"How is his relationship with the boyfriend? Did it weather the storm?"

"Better than me and Ryan's. It weathered the storm but took a few dents and dings."

"So he's still a suspect. What about the wife?"

"She's played up the wronged wife act to the hilt. She now has more name recognition than ever. Her likeability ratings are through the roof. I think every woman who's ever been wronged by a man is on her side. Even I'd almost be willing to buy whatever she was pitching."

"Or whomever."

"I said *almost*. She's pitching your dad like it's opening day at Wrigley. No offense, but the thought of him running this country makes me..." She clenched her fist and gave an exaggerated shudder.

"I'm not offended. I'm not my father."

"He doesn't like that, does he? I mean, he hasn't exactly been eager to help you."

"That's because I won't dance to the politics as usual tune he and his cronies are playing."

"And that's why I could see you someday being president."

"Let's just get me elected senator first. Actually, let's just make me win this primary."

"It would be a much easier task if you had more party support."

"You mean if I had *any*. They wouldn't even help me pay for you." As soon as he said it, he remembered she didn't know that truth.

"Then how are you paying me?"

"From my trust fund."

"Why?"

"I was the only one who wanted to hire you. They refused to contribute unless I hired Richard Tucker.

"He's a hack. Why him?"

"I don't know if he's a hack or a very gifted hatchet man. They send him to manage careers they want to bury. Mrs. Layton suggested him."

"Really?"

"I think she sees me as a threat to my dad's potential presidency bid."

"Because you're not a team player? Not a mini Will Bedloe?"

"Pretty much. I think for myself. I disagree with my dad's position on some key issues which wouldn't look good on the nightly news when my sound bites contradict his."

"I didn't know Mrs. Layton and your dad were so close."

"They have been ever since she became the regional director. She has power and wears skirts—both things my father has a weakness for."

And with those words, Amara had no doubt who the source was.

"RYAN, YOU WANT TO play twenty questions?" Amara said later that evening as she sat on the couch next to her husband eating takeout while watching TV.

"Are we seven?"

"No, but I have some questions for you and thought game form may be the easiest way to get answers.

"Okay, but for every question you ask me, you have to take off an article of clothing before I answer."

"What kind of games were you playing at seven?" He answered her question with a raised eyebrow. "For every question I ask you, you get to ask me one," she corrected him. "Those are the traditional rules."

"All my questions will be requests for you to remove an article of clothing."

"Let's be serious here, Ryan."

"You want to be serious about a game?" He shook his head. "Okay, I'll be serious. What's your first question?"

"First you have to promise you'll answer honestly."

He put a hand over his heart and one in the air. "I promise."

"Do I know your source?" She didn't go straight to the center bull's-eye by asking if Mrs. Layton was his source, but she did hit the outer ring.

His fork paused on the way to his mouth. "I told you I didn't have a source," he said before continuing to eat.

"You said you were going to be honest. Both of us know you didn't find out Layton was gay from me."

"I don't want to play this game."

"Why not? Is it because I might find out the truth, and you don't want me to?"

"You know the truth. I told you the other day. You were right all along—I ruined your career to further mine." He sounded like a prisoner of war repeating name, rank, and serial number. He wasn't going to stray from his current statement of utter guilt.

"Or you were played just like I was played, but once you figured it out, it was too late. Maybe the person who played us is powerful. Powerful enough to make you feel you have to protect me from a threat."

He got up from the couch and threw his plate, food and all, into the sink. "Please just drop it." He pinched the bridge of his nose before turning away from the sink. "I'm tired. I'm going to bed."

"It was Mrs. Layton, wasn't it?"

He stopped on the stairs. "Good night, Amara."

This wasn't how she had expected the night to go. Actually, it was exactly how she expected it to go. She didn't really expect him to pop a cork and make a toast, but it would have been nice if he'd stayed and denied it.

Or kissed her until she forgot about it—his kisses did that. Making love to him would wipe her mind clean of everything but him. Who was she kidding? Just being near him wiped her mind clear of everything else. Usually. But this time she needed to know she was right. Not because she was competitive, which was generally true, but because she wanted to know if he was trying to protect her.

Mrs. Layton struck her as the type of woman who thought in order to get ahead, you had to run with the boys, which usually meant stepping all over the other women in your path. Amara wasn't that kind of woman. She fell more into the category of women who got through the door with their looks then took over with their skills. Men were just like sixteen-year-old boys, easily distracted by a pretty face and in too deep before for they realized it. She had cultivated her wardrobe to be professional yet sexy and stylish, sedate enough to be non-threatening to wives and girlfriends.

There was a time when she'd admired Mrs. Layton. But that was before she met her. Mrs. Layton had opposed her every step of the way. Until yesterday, she thought it was because the woman thought she knew better than her. Now she realized it had been sabotage because she didn't want her husband to have a serious shot at the White House. She knew that the higher his poll numbers got, the harder the fall would be when it came out—or when he was forced out of the closet.

Unlike Amara, Mrs. Layton had her own political ambitions, but they hadn't panned out. As a result, she'd attached herself to someone who could gain the spotlight. That way she could have power by association. Amara didn't crave the spotlight. She craved the exhilaration of out-strategizing an opponent and the elation of victory. The thought of actually doing the job was tiresome.

She wanted to go upstairs to Ryan to finish their discussion, but she knew he needed his space. He liked to be in control, a side effect of growing up with a mother who had controlled everything—sometimes even trips to the bathroom. Freedom for him had meant being in control of his own life. Whenever he felt he was losing that control, he had to pull himself together and make a plan to regain it. She'd let him do that tonight. Let him think of a way to be in charge, or at least let him think he was. She was good at that.

AMARA WAS ALREADY ON her second cup of coffee when Ryan came down. He looked handsome in his three-piece suit. It was the suit he looked best in, especially when he took off the jacket, letting the vest emphasize his broad shoulders and highlight the way his crisp cotton shirt stretched over his biceps. It was his feel good suit.

"I'm not afraid of her." Amara greeted him as though last night's conversation had merely been put on pause and hours of restless sleep hadn't ensued.

Without asking, Ryan knew exactly which "her" his wife was referring to. "That's because you don't understand the importance of healthy fear. She's a very powerful woman."

Amara bit her lips to hold back her joy at his admission. Well, it wasn't an admission per se, but she knew it was as close as she was going to get. "She may be powerful, but she has no power over me. She's already done the only thing she could do to hurt me."

"No, she hasn't. She only set your career back, she didn't destroy it. But she could easily do that."

"I wasn't talking about my career. I was talking about you. Us. Our marriage. My career is important but not as important as you." She'd done it again, put her heart out there on the line. The last time she'd done that, they ended up married, and then he broke her heart. The first time was back in college.

Eight Years Ago

RYAN HAD ONLY BEEN out of school for about a year, so going back for homecoming was still an absolute must. Some of his fraternity brothers who were freshmen when he was a senior were still there. He'd missed the freedom and limited responsibilities of college. College had gotten him away from the rule-laden house his mother controlled. He had a full college experience—he partied hard and responsibly. It was so much easier to pick up a girl at a party than it was in a bar or a club. In high school, he was the top dog. In college, he was a big dog. In the big city of Chicago, he was barely a pup.

To be truthful, the main reason he came back was because Amara was there. He'd had a couple of friends keeping tabs on her and reporting back to him. He knew how upperclassmen preyed on pretty young freshman, and he didn't want his sister's friend to fall victim. Early on, he knew he didn't have much to worry about, Amara had proven she could handle herself. That's why he was surprised when someone approached him within minutes of arriving to tell him she was getting drunk by eating the fruit from the punch. Common rookie mistake. Eating the fruit that had been soaking in alcohol for days was worse than doing a keg stand.

When he found her in some back room, she was sitting on a guy's lap. He knew the guy and didn't like him. He was a sixth-year senior because he spent more time trying to get up a girl's skirt than going to class. He was that guy who always went after the weakest one in the pack—the girl who thought she wasn't as cute as her friends and was usually easier because of her low self-esteem or the drunkest friend who'd lost track of her friends and had already begun to display poor judgment.

Ryan didn't want to have to fight the guy, but he would. Fortunately, Amara saved him from that fate.

"Ryan! I knew you would come." She tried to stand, but the guy didn't release his arm from around her waist. She had to be drunk because she couldn't figure out why she couldn't get up. After a second attempt, she looked puzzled.

Maybe he would have to fight the guy after all. "Let her up," Ryan told him.

"You need to find your own. She's mine. I've been priming her all night, and she's almost ready to go."

"That wasn't a request," Ryan said, taking his jacket off so it wouldn't impede him throwing a serious punch. He didn't turn, but he could see from the corner of his eye that a couple of his frat brothers had silently joined him. They didn't need to know what was going on—they had his back and would get answers later, if at all.

"I had to ply little Miss Good Girl with fruit all night to get her drunk. And you think you can just waltz in here and get lucky? This is my fresh meat freshman. Go find your own. Mary is mine."

"Who is Mary?" Amara asked.

"Let her go," Ryan said with so much bass in his voice that half the people at the party stopped what they were doing to see what was happening. The guy saw he was outnumbered and gave up. He moved his arm from around her waist.

She stood and stumbled into Ryan's arms. "Who's this Mary that's his? I hope she won't try to kick my butt. I didn't know he had a girlfriend."

"He was talking about you. You're Mary."

"But that's not my name."

"I know. Let me take you home." He wrapped an arm around her waist, and she leaned on him.

"But he said Mary was his. I'm not his, so I can't be Mary. He can have this Mary chick because I'm yours. I can't be his because I've always been yours."

"I know."

She stopped walking and looked at him. "No, you don't. You don't know that I love you."

"I do know. I love you too."

"No you don't." She leaned back onto him and started walking. "You don't love me like I love you. You love me like you love Diane."

"Just trust that I love you. Have you eaten?"

"Yeah, I ate fruit. I think it was bad. I feel funny."

"Did you eat anything before the fruit?"

"I had lunch. I feel really funny."

"You're drunk."

"But I haven't had anything to drink. I don't drink."

"If they did it right, that fruit you ate had been soaking in alcohol for probably a week."

"Oh. That would explain it."

He drove them back to his hotel after stopping at a drive-thru. He got her a supersized meal and bottled water instead of a soft drink. He knew that dehydration was what caused the worst part of a hangover.

"Thanks for the food." She gave him a hug, and her hands began to caress him through his shirt. "Have you been working out? You feel like you've been working out. Take your shirt off." Her fingers began to fumble at undressing him. "I haven't seen you shirtless in a long time, and my fantasies are becoming foggy."

He took her hands and kissed them. "You need to eat."

She took her hands out of his. She looked disappointed. "Since you won't take your shirt off, you have to give me a kiss."

She took his shirt in her fists and pulled him to her. She was up on tiptoes, and her mouth was on his before he could say anything. At first he resisted, and then he gave in, kissing her back and tasting a mixture of sweet fruit and alcohol. Her talented mouth moved on his with expert precision. He had thoughts of granting her request and taking his shirt off to feel her roaming hands against his skin. The thought of removing her shirt made him break the kiss.

If she were sober, he'd be all for this. Well, mostly for it. Even though his eyes were opened to the fact that she was more than his little sister's friend with a crush on him a couple of years ago, there was part of him that still saw her that way. That kiss made that part a little smaller. It stirred feelings in him, feelings he'd learned to suppress. This just wasn't the right time. She still had to finish college. He had to get his career started and become financially stable. Right now, his parents were supplementing his income.

Those things were a concern because Amara wasn't just a freshman you took advantage of because she didn't know the fruit was spiked. She was the kind of woman you married. And that wouldn't happen if they started dating now. The distance and his workaholic schedule would doom them. She'd become the one that got away. There would be awkwardly pleasant small talk when she came to visit Diane with her new boyfriend in tow. Then there'd be their individual weddings to other people, and babies, followed by a divorce because they'd married the wrong people. That was the future as he saw it if they weren't patient.

She turned away from him, but not before he saw her wipe a tear from her eye. "I told you that you only love me like your sister's best friend."

"That's not true."

"It is." She opened the bag of food and began to eat.

He turned the TV on and sat in the chair. They ate with the TV as background noise to their thoughts. After she finished, she just sat there with a sad look on her face. He hated that she thought he was rejecting her. He wanted to kiss the disappointed look off her face.

"Are you feeling any better?"

"A little."

"Why don't you take a shower? It'll help. Then I'll get you back to your dorm."

"I don't want to go back to the dorm."

"Where do you want to go? I'm not letting you go back to that party."

"I don't want to go back. I want to stay with you. Can I stay here with you tonight?" There was a glint of hopefulness in her eyes.

"Why?"

"Never mind. I'm going to go take that shower."

Words were no longer falling from her mouth haphazardly. Her perceived rejection must have sobered her up. He stretched across the bed while she showered, trying to not think about her naked body glistening in the shower in the next room. Being patient was going to drive him crazy.

SHE LOVED THAT HOTELS had a seemingly endless supply of hot water, and she stayed in the shower far longer than it had taken her to regain her wits. She dried off and put her underwear back on. She was about to put her dress back on when she caught a reflection of herself. She'd bought this bra and panty set special for tonight. The plan had been to seduce Ryan.

That was the only reason she had gone to the party— Diane had told her Ryan would be there. Otherwise, she would have been in her dorm room watching Netflix. She never went to parties out of habit. She'd become a homebody, spending almost her entire life with her

THE NEARNESS OF YOU

sheltered best friend. Her new college friends were shocked when she said she wanted to go. They were even more surprised when she convinced them to go to the mall with her to shop for new party outfits.

The dress she picked was supposed to show Ryan that she was all woman now. That the little girl he still pictured was gone. She'd bought the lace and satin underwear in hopes he'd bring her here and make love to her. But she got drunk. How was she to know the fruit had been spiked? Who soaks fruit in alcohol anyway?

So much for her plan of seduction. Or maybe not. She could give it one last attempt. She'd lean against the door in her lingerie and show him what he was missing out on. It worked in movies, so maybe it could work for her. She took a deep breath to steady her nerves and opened the bathroom door only to be let down. Ryan had fallen asleep during her lengthy shower.

She quickly switched to plan B and went to lay next to him. She slipped a hand under his shirt. He stirred but didn't wake. Blame it on the alcohol, or a desperate desire, or a combination of both, but she became bold. She slipped her hand down to just below his belt. She planted her mouth on his. Her hand began to stroke back and forth. He moved into her touch, and his lips began to return her kiss. His hands began to touch her body. She thought she would explode from the sensation and utter joy. She felt that her dream was finally coming true.

He rolled on top of her. The hardness between his legs pressed against the softness at the apex of her thighs.

His mouth had moved to the hollow just above her collarbone. One of his hands was squeezing her butt as he ground into her. Her lace-clad, erect nipples brushed against his chest as she moved underneath him. His fingers slid under her panty, greeted by her desire.

"Ryan," she moaned.

"Amara," he grunted before his body went completely still. His eyes flew open for the first time since she'd joined him in the bed. He looked down at her, confused, then leaped from the bed. "I'm so sorry, Amara." He covered his face with his hands then ran them back over his head. "I'm sorry. I didn't think that was really happening. I didn't mean to do that."

"But I did."

"No, you didn't. You're drunk."

"Maybe I'm a little drunk, but I know what I'm doing. The only effect the alcohol had on me was giving me enough courage to try again." She looked away from him and hugged one of the pillows in front of her. "But I understand. You don't want me like that."

She avoided looking at him for fear the tears would start falling. Or that she'd go back on the promise she'd just made and try to kiss him again.

"Amara, please stop telling me how I feel and what I want because you don't know."

"I do know. You just hopped off the bed like I was radioactive when you realized it was me. That's not the behavior of a man who wants a woman."

"It's the behavior of a man who doesn't want to take advantage of a drunk girl."

"And there's the problem. You see me as a girl, but I'm not. You weren't taking advantage of me. I was seducing you." She pinched the bridge of her nose to stop the tears and anger from pouring out.

"Amara, I want you. Now is not a good time to start a relationship."

"I'm not asking for a relationship. There are so many reasons it would be doomed."

"If you don't want a relationship, what do you want?"

She took a deep breath and locked eyes with him. "I want you to be my first."

"You mean you haven't...?"

"I want you to be my first," she repeated.

He turned away from her. "I can't."

Even though he couldn't see, Amara nodded her understanding and went back into the bathroom to finish getting dressed. When she came back out, Ryan was still standing there as if he hadn't moved. "I'm ready to go," she said, standing by the door.

"I'll take you back to the dorm."

"Drop me back at the party."

"No. You shouldn't go back there."

"Yes I should. You can't be my first, but I know at least one guy there who will be more than willing."

"I'm not going to let you—"

"Stop right there. I don't need permission from you."

"You need someone to think rationally for you because you're definitely not doing it."

"I know I'm not thinking rationally. A rational woman would have never wanted you to be her first. A rational woman wouldn't want you at all. I guess I did because, according to you, I'm not a woman, just a girl. Just take this irrational girl back to the party."

"I don't want you to go back there."

"You've made it abundantly clear that you don't want me at all."

"That's not true, Amara. I want you. I just want to be more than some guy you slept with in college."

"You wouldn't be just some guy. You'd be the guy who made sure my first sexual experience was special and enjoyable."

"Amara, if I made love to you tonight, do you think I could just walk away and leave it at that. You're not the kind of woman I can have a one-night stand with. You're the kind of woman that I would want something more permanent with."

"Ryan, I would like something permanent with you someday. I have imagined you as my forever guy for what seems like forever, but I don't want that forever to start now. Now, tonight..."

"Tonight what?" He stepped closer to her.

"I know you won't be my only, but I was hoping that you'd at least be my first—and hopefully my last."

"Why me, Amara?"

"I know you think it's just a stupid little girl crush that I should have outgrown by now, but it's not. As a little girl, I saw in you kindness and generosity. Most big brothers wouldn't choose to read to their sister over riding bikes with their friends. I can go on and on about all of the attributes that make you perfect."

"I'm not perfect, Amara. You deserve perfect."

"I figured that out when you literally cried on my shoulder last Christmas. Then you asked for my advice and you took my opinion seriously. You showed me you had vulnerabilities and made me feel like I mattered. No, you're not perfect, which is what makes you perfect for me. There's only space for one perfect person in a relationship, and that's me."

"You are perfect, Amara. That's why I don't want to mess this up. If we make love tonight—"

"We'll be able to tell our grandkids about it."

He raised an eyebrow. "Why would you talk to kids about sex?"

"I wouldn't. I'd tell them how you came back to Butler for homecoming and whisked me away from a party, and we confessed our love to each other for the first time. We talk all the time about everything except how we feel about each other. Or maybe I'm wrong. Maybe you don't love me the way I love you, which would make this entire night pretty pathetic."

"I do love you, but I don't want to take advantage—"

His words were cut off by Amara's lips on his, and he was suddenly having a difficult time trying to remember his rationale for not making love to her.

"Ryan, can't you see what's happening?" she said as she unzipped her dress and let it fall to the floor. "I'm not some young girl with a crush. You're not taking advantage of me." She unfastened her bra and slowly pulled it down, revealing her full breasts and erect nipples. She was standing an arm's reach away from him in nothing but black lace panties and six-inch heels. "I'm a woman who knows exactly what she's doing and exactly what she wants. I'm trying to take advantage of you."

"But Amara..."

She took the final steps toward him until there was no space left between them. She put her finger on his lips to silence him then trailed that same red-tipped finger down his chest. "No buts, Ryan. All that matters right now, in this moment, is that you want me. Do you want me, Ryan?"

She lowered her hand to below his belt to get an answer. The alcohol in her system hadn't clouded her judgment, but it had made her bolder. There was no hesitation as she cupped his hardened length through his pants. Her eyes were locked with his. The desire in his brown eyes matched hers.

"You do want me," she said, caressing him and eliciting a groan, "so have me. I'm yours."

The feel of her touching him, the sight of beautiful bare body before him, and the lusty sound of her voice offering herself to him broke the last of his resolve. He was only human. He was trying to be a gentleman, but he wouldn't be a man if he continued to resist the nearly naked woman in front of him.

He crushed his mouth to hers, kissing her with more passion and force than he ever had before. His hands explored her curves. His fingers slipped beneath the delicate lace, and he almost lost himself at the feel of her desire for him. He somehow found the will to keep his head. This was her first time. He had to remember that.

He didn't rush it. He loved her slow, reveling in the perfection of her body while bringing her pleasure with his touch and his tongue before finally making love to her. That first time was for her. The couple of times he woke her in the middle of the night was because it just felt so good. But that morning, that was for him. He was claiming her as his. Ensuring that every other man would fall short of making her feel the complete and utter ecstasy that he could make her feel. A relationship now wouldn't work. He needed to make sure that every other guy was merely someone to pass the time with until the time was right.

Present Day

ONCE AGAIN, AMARA FELT bare and exposed to this man. She really wasn't concerned about her career.

If he'd come to her and told her what was going with the Laytons, she would have gladly sacrificed her career for their marriage. She was beginning to wonder if there would ever be a time she didn't have to cajole him into loving her.

"Amara, I love you. You're the most important thing to me too."

"You don't have to say that."

"It's the truth."

"Then why did you do the story, even if you had a source. You had to know it would hurt me."

"I didn't know who my source was right away. Our communication was very cloak and dagger at first. My first thought was to just sit on the story—which I did for a couple of days. Then I was told that the story was going to be broken by me or by somebody else, but it was going to break. So I planned to tell you all this the night before it was planned to air. But that got messed up when the network got wind of the story, and it went live a day early."

"When did you find out who your source was?"

"A couple of weeks later. She must have thought I had known, and she wanted to be sure you never found out. She wanted to be sure no one did."

"She played both of us. Without us even knowing."

"Maybe she did, but Amara, I need you to let it go. Don't take her on."

"I can only fight one battle at a time."

"What other battles are you fighting right now?"

"Chinese wall. I can't say."

"Okay, but promise me you won't try to prove you've got a bigger pair than Mrs. Layton."

"You should know I don't have a pair at all. But my heels are higher than hers." She kicked up her heel to prove it.

"You want to play hooky today? We can spend the whole day making up with you in those shoes?"

"That sounds very tempting, but I have some important things on my schedule today."

"How about I make us dinner tonight?"

"That sounds good. When did you become so skilled in the kitchen? I know you didn't learn all of this from a handful of secret rendezvous with your dad."

"While you were gone, I worked out and watched a lot of Food Network. I figured knowing how to cook might help get you back. I knew the six pack would keep you."

"Is that why you can't seem to find a shirt when you're home? It is pretty irresistible."

"You seem to be doing just fine resisting me."

"If you only knew. It's taken every bit of my willpower not to sneak into your room in the middle of the night and have my way with you."

"I'll leave the door open so you don't have to sneak."

"Maybe I'll leave mine open." She blew him a kiss and picked up her travel mug of coffee. "I'll see you after work."

chapter 15

A MARA PULLED INTO THE DRIVEWAY. As the garage door rose, she had the hope of locking herself in her room until the morning— or at least until she figured out how to handle the situation. She was still shaken and couldn't think. She didn't know how she would end up handling it, but she knew she couldn't let Ryan see her. He wouldn't give her a chance to figure things out. He'd just react, like that time he ran into her at a bar and a guy was getting more intimate than Amara cared for. He went into protective mode, ready to beat the guy to death had security not intervened. There was no security to stop him now, which likely meant the result of him seeing her like this would be bad. It might even result in prison time.

Ryan's car had pulled into the drive before the garage door had completely raised. Her only option now would be to get into the house before him and lock herself away.

That would have been acceptable behavior a few weeks ago when he first arrived, but this morning they had taken a huge leap toward reconciliation, and ignoring him would alienate him. It was now a real possibility that they could actually be a real married couple, sex and all.

She would have to dig deep and sell it. What she wanted most was to run into his arms and have him reassure her everything would be okay. But if she did that, Neanderthal Ryan would appear and run off to club somebody. So sell it she would. There was no reason for her to be mad at him, but she was a female and as such didn't need a reason—at least she knew that's how he thought. He'd spend the night trying to figure out what he'd done, and she'd have time to strategize.

She got out of the car and slammed the door with as much force as she could. She could see in her periphery that he looked toward the sound, but she didn't look his way. She was prepared to close the door to the house with equal force and exuberance, but it was locked. He was out of his car and behind her as she fumbled to get the key in the lock. He put his hand on her waist and pulled her coat collar down to kiss her neck. The door finally opened, and she flew through before his lips made contact with her. More importantly, it was before he could see the developing bruise on her face. She tried to close the door on him, but he stopped it with his hand.

"Amara. What's wrong?" His question was met by silence. He tried a different route. "What do you want me to cook for dinner?"

"I don't want you to cook me anything for dinner." Her voice was cool, but had an edge to it. It didn't deter him.

"But I thought—"

She headed up the stairs with her coat and shoes still on, not bothering with her normal ritual. "I'm not hungry."

"Amara, slow down." She continued up the stairs until she felt his hands encircle her wrist. She stopped but didn't turn. "What's wrong?" he asked, standing a couple of steps below her.

"It was a long day at work."

"Okay, then tell me about it."

"Can't, Chinese wall," she snapped back, trying to free her wrist.

"If it's just work, why won't you look at me? I thought we were good again."

"You thought wrong."

"We were at least better. Better than you not even wanting to see my face."

"Ryan, just let me go upstairs." Her edge had softened

"We agreed to try, Amara. That means you can't just shut down. You need to talk to me. Please." He looked down to where his fingers had begun to caress her wrist. There were two circular stains on her shirt cuff that was peeking out from her coat. He leaned in closer. "Is that blood?"

She snatched her arm out of his grasp and ran upstairs. She was quick and made it to the room in enough time to shut the door. He was quick, too, reaching the door before she could lock him out. He pushed it open, causing her to stumble back. He stood frozen when he saw her face. The left side of her lower lip was split and red. Her eye was only swollen now, but the light brown skin around it would be shades of blue and purple by the morning.

"Amara, are you okay?"

She looked at him for the first time since he'd seen her. The anger that she'd expected wasn't there, only concern. Seeing how worried he was caused the tears she had been holding back, the tears she'd planned on shedding alone, to fall.

"Oh Ryan," she whimpered through the hand that covered her mouth.

He pulled her to him, careful not to hold her too tightly in case other areas were hurt. She rested her head on the rough wool of his coat that was still cool from outside. He stood there and held her, rubbing her back while she cried. He didn't say a word. The rapid rise and fall of his chest let her know that he was angry but holding it in.

Once the tears stopped, he released her and unbuttoned her coat. He gestured for her to sit on the bed. He kneeled before her and took her shoes off. When he stood, he shrugged out of his coat and tossed it on a chair.

"Were you mugged?" he asked, sitting on the bed next to her.

For a moment, she thought of saying yes. It was an easy way out of explaining what had actually happened. But then she'd have to file a fake police report. She shook her head.

His eyes closed tightly, and he shook his head as if trying to deny a thought. His hands clenched into fists at his side. "Were you raped?"

"Fortunately no. Nothing like that," she said to soothe his mind. "It looks worse than it is. I just want to rest."

"What happened?" His hands were still balled tightly into fists.

"I can't say." She wasn't afraid he'd use this in a news report. She trusted him now that she knew the entire story of what happened. The reason she didn't want him to know was because, although he was holding in his anger right now, she knew he'd blow like Mt. St. Helen's.

"If this is about the Chinese wall, your health is more important."

"You know how not telling me about Mrs. Layton was to protect me."

"Can you tell me if it's somehow related to your job?"

"Ryan." Her brown eyes pleaded with him to accept her silence.

He smiled and nodded. "If you think it's best I don't know." He disappeared into the bathroom, and she heard the water come on a few seconds later.

The soothing hot water of a bath sounded nice. She began to undress. A long soak would relax her mind, and she could decide what to do. The fact that Ryan had saved her wasn't the only reason that night at the bar came to mind. After that night, Ryan had insisted that she take some self-defense courses if she was going to be a single woman in the big city. It was those classes that had stopped unwanted advances before they'd escalated to sexual assault. She didn't want to borrow worries by thinking about what might have happened.

She was down to her underwear when Ryan came out.

"The bath is just how you like it—lots of bubbles, those crystal bath things, and hot enough to cook a lobster."

"Thank you."

He smiled. "I even lit the vanilla and sandalwood candle for you. You just relax while I go make dinner."

She went into the bathroom, finished undressing, and sank down into the inviting waters of the bath. Her head and knees were the only parts of her body that weren't immersed in the tub. Ryan opened the door and put her phone on the bathroom sink. It was playing the relaxing music of one of her favorite singers, Goapele. The soft glow of the candle, the music, and the warm water had her immediately in a more relaxed mood. Her mind was no longer a flurry of panicked thoughts.

She didn't know what she was going to do, but she did know what she wasn't going to do. Going to the police was out of the question. It was her word against his. He had the power, and she had the bad reputation, so most would believe his version of events—especially the police.

It was a good thing that Ryan knew she'd been attacked. He could help figure out what, if anything, she could do. He had reacted much better than she'd expected. Unlike the rest of his family, Ryan could be hot-tempered, wanting to throw punches rather than razor-sharp words. How calm he was tonight was almost out of character. It was also abnormal that he hadn't even seemed to notice when she stripped down to her underwear. Maybe he hadn't said anything because the timing would have been a bit off, but he didn't even raise an eyebrow in interest. It was almost as if he hadn't noticed at all.

Sometimes he couldn't see what was right in front of him when he was focused on something. Perhaps he'd already started to hatch a plan. How could he when he didn't know the details of what had happened? Ryan was good at working on instinct and hunches. Most of the time they were right, but when they were wrong, they were really wrong. She sat straight up in the tub. Wait. He wasn't keeping calm, he was *acting* calm to placate her until she couldn't stop him from flying off the handle and doing something foolish.

Just as she had that thought, the sound of the garage door raising filled the bathroom. "Crap!" she yelled. She hopped out of the tub and ran to the window. Ryan was pulling out of the driveway. She knew she had to stop him. Nothing good could come from him bashing heads. She'd already done that.

Dripping wet, she didn't bother to towel off. She threw open a drawer and grabbed a pair of pants and a shirt. She didn't even take the time to put on underwear. Pulling the clothes on over her wet skin took more time than if she had taken a couple of minutes to dry off. The first pair of shoes she saw were the ones that Ryan had so lovingly—or more like calculatingly—taken off her feet earlier. A coat completed her haphazard ensemble.

She grabbed her phone from the bathroom sink, the music coming from it she now found to be annoying. She shut off the music. When the phone switched back to the home screen, a picture of her appeared. This wasn't her phone. Who used a picture of themselves as their own wallpaper? She took pride in how she looked, but vanity was not one of her flaws. This was Ryan's phone. And that meant he had hers—and therefore Ethan's address.

chapter 16

A MAN WHO HIT A woman deserved to have a real man show him how much of a coward he actually was. Ryan would be the one to teach Ethan that lesson. He knew there would be consequences for beating the living daylights out of the governor's son, but he didn't care. No one was going to assault his wife and get away with it just because of their last name or who they could afford to pay off.

Every red light in the city seemed to be plotting against him. He was sitting at yet another, still fuming. He was tempted to run it but didn't want one of those traffic cameras catching him in the vicinity of the nearly fatal beating that was about to take place. There was a time for talking, and then there was a time for action. His wife thought it was the time to talk and think. He thought it was the time to let his fists teach a lesson.

He never liked the idea of Amara working with Ethan Bedloe. His father was a notorious womanizer. Accusations of indiscretions and sexual harassment had been flung his way for decades. Between his power and his wife's family money, those accusations had all but vanished. The apple usually didn't fall too far from the tree, or in this case the snake didn't slither too far from its hole. At least he had the decency to stay single and not put a wife through the humiliation of wearing the mask, smiling in the background at press conferences while he told the obligatory lies about being a loving and faithful husband and a dedicated father. It had always baffled him how that man could continue to get elected when he didn't have a sincere bone in his body. He also didn't understand why Jacqueline stayed. Did she really want money and power that badly?

Operating on the adrenaline of pure rage, he parked in the center of the driveway and got out of the car. A high-pitched beeping emanated from the open door, reminding him that the keys were still in the ignition. He ignored it and walked to the door, jabbing his finger at the doorbell and then pounding on the door so hard it shook in its frame.

The door opened, and Ethan Bedloe appeared with the fake smile politicians wore when they were annoyed but didn't want to look it.

"That was quick," Ethan said. "Oh, you're not pizza delivery, but I do recognize you. You're Ryan Clark. Amara's not here."

"I know. She's home resting. I'm just here to tell you to keep your hands off my wife."

"I don't know what you're talking about." Then he appeared to remember and said, "It was just a kiss, and it didn't mean anything."

Ryan responded by jabbing him in the abdomen. Ethan doubled over in pain from the unexpected blow. He waited for him to stand back up so he could finish him off. The punch must have been harder than he'd intended, or maybe the woman beater could only give blows and not take them. Either way, Ethan was still doubled over, profanity streaming from his mouth.

"Ryan, don't do anything stupid," Amara said. Ryan turned at the sound of her voice, revealing a partially upright Ethan.

"Defending you isn't stupid."

She brushed past him, berating him with a look. Ryan was confused. Why was she going to her abuser's side?

"It is stupid if you're defending me against the wrong person." Ethan put his arm around her shoulder, and she helped him to the couch. She threw her car keys at Ryan. Unprepared for the toss, they hit him and fell to the ground. "Go park your car correctly and pull mine into the driveway before a neighbor complains or calls the cops."

He picked up the keys and followed her instructions.

"Thanks for rescuing me," Ethan said and looked at Amara for the first time. "What happened to you? Did he hit you when you told him we kissed?"

"No, he would never hit me. And I didn't tell him we kissed."

"So he must have thought I did that to you when he told me to keep my hands off of you. Well, I'm sorry, but he knows about the kiss now."

"You told him about it? Oh Ethan, really? You're a politician! You should really be better at keeping secrets and telling lies. I'd hit you if he hadn't already. Let me check to see how badly you're hurt."

Ryan walked back in as Amara was unbuttoning Ethan's shirt. "He's fine."

"He's right, I'm fine. If bleeding internally is fine."

"It was just one little punch."

"Yeah, but these muscles are for show, not for combat." Amara was gently pressing on his abdomen, and he grimaced when she touched the spot sore from the blow.

"Would frozen peas or raw meat help?" Amara asked.

"You should use those things on that eye of yours," Ethan said, looking concerned. "Hitting him back will make me feel better. It would at least help my bruised ego."

"There will be no more hitting. There's been more than enough of that today," Amara said. "He will apologize, and you will accept. If that doesn't help your ego, too bad."

"I don't want an apology, I want to hit him."

"I'm glad you don't want an apology because you're not getting one. You may not have hit my wife, but you did kiss her. Consider us even. And if you hit me, we're going to have a *real* fight."

"I kissed a woman I thought was single. Maybe if you were a better husband, she'd have been wearing her ring and telling people about you before I had the chance to kiss her."

"Stupid little boys, enough." Her stomach made an inaudible gurgle. She hadn't eaten anything since breakfast. "Actually, you know what. You two fight it out. Reenact a WWE Smackdown for all I care. I'm hungry. I'm going to get dinner."

"Let's go home. I can fix dinner while you tell me who did this."

"I ordered enough pizza for all of us. I think it's only fair that I know who did this since I was wrongly—and painfully—accused."

Amara thought for a moment. "Pizza sounds great, but I think it's best that neither of you know who did this."

"You can tell me—or I can figure it out," Ryan said.

"Why? So you can go and beat someone else up? You don't need to because I already did. I know I look bad, but trust me, he's worse off than me."

"I've gotten the anger out of my system. You can tell me, and I promise I'll respond like an adult, not a stupid little boy," Ryan said, using her own words to try and soften her up.

"I don't trust you on that. Even if I did, I can't tell you because of the—"

"Chinese wall," he finished for her. "I've learned my lesson. You are my priority. Making whoever did this to you pay is much more important than ratings. Chinese wall or not, I'm not going to report this because it would hurt you more."

"I know you don't care about the wall. If you did, you wouldn't have stolen my phone to get Ethan's address."

"I could have gotten his address without your phone. Your phone was just the quickest way to do it." He had to act quickly because he had known it wouldn't take her much time to figure out what he was up to. Even with the advantage of her phone, he barely beat her here. "What does the wall have to do with this anyway? Ethan is your candidate. If it's not him, then why would there be a need for any wall?"

Ethan mumbled an expletive then said, "Because it was my father."

Ryan knew from the look on her face that Ethan was right.

chapter 17

"**I**T, IT WASN'T YOUR FATHER," Amara lied. The uncharacteristic hitch in her voice gave away the fact that she wasn't telling the truth.

"As someone recently told me, you need to be better at lying if you're going to work in politics," Ethan said.

"That's not what I said, and what applies to you, does not apply to me. I wasn't lying."

"Why do you think it was him?" Ryan asked Ethan.

Amara slipped her coat off. Ryan had gotten a whiff of the truth, and she knew he wasn't backing down until he got the full story. She plopped down on the couch, too tired to fight the inevitable.

"She left early because she said she needed to handle some campaign funds business. I thought she meant finalizing all the transfers."

"What transfers?" Ryan asked.

"We transferred the management of my campaign funds over to her cousin's accounting firm. We did that because Amara found—"

"Ethan," she interrupted, "do you really think you should be telling this to a reporter?"

Ethan looked at Ryan. "Are you a reporter right now, or are you just another guy concerned about Amara's well-being?"

"I'm not a reporter right now. But I'm more than just another guy. I'm a husband looking out for his wife's well-being."

Amara felt like a tree being marked by two dogs. Did Ryan really think Ethan had attacked her or had his somewhat unfounded jealousy caused him to jump to that conclusion so he'd have an excuse to hit him? "My being is quite well."

"Yeah, your face looks quite well," countered Ryan.

She narrowed her eyes at him. "You know what, Ethan? Go ahead and tell him everything. When you lose the primary because he's spilled his guts on national TV, remember you told him, not me." She sat back and folded her arms.

"What's said doesn't go beyond this room," Ryan said. He took his coat off as well and sat next to Amara.

Ethan explained about the missing money Amara had discovered which led to them changing accounting firms. "When she told me, I thought she thought it was the firm, but she must have thought it was my father, too."

"Wait," Amara said, "you thought it was your dad?"

"Of course! That man can't be trusted around women or money."

Amara had never heard him talk negatively about his father. He disagreed with him on policy issues, but he'd never had he said anything negative about his character. This entire mess could have been avoided if she had known he wasn't the loving son she'd thought him to be. Instead of confronting his dad, she would have discussed her suspicions with him first.

"When she left here, she must have gone to talk with him about the money," Ethan continued. He shook his head. "I thought you were smarter than to face my father alone."

"Thank you, Ethan. Not only am I a weak woman who needs a man to look after her well-being, but I'm a stupid one too."

"I don't think that's what he meant," Ryan interjected.

She cut her husband a look and leaned away from him.

"I didn't. Not at all. You're one of the most intelligent people I know. It's just that my father, at his core, is a vile excuse for a human being. The fact that all you have is a black eye and a busted lip proves that you aren't weak."

"Then it *was* him?" Ryan asked, taking her hand.

"What difference does it make? It's my word against his. I don't feel like fighting that fight when I know I'll lose."

"You don't have to fight the fight alone," Ryan said.

"And you don't have to fight with words," Ethan said. "You can fight with your numbers. He embezzled. Or as the media is fond of saying, he misappropriated campaign funds."

The doorbell rang. "I'll get it," Amara said.

"Not looking like that," Ethan said.

Amara touched her eye. She'd adjusted to the pain and obscured sight, forgetting what she must look like.

"Or with that black eye," Ethan added. "It wouldn't be good for my poll numbers for Tim to see a battered woman answering my door dressed like that."

"Ethan, do you want me to post a picture of your Babylon 5 doll collection on Facebook?"

He smiled. "I keep telling you, those are collectible figurines, not dolls."

"I keep telling you they're not collectibles. I'm fairly certain you made them because no one else has even heard of that show. I doubt it had any merchandise."

"Collectibles or not, they are very valuable."

"And quite embarrassing. It's also a bit disturbing that you're on first name basis with the pizza delivery guy."

"I'm a bachelor. I'm supposed to eat pizza and drink beer every night. He's also over eighteen, which makes him an eligible voter."

She shook her head but smiled. "I'll get plates and some wine," Amara said and headed toward the kitchen. Ryan followed her to help.

"You two seem to have a pretty friendly relationship."

"We do." She moved around the kitchen familiarly.

"You seem to know the kitchen pretty well too."

"I spent a lot of time here early on. He didn't have enough money for a campaign office and my salary. I was sleeping on Serenity's couch, so we worked here."

"Is this where you kissed?"

"Is it where he kissed me? It doesn't matter because it didn't mean anything."

"Was it just a kiss, or was it more?" His hands were in his pockets as he asked.

She sat the bottle of wine she'd pulled from the refrigerator on the counter next to the plates, glasses, and utensils she'd already retrieved then moved to stand right in front of him. The confidence Ryan emitted sometimes made her forget about his vulnerable side. It was the side hurt by his mother because he was still that little boy looking for her approval. There was a part of him that was very vulnerable where she was concerned.

Ryan was her prize, the person she'd always wanted. In her mind, she was always loving and wanting him more than he loved or wanted her. She had always felt like the pursuer. Even when he proposed, she saw it as her finally catching him. That's why it was so easy for her to believe he'd married her to get the inside scoop. She had never thought he felt the same way—that she was the prize he wanted to obtain. She had always been the driving force in the evolution of their relationship. Or was she? In retrospect, maybe there had been times when he was the pursuer. His jealousy brought that into focus. He thought of her as a prize he could lose.

"It was just a little kiss." Okay, it was slightly more than a little kiss, but she didn't need to tell him that. "He kissed me, and I stopped it because I don't feel that way about him. I only feel that way about you."

"For the record, I've not kissed anyone—or allowed anyone to kiss me."

"I have no control over someone else's feelings."

"Does he still feel that way about you?"

"No, married women are off the table as far as he's concerned. I don't really think he felt that way about me anyway. We're friends, and he was lonely—and I'm a pretty cute chick." She scrunched her nose on the last one.

"You are. Even with a black eye, a swollen lip, and the unfortunate combo of hot pink yoga pants, a Halloween T-shirt and tan suede stilettos you're still the most beautiful woman in the world to me."

"I will hurt you and him both if you mention what I'm wearing one more time. If I hadn't been trying to save him from being beaten and you from jail time for assault, I could have put effort into my outfit."

He pulled her into him. "You're beautiful no matter what you have on."

She placed a kiss on his cheek, flinching when her still sore lip made contact with the stubble there. They gathered up the items she'd gotten out and joined Ethan in the living room.

"What happened with you and my dad?" Ethan asked after they'd enjoyed a few slices of pizza.

"He laughed at me when I brought up the missing funds. Then he told me I didn't need to make up an excuse to get him alone. I told him I'd rather schedule a waterboarding than spend time alone with him, and I was there to discuss the money. He came and stood right in front of me. I thought it was to intimidate me, but then he said I'd have as much luck proving he took a dime as I would proving I hadn't come there to get my career back on track by lying on my back. Before I knew what was happening, he'd grabbed me and held me to him with one arm." She paused. Her heart was beating as rapidly as it had at that moment.

"You don't have to go on if you don't want to," Ryan said, holding hand.

The feel of his hands on her butt, pulling her to his groin, and his tongue slithering over her ear flashed back, and she couldn't manage to get the words out to tell them. It would make it all too real again. She skipped ahead to her escape from his fat-fingered clutches.

"I angled a foot and brought my heel down on his toes as hard as I could. The pain caused him to let me go enough so I had room to knee him in the groin. He doubled over from the pain, but he still had a tight grip on my wrist. I pulled but couldn't get away. I tried to pry his fingers off. He called me a name I won't ever dare repeat before smacking me across my face with the back of his hand. Before he could bring it back across my face,

I swung my fist with all my might, landing a left hook. Then I brought my elbow back and jabbed somewhere—I really wasn't paying attention. My wrist was free, so I ran out."

"I'm so sorry," Ethan said.

"It's not your fault. The most damage was to my eye. I'm fine." She cuddled closer to Ryan on the couch. She said she was fine, and she was, but she wanted the security his warmth provided.

"We may not get him for what he did to you, but we'll get him for the money," Ryan said

"Going after him will hurt you in the primary. That much negative publicity about a Bedloe will hurt you both," said Amara. "Especially since it was your money he was taking. I don't want you to make that sacrifice for me."

"Amara, let's face facts. I'm a long shot anyway. It wouldn't really be a sacrifice. It could even help if people see I'm willing to do the right thing, even if it means bringing down my own father."

"He's got a point. It could work to his benefit. Especially if he gets out in front of it," Ryan said. "But there's something I don't understand. Why would he risk getting caught by taking your money? Why not his own campaign funds or the hundreds of millions he has in the bank?"

"He's not up for election this year. The only campaign funds he has are for his potential presidential bid, and that money's watched more closely," Amara explained.

"He doesn't have hundreds of millions in the bank, my mother does. When my grandfather died, the easy flow of funds to support his lifestyle of multiple mistresses dried up."

"Isn't he from money too?" Ryan asked.

"No. He doesn't talk much about his family because they're not much to talk about. He was raised by his grandparents. I think his mother was unmarried when she had him, but his father was married. But that's all rumor. I don't even think my mother knows the truth of his life before college," Ethan said.

"Did you know that Ryan's parents went to school with your dad?"

"I didn't," Ethan said.

"It was more like they were there at the same time than they went there together," Ryan clarified.

"That's true—his mother said they didn't even cross paths," she said then yawned.

"You've had a long day. We should get you home so you can get some rest."

"You should rest tomorrow too. In your condition, you probably shouldn't be campaigning," Ethan added.

"I know you're more concerned about how a black eye will affect the poll than you are about me, but there's no need to worry. Tomorrow, we're going down to where my friend is. I'll avoid the campaign and visit with her."

"You're going to see Diane tomorrow?" asked Ryan. "Will you be sure to tell her I wasn't the one that did this to you? I'm fairly certain she'd waddle up here and kill me if she thought I hurt you."

chapter 18

THE SUN CREPT IN THE next morning. Ryan was already awake because his internal alarm clock always woke him up at the same time. Despite the stress of last night, he slept well. It was because for the first time in months, the woman he loved was in his arms, and she'd been there all night. The previous morning, he'd had hopes that they would get to share a bed while still awake. That evening, those hopes had been dashed, and he thought she'd want her space. He was pleasantly surprised when she stopped him from going to his room and invited him to hers.

He wanted to enjoy this moment because he didn't know if she'd feel the same way tonight. Her moods were fickle. She said she had forgiven him but that things wouldn't just change overnight. That was her way of saying she forgave him but reserved the right to still be mad at him over it. Amara was stubborn, which could be both a good and a bad thing.

The good part of it was that she was persistent and loyal. When faced with a challenge, she would fight tooth and nail, even when most would give up. That and her loyal nature was what kept his hope alive for a reconciliation. After all she'd done and how long she'd waited for them to be together, he knew she wouldn't just give up at the first bump in the road.

The bad part of her stubbornness was that she could hold a grudge for a very long time before her loyalty kicked in. That's why he had forced her hand by buying the house. He knew she would stay and eventually talk with him so that he could fix things. So far his plan had worked. Now he needed to resolve things with Mrs. Layton to ensure Amara wasn't persistent where she was concerned.

Then there were the new Bedloe issues. Ryan wasn't going to let Will Bedloe get away with what he had done to Amara. One way or another, he had to pay. Digging up something that would squash his presidential dreams would be good. The other issue was Ethan's feelings for Amara. While he trusted her when she said she didn't feel that way about Ethan, she didn't trust the man to not try to change her mind.

She began to move in his arms. "Good morning," he said and kissed her on the top of her head.

"Good morning to you too. Thank you for staying with me last night."

"Believe me, it was my pleasure."

"It was your pleasure to have me tossing and turning next to you all night? I'm sure you'd rather we were doing something else."

He turned her so she was facing him. "I enjoy making love to you. I enjoy it a lot. Last night, I made love to you by holding you when you needed to be held."

"If I hadn't just woke up and wasn't afraid of forever turning you off with my morning breath, I would kiss you right now."

"If that's the only thing that's keeping you from kissing me, the bathroom is just a few steps away."

"The busted lip is keeping me from kissing you too. It's still kind of sore."

"I can work around both." He brushed his lips against the side of her lip that wasn't injured. He continued on to her neck where he took up residence until she moaned for him. He continued down, kissing the skin between her breasts, becoming reacquainted with every delightful inch of her body, eliciting moans and breathless cries of his name. He settled his body between her thighs.

"Make love to me Ryan." Just in case her grinding against his thighs didn't get the point across, she added, "The sex kind, not just the holding me kind."

"Are you sure? Is our marriage still a crap cake?"

"What are you talking about?" Her words were shaky and her thoughts foggy because her legs had found their way around his waist, and her hips had increased their speed.

It was a struggle for him to remember what he was talking about. Only one part of his body was communicating with his brain, and it was telling him to shut up and concentrate on how good she felt writhing beneath him. He forced himself to focus because he didn't want to lose her. He wanted her body to feel this pleasure for the rest of his life, so this had to be right. "You said sex would be the, umm, the caramel icing on our crap cake marriage and leave a, umm, a bad taste later on. I don't want this to, umm, to be that."

"What?"

Her eyes were closed, and he was pretty certain she didn't hear anything he said. He cupped her face in his hands. "Baby, this is important. Look at me." Her eyelids were heavy with desire. "If we do this, the trial period is over. We're married, and there's no more talk about divorce or annulment. Is that what you want? Do you want us, or are you just horny?"

She nodded. "I want to make love to you because I love you."

Hearing her say I love you was all he needed. He couldn't hold back anymore. His hands grabbed her hips to stop their scintillating motion. "You need to stop that or this will be over before it starts. We can take our time." He dispensed of their clothing so there was nothing between them, and proceeded to slowly make love to his wife. The sex kind, not the holding through the night kind.

♡

AS USUAL, AMARA SHOWERED in the master bath while Ryan washed in the hall bath. He'd offered to share a shower, but she declined. If they got in the shower together, they'd never get clean and be even later getting to work than they already were. They'd made up for lost time this morning, making love several times. The first time was quick for both of them, despite him trying to take it slow. Their bodies had missed each other, and when they were reunited, it felt so good that it took only a few minutes for them both to climax. Ryan felt he had something to prove to make up for his hasty performance. And he did. Two more times, giving her countless orgasms.

When she stepped out of the bathroom, Ryan was waiting. He'd prepared a travel mug of coffee for her, and he sat in the chair sipping his own. The way his eyes roamed her towel clad body made her want to call in.

"How did you get showered and dressed so quickly?"

"I wasn't quick. I just didn't try to test the limits of the water heater."

The cold water kicking in had been her indicator that it was time to get out of the shower. If she had a larger heater, she'd stay in there all morning. "Thanks for the coffee. You know I need this pick-me-up to start my day."

"Didn't you already have a morning pick-me-up?"

"That pick-me-up made me want to take a nap. Are you going to just sit there and drink?"

He nodded "A little coffee and a show sounds good."

"What show?"

"You putting on lotion. And I want to see you put on the panties I'll be taking off tonight."

"You didn't give me a show, so you're not getting one."

"I'll give you one right now," he said as he loosened his tie.

"I have to get to work, and so do you." She selected a bra and panty set, grabbed the lotion, and walked into the walk-in closet. "Sit there if you want. I'll get dressed in here." She shut the door slowly so he could see her dropping the towel.

"No fair. I want my money back for this show."

"Maybe that's the problem—you didn't pay."

"Seriously, I wanted to talk to you about this morning." The lightness was gone from his voice.

She suspected he wanted to make sure she didn't have any regrets. "I don't regret it if that's what you're worried about," she called through the closed door.

"I'm glad you don't, but that wasn't what I wanted to talk about."

"Oh."

"I forgot to use birth control."

"Don't worry, I had us covered. I went back on the pill when you moved in."

"You did?"

She could hear the cocky smile in his voice. She opened the door a crack and peeked her head through.

"Wipe that smile off your face or there will be no repeat of this morning."

He began to laugh. She looked at him menacingly and shut the door hard.

"I knew all that no sex talk was just that, talk. You think I'm irresistible."

She didn't say anything as she finished getting dressed. Today she opted for a form-fitting navy dress that stopped at the knee. It had a crossover sweetheart neckline and a kick pleat in the back. She added a thin white belt at the waist and slipped into a pair of navy and white T-strap spectator pumps. It was one of her favorite outfits because it emphasized her small waist, made her breast seem fuller than they actually were, and hugged the curve of her posterior. Considering she was sporting a black eye, she really needed the boost in self-confidence she got from wearing this dress.

"Woman, you look amazing."

"Thank you," she smiled. Her insides began to warm from the way he was looking at her. It felt good to know he thought she looked as amazing in this dress as she felt wearing it. She went into the bathroom and began to try to make the bruise on her face less obvious.

"Is it just you and Ethan today?"

"Yes."

"I see."

She paused in the middle of covering the black eye with layers of concealer and foundation to look at him.

She didn't like his tone. She especially didn't like the look that went with it. "You see what?"

"Nothing."

"If it were nothing, you wouldn't have said you see. What is it you think you see?" She could have let it go. She should have let it go. Truth be told, it didn't even bother her that much. She'd gotten so used to directing her anger toward him, and sometimes even new habits were hard to break. Amara wasn't even upset with Ryan. It was the father of her boss that had her in a foul mood.

"I could see why Ethan kissed you. You joke with him. You spend most of your time with him. You dress like this for him."

"Stop right there." Amara put a hand on her hip and the other in the air to emphasize her words. "I dress for me and no one else. Not Ethan. Not you. *Me*. I'm not going to start dressing dowdy because you're jealous that someone else might find me attractive."

She was gearing up for a fight, but he didn't give her one. Ryan put his hands up in silent surrender and came to stand right in front of her.

"You're right. I'm sorry. You've always dressed like this. I don't want you to change your style." He put his hands on her waist. "I just wish you weren't so incredibly sexy in these dresses."

"Not everyone thinks I'm as incredibly sexy as you do."

"Ethan does. And he's more your type," Ryan said.

"I don't have a type. If I did, that type would be the Ryan Clark type." She looked directly into his eyes so he had no doubt that what she was saying was true. "You're the only man I have ever loved. By ever, I mean I have been in love with you for twenty years. I've compared every guy who has asked me out, or dated me, or shared my bed, or even shared a pencil with me, to you."

He raised an eyebrow. "Let's get something straight, you've only shared your bed with me."

"That's not true."

"It's a fact in my mind, so let's not dispute it."

"Fine, if that's what helps you sleep at night, but that's not the point. My point is that I can give you dozens of ways Ethan doesn't compare to you and is, therefore, not my type."

"Like what?"

"This morning has not been declared National Boost Ryan Clark's Ego Day."

"You don't have to give me dozens, just one or two will do."

She just shook her head and went back to applying her makeup.

"There is one thing that can boost my ego. Well, maybe just make me feel more secure."

"That would imply that there's something you're insecure about. I don't believe you're insecure about anything."

"I didn't used to be," he said, coming to stand behind her and making eye contact with her reflection in the mirror. "That is, not until the day I came home and saw these sitting on the counter." He dug into his pocket and opened his hand. She looked at his reflection in the mirror and saw her wedding set. "The day I saw you'd taken these off, I doubted I would ever get you back. Especially since I knew I didn't deserve you in the first place."

She turned to look at him directly. His feelings sounded foreign. This was all so new to her. She really thought he had settled for her because he was tired of her chasing him. She married him hoping that he would grow to love her as much as she loved him. Now she understood he already did. She placed a soft kiss on his lips.

"I love you, and I would love to put them back on." He smiled and lifted her left hand. "But," she said and pulled her hand back, and his face fell.

"You can't still want a divorce."

"No. That's not it at all. As long as you're giving me orgasms and coffee in the morning, I'm not going to get rid of you."

"It'll be my pleasure to do both those things for you each and every morning. What's the problem then?"

"Most people don't know about us. I think more than your sister and my boss should know first."

"And my dad."

"You told your dad?"

"Not really, he figured it out, and I didn't deny it."

"We need to tell everyone, or at least my parents and your mom, and then I'll wear them." She reached for the rings.

He pulled his hand back. "I'll hold on to them until I can put them back on your finger. Maybe in a ceremony bigger than a chapel in Vegas."

"Let's make plans to go home and tell our parents, then we can have a small renewal ceremony after the primary elections."

"We can play hooky and go tell them today." He nuzzled her neck to try and convince her.

"I don't want to have to explain my eye. The makeup made it look better, but it's still visible. The only way to cover this up is to put on enough makeup to be mistaken for a drag queen. I'm fairly certain my father would give you two black eyes before we could explain you didn't do it to me."

Ryan wrapped one arm around her and pulled her against him as he slowly caressed her body with the other. "We should still play hooky and get reacquainted with each other as husband and wife."

Between the hardness of his body pressing against her and his hands sending waves of heat through her, she was ready to say yes. Before she could have one good erotic thought about what she wanted him to do to her, the doorbell rang. It was probably Ethan. He was picking her up because they would usually only take one car on the campaign trail.

"Let me guess, that's Ethan." Amara nodded. "He's not giving me much reason to like him."

"Here's an opportunity to bond. Go let him in while I finish getting myself ready."

When Amara arrived downstairs, she found Ryan and Ethan standing in a silence laced with palpable tension. Ethan was glancing nervously at Ryan, probably afraid of another punch. Ryan was staring at Ethan with a look that said he was, in fact, considering punching him. Both men were holding cups of coffee.

"You look nice. That dress is one of my favorites," Ethan said.

"Yes, my wife does look beautiful," Ryan said, looking at Ethan and not Amara.

"I...um...I brought you coffee."

"And I prepared this myself, especially for you, but if you want the overpriced chain store—"

"Thank you," Amara said, breaking Ryan's words off. She kissed him on the cheek then whispered in his ear. "You're jealous. I can't lie, this pissing contest you're having with Ethan is kind of turning me on. I'll see you this evening."

She turned to go, but Ryan turned her back toward him. He lowered his mouth to hers and kissed her thoroughly. The lipstick she'd meticulously applied just minutes ago was smeared on both their mouths. She had no idea why she was about to walk out the door with Ethan instead of climbing back into bed with Ryan.

"You two have gotten back on track."

"We're headed that way. You spilling the beans about the kiss didn't help."

"I'm sorry. At the time, it was the only reason I could think for why he'd be angry with me."

"I'm going to give you some advice that you can use in both your professional and personal life. When accused of wrongdoing, even if you feel one hundred percent certain you know what you've done, let them tell *you*. Never—ever—volunteer your sin."

"I'll take note of that. Any more words of wisdom, all-knowing one?"

"Actually yes. I've decided that the way we will gain ground in this campaign is not by raising more dollars than the other guys. Instead, we're going to out-data them."

He glanced over at her, waiting for her to elaborate on what that meant because he was clueless. "Out-data them? Like polls and stuff?" he asked before she got too caught up in what she was looking at on her laptop.

"You say stuff like that, and it explains why I'm the campaign manager and you're the candidate. Just promise me when you're POTUS, I'm your press secretary or maybe chief of staff."

"The offer still stands for First Lady."

"I think my husband would have a problem with that."

"The Secret Service would get him before he got to punch me."

"Back to the data. What I'm talking about is the vast amounts of information on voters at your disposal. We use that info to tailor your message to each place we go and each email we send."

"That's flip-flopping. I'm not a flip-flopper."

"That's not what I'm saying. I didn't say change your message, I said tailor your message. You don't want to talk about taxes to people who are concerned about losing their houses. We target specific parts of your platform that will sway the most voters at the time."

"Who are we going to use to get this data? More importantly, how much will it cost?"

"I told you when you were interviewing me that I'm the only person you need."

"You really are. I wish I'd met you before Ryan."

"I met Ryan when I was five."

"Well, I wish I'd met you before you married Ryan."

"If wishing were money, I'd be rich," Amara said, still looking at her computer. The part of him that wanted her was the part that just wanted someone. She wondered what her life would have been like if she hadn't known, by age five and a half, the man she would marry. She shut her laptop. "I know you'll find someone way better than me. Maybe not better than me, but better for you than me. Like a preschool teacher or someone that LARPs. You don't want me running your private and professional life."

"You're probably right. Not about me marrying someone that live action role plays, but about me not wanting you controlling every aspect of my life. "So back to this targeted message thing, you'll tell me what I need to say and where I need to say it?"

"I'm not controlling, and stop saying so."

"That sentence didn't contradict itself at all."

"I think I'm going to up the ante. Every time you say 'so' you have to buy me a new pair of shoes."

"From Payless?"

She gave him an incredulous look.

"Then I need to stop saying that word because I can't afford that."

"When we get there, I'll make sure that everything is set up, then I'm going to disappear. I really don't want anyone to see me like this with you. It would lead to questions that we don't want to answer yet. Or people will jump to the same conclusion as Ryan."

Amara was glad she had Ethan wait in the car. Both Noli and Cooper's response to her black eye was similar to Ryan's, with the exception that they thought it was Ryan who had done it to her. Relative or not, Noli was ready to give her cousin a black eye, and her new husband was ready to follow suit. After she had convinced them it wasn't Ryan, she had to convince them that it wasn't Ethan, either. It was about twenty minutes before she gave Ethan the all-clear to come out of the car. Amara made introductions but was hesitant to leave Ethan on his own. Cooper at well over six feet tall and one hundred percent muscle was intimidating when he smiled, but when he scowled, he was downright frightening. Before she left, Amara told Noli to keep her husband under control.

Amara took Ethan's car and drove to Diane's law office. Fortunately, it was lunchtime, and there was no one there but her friend. She wasn't ready for the stares from complete strangers about her appearance. She was looking forward to talking to her friend and telling her everything that had happened.

"Knock knock," Amara said at the open doorway.

Diane looked up from the papers on her desk. "Amara," Diane's voice trailed off with each syllable. When she spoke again, her voice was a couple of octaves higher. "What happened to you?" Diane had one hand on her belly and the other hand raised in the air. "So help me God, if my brother did that to you, I will kill him if you haven't already. If you have, I will help you bury the body."

"It wasn't him."

Diane let out a breath. "Good because it's really hard to dig a shallow grave with this belly in the way."

"You have been pregnant for five years," Amara said, walking to Diane. They gave each other a hug.

"It really does feel that way, but I still have at least five more weeks to go." Diane eased herself back into her chair, and Amara took the chair across from her.

"Well, I suggest you get your absentee ballot in case you go into labor on Election Day."

"About that, what happened to you? If it wasn't Ryan, who was it? Did Ethan do this to you?"

"I feel like I'm on the witness stand."

"You walked into my office with a black eye. What do you expect? Now answer the question, witness."

"It wasn't Ethan." She paused. "It was his father." Amara braced herself for the storm to come, but there wasn't one.

Diane mumbled something under her breath that Amara couldn't make out. Then she said, "Why? What happened?"

Amara explained about the missing funds from Ethan's campaign and her confrontation with Will Bedloe. With her friend, she didn't have to put on the brave face that she wore when she explained what happened to Ryan and Ethan. By the time she'd reached the end of the story, Amara was in tears, and Diane was hugging her, belly and all.

"I don't know what to do. Pressing charges will get me nowhere. Even if it would, I have no proof. It would just be his word against mine. It would also be the end of my career, and Ethan would definitely lose the election."

"You shouldn't be concerned about your career or the election right now."

"That's exactly what both Ryan and Ethan said. Oh! I left totally left out the part where Ryan sucker-punched Ethan in the stomach. I had never been so angry and turned on at the same time in my life."

"You're weird. And eww."

"That's precisely how I feel when you and Jack are making kissy face and talking about going home to have sex."

"Fine. Friend rule number 1209, you don't talk about being intimate with my brother, and I will stop making kissy face in front of you."

"New rule accepted."

"It would be your word against his on the assault, but what about the money?"

"There's not much there. The money was gone, and then the bulk of the money reappeared without a trace of having ever been gone. That's why I went to confront him. He must've somehow gotten wind that we were looking into it and put the money back before we could see that it was gone. Ethan suspects his father was using the money for a mistress. Apparently, stepping outside of his marriage is a common occurrence."

"Is that so?" Diane began to shuffle the papers on her desk, no longer making eye contact with Amara.

Amara leaned forward in her chair. "What's going on, Diane?"

Diane continued to stare at her desk. "I know something that might be able to help you, but client-attorney privilege prevents me from telling you."

As if there was some type of psychic connection, Misti burst in, dragging a stroller behind her. "Diane I don't know why thought you would be a good attorney," Misti said in her annoying, nasally voice. "I thought you would've nailed that bastard Bedloe by now, and I would have my money back in the bank."

The blonde was about to continue, but Diane interrupted her. "Misti, this is Amara."

Misti noticed Amara for the first time. She looked her up and down, making an assessment, lingering, of course, on the black eye. "Sorry, but you'll have to come back later for your little domestic dispute." Misti waved her hand around as she spoke, dismissing Amara. "You'll have to come back. My paternity case is far more important than your little domestic disturbance."

"I'm not here to see Diane as an attorney. I'm here to see her as a friend." Amara's glance shifted from Diane to Misti. The tense look on Diane's face had increased since Misti arrived. The surgically enhanced woman stood with a hand on her hip, looking annoyed that Amara was still present. "Misti," Amara said under her breath. "Misti as in Jack's ex-wife?" Amara asked Diane.

"I prefer first wife," Misti said. "Diane is his second wife. She's a silver medalist, someone who eats someone else's leftovers. Irregardless," she continued as though she hadn't just insulted Diane. Diane and Amara mouthed 'irregardless' to each other, making fun of the bad grammar. "Where are you on getting me my child support? I need to get a manicure, and like formula or something."

"Misti, as your attorney, I would advise against you talking about your case any further in front of a third party."

Amara hadn't gone to law school, but she had watched every episode of *Law and Order*—which was almost the same. If she remembered correctly, she knew that Misti was waiving client privilege by discussing this in front of her. She also knew that her friend had just cleverly reminded her of that. More importantly, if she could get Misti to divulge information, it wouldn't even matter.

"You mentioned a Bedloe? Are you talking about Ethan?"

"I wish. I might've actually enjoyed having sex with him. I'm talking about the governor, Will."

Amara used all the strength she had and every ounce of acting in her to curl her mouth up into a smile. She touched the woman's arm as though she was about to betray a confidence. "What a relief. I'm Ethan's campaign manager, and I couldn't deal with the scandal of a child out of wedlock this close to the election."

The annoyed look Misti had had when regarding Amara went away. It was replaced with the calculating look of a woman trying to figure out the best way to get what she wanted from her mark. The woman was so self-absorbed she had no clue Amara was doing the same.

"Did Ethan do that to you?" Misti asked, indicating the black eye. "His dad likes it rough too."

Amara was glad that she only had coffee in her suddenly upset stomach. "No, it wasn't him. How I got this black eye doesn't matter. What matters is you getting the child support you deserve to take care of your child. I might be able to help you."

"I can't ask you to do that."

Amara recognized that her friend was trying to protect herself from a malpractice suit, but Misti didn't. "You really are a horrible lawyer. She's willing to help at no charge." Misti turned toward Amara. "You're not trying to take a cut are you?" Amara shook her head. "Then I would love your help."

"I'll just need some details from you," Amara said.

With that, Misti started to divulge everything about her relationship with will Bedloe. Sometimes the details were too vivid. Amara took copious notes. Diane jotted down some of the more appropriate things that Misti had not told her before. Amara left Diane's office then. She had to do two things. First she needed to get proof to back up Misti's story. The second task was more challenging—she would have to try to keep Misti at bay until the end of the primary elections.

chapter 19

"LISTEN ETHAN, I'M GOING TO tell you this for the last time—if you want a chance at winning constable of a township, you need to drop her."

Ethan had lost patience with the woman sitting across from him. He wanted her out of his office, but she wouldn't leave. No matter how many times he said no, she still stayed. This was almost as bad as that time he'd tried to cancel his cable provider. He got up from his chair and sat on the corner of his desk in front of her. This allowed him to tower over her, giving him a non-verbal edge. Thank heavens Amara had taught him so much about body language and how to use it to his advantage.

"Why would I drop Amara? When suddenly and mysteriously no one would run my campaign or contribute to my account, she came along, took the job, and found me money. With her, I can make it to DC, and I'm talking Pennsylvania Avenue."

The woman chuckled, but it lacked conviction because it wasn't genuine.

"There are only two ways you'll make it to DC. One is by buying a plane ticket, and the other is on your daddy's coattails. On your own, you don't have what it takes to make it as a politician. You're too soft, just like your mother. Neither of you can stand up for yourself."

"What is that supposed to mean?"

"We both know that there was no mystery in you not being able to find someone to work on your campaign. We both know that I made sure no one would. Did you confront me? No, you found the one person desperate enough to take the job."

"What you thought was a weakness was intelligence. If she hadn't been desperate, I wouldn't have been able to afford her."

"If it were your father, he wouldn't have been grateful to get my scraps, he would have confronted me directly. I know this because that's exactly what he did. I want to be First Lady, and I don't care who my POTUS is."

It was Ethan's turn to laugh. "You figured you'd have a better shot with my father, even though he already has a wife, than you would with your gay husband."

"Your poor father has had to live decades with your mother's substance abuse," Mrs. Layton said, shaking her head in mock sympathy. Ethan looked confused. "Kind of similar to me living all that time with a gay husband. Two political powerhouses who kept their spouse's secrets and pasted the smiles on for the public—until the day the truth hit the fan and they found comfort in each other."

"Was your husband gay when he married you, or was being married to you what made him gay?" Mrs. Layton moved to stand, but Ethan extended his legs, blocking her in. "As far as my mother is concerned, she doesn't have a substance abuse problem."

"Of course you'd defend her. You're in denial yourself. After all, substance abuse is genetic. Wouldn't it just be a shame for your mother to take you down with her when the world finds out how she was buying drugs from the very streets your father was trying to clean up?"

"Am I going to be the scapegoat for that headline as well?" Amara asked sweetly.

Mrs. Layton smirked at the sound of Amara's voice. She didn't even turn or throw a look over her shoulder as she answered, "The idea had crossed my mind."

Amara came to stand next to Ethan. "I really don't know why it took me so long to figure out it was you who leaked the story about your husband. All the pieces were there, but I was too heartbroken to see them."

"You were too distracted to figure it out when it counted."

"You played me like a concert pianist. How does that saying go?" Amara snapped her fingers. "Oh yeah. Fool me once, shame on you—and start sleeping with one eye open and a finger on the trigger because I'm coming with both guns blazing when you least expect it."

"You're so cute. Like one of those Chihuahuas, all bark and no bite," Mrs. Layton said as if she were talking to a child who was showing off some artwork.

"I wouldn't underestimate her if I were you," Ethan interjected. "While you're at it, don't underestimate me, either. Bears are angriest after they've been hibernating."

"At least her threat made sense," Mrs. Layton said.

"Mine makes sense as well. You just poked this sleeping bear by threatening my mother, so I suggest you figure out how to sleep with both eyes open."

Mrs. Layton laughed a hearty laugh that lacked sincerity. "I'm shaking in my Manolos."

"No need for you to shake—the foundation you built your pipe dream on is riddled with cracks and will crumble right from under those knockoff Manolos." Amara held a hand out toward the open office door. "Thank you so much for dropping by with your," she searched for the right words, "campaign advice. We will take it under advisement. Goodbye."

The two women locked eyes with one another. Amara could see through Mrs. Layton's cold gray eyes to the scheming gears turning at warp speed in her head. Amara accepted the challenge. Mrs. Layton stepped on Amara's toes as she stood. The younger woman didn't flinch, but she did begin planning her victory outfit, right down to a pair of genuine Manolos. Amara watched until Mrs. Layton was out the front door and her Mercedes was no longer parked out front.

"Ethan, understand that I meant what I said. That woman is going down, and your father may be collateral damage. If you're not okay with that, I'll go pack up my desk now."

"I want you to understand that I'm taking my father down, and Mrs. Layton may be collateral damage. Or we can work together and make a direct hit, take them both out."

"She did poke the sleeping bear. I don't know if I'm scared or proud."

"Perhaps you should be both."

Amara's expression turned serious. "The stuff I heard her saying about your mother...?" she asked her partial statement as a question.

"None of it's true. The closest my mother has come to rehab is an all-inclusive resort in the Caymans to escape from life with my father."

"Maybe that's what you were told as a cover."

"She's not the only one that's needed time away from the not-so-honorable Will Bedloe. As an adult, I went with her to the resorts. As a child, it was usually Disney World or surfing in Hawaii. About every seven months, we went on a get-away-from-Father getaway."

"I wonder if Mrs. Layton knows your father has no money of his own."

"Not if she believes the reheated heap of bull he's feeding her about leaving my mom. They have an airtight prenup. He's not going anywhere. He likes power and wealth. Without my mom, he only has power, and that would disappear as soon as the wealth does."

"Why does your mom stay?"

"The best I can figure out is at first she stayed for love, then she stayed for me, then she stayed because my grandfather strong-armed her to keep her from leaving."

"I'm sure there's little if any love left, you're a grown man now, and your grandfather is dead, so why's she staying now?"

"Habit? Fear of the unknown? I don't know. My mom is a planner. She's probably planning an exit strategy as we speak."

"Your mother files for divorce, and then the allegations of embezzling campaign funds to pay for one of his mistress's apartments and a possible love child surface. The only chance he has to get in the White House is on tour."

"Did you say possible love child?" Ethan asked.

"I did. The woman your father has been keeping may have had his child last year. I found out today while I was visiting Diane."

Ethan got up from the edge of the desk and plopped in his chair. "I may have a half sibling out there?"

"Probably. You should pray for him, his mother might be worse than your father. Are you sure you want to do this?"

"There's no love left in my relationship with my father. Affairs were bad enough, but to start another family..." Ethan shook his head. "You know I don't think

I've ever seen my mother truly happy. She deserves to be happy."

"So do you. I was thinking of enlisting Ryan's help. Ever since this," Amara pointed to her black eye, "he's been eager to retaliate somehow against your father. Ruining his lengthy political career might be retaliation enough to satisfy him."

"I think it might be best if it were Ryan who did it. I learned from Mrs. Layton to make it look like your hands are clean even when you're elbow deep in the thick of the muck."

"I hope you didn't learn to use me as your scapegoat," Amara said.

"I'm not stupid enough to think you're dispensable." He raised the right side of his mouth in a lopsided smirk. "Were her Manolos really knockoffs?"

"They were. That style didn't come in that color, and for good reason." They shared a laugh. "Severe storms are supposed to roll through this evening. I'm going to head home. I have a Chinese wall to knock down."

"Is that code for something sexual?"

She was about to answer when she realized he was joking.

AMARA MOVED AROUND HER husband, cutting her eyes in his direction as she passed. She took the pot of pasta off the stove and dumped it into the waiting colander in one of the double sinks before slamming the now empty pot into the other side with more force than was necessary. Frustration had turned into anger as Ryan continued to doubt her. "Ryan, I'm done explaining that Ethan is my boss and my friend and nothing more. Why do you keep insinuating there's something more between him and me?"

Ryan put his hands in his pockets and continued to give her a wide berth. "I know I hurt you." She raised one very well arched eyebrow at him. "I know that doesn't begin to describe how I made you feel. Even though you've said you forgive me, I would understand if you haven't. If you wanted revenge, if you wanted to hurt me the way I hurt you, having an affair with one of *Indianapolis Monthly*'s most eligible bachelors would do it. I would be devastated."

"Unlike someone in this marriage, I took those vows seriously even if they were said in a dinky chapel in Vegas after midnight."

"I took our vows serious—"

Amara slammed her hands on the island's counter at the same time thunder sounded outside. "The alcohol from our wedding toast wasn't even out of our system before you broke those vows, so don't you dare utter a word about taking our vows as seriously as I did."

"I didn't mean to upset you. I was just trying to explain why your friendship with Ethan makes me feel insecure."

"My friendship with him doesn't make you feel insecure. You choose to feel insecure by thinking I'm a liar. How am I supposed to trust that you love me when you don't trust that I love you?"

She was scrubbing at the already clean pot so he wouldn't see the tears beginning to fall. When she felt his hands go around her waist, she knew she hadn't kept the emotional hitch out of her voice. She elbowed him, but he didn't let go. He held her tighter and kissed the top of her hair before resting his forehead on the crown of her head.

"Please don't cry, Amara. I will be his best friend if that's what makes you happy. I trust that you love me. I just don't know why you do. I don't deserve your love, and I'm scared you'll realize that someday."

Amara leaned back into his embrace. "Someday?" she asked, smiling, as she wiped away her tears. "I realized a long time ago that you don't deserve me, but for some reason I love you anyway."

"I don't know if this is the reason, but I know you love it when I kiss you here," he said, pulling her hair aside and kissing her neck. "You always moan 'I love that' when I touch you here," he whispered in her ear as he slipped his hands inside the waistband of her yoga pants.

It took only a few skilled maneuvers of Ryan's fingers to make Amara tremble. He had to support her weight as she climaxed from his touch. Her loud moans were drowned out by house-shaking claps of thunder. As her breathing began to even back out to a normal rhythm, he turned her to face him. They looked deep into each other's eyes, and in the moments before his mouth claimed hers, she saw the depth of his love for her.

"I'm not hungry for dinner anymore," she said when they managed to pull out of the kiss.

His hands were still exploring her body as he smiled down at her. "Really? What are you hungry for?"

"You know." She bit her lip, raising and lowering her leg so that her thigh caressed his arousal.

He shook his head. "I think that's more dessert. I know exactly what I want for dinner."

In one swift motion, he pulled her yoga pants down and lifted her onto the island. She kicked the pants from around her ankles. He lifted one of her legs and began to kiss and nibble his way up it. He had almost reached the apex of her thighs when the chime of the doorbell sounded just loud enough to be heard over another violent crash of thunder. He continued his journey until he felt Amara's hands pushing his head.

Ryan nipped the soft flesh of her inner thigh before standing. He helped her down then moved the pasta out the sink and washed his hands.

"My mother didn't say she was coming to town," Ryan said.

"Why do you think it's Catherine?"

"No one else consistently interrupts us at exactly the wrong moment. I'll get the door while you pull yourself together. You look like a woman on the brink of some great makeup sex."

Ryan looked through the peephole and bit back a groan. This was worse than his mother. He pasted on a close facsimile of a real smile and opened the door. "Ethan, good to see you. Come on in out of that storm."

"Is Amara home?" Ethan asked, remaining on the porch. He was still wary of Ryan from their first meeting, and Ryan's enthusiastic greeting only intensified that feeling.

"She is. Come on in, and I'll get her." Ryan opened the door wider for Ethan to enter and then went back into the kitchen. "It's not my mother, it's my new best friend."

Amara was surprised to see Ethan, who was dripping rainwater from every inch of his body onto the tile flooring just inside the entry. She was surprised that Ryan hadn't followed her back. Maybe their talk had resonated and he was trying. It was more likely he was just out of sight, eavesdropping.

"Ethan, what are you doing here? You shouldn't be out in weather like this. You're drenched."

"I was at the mansion, but it's a monsoon out there. I couldn't see a foot in front of the car. Half the streets look like rivers. I don't see myself getting home or back to my parents' without an ark. You were the closest place I could get to. Is there a possibility I can wait out the rain here?"

"I don't see why it would be a problem, but let me double check with Ryan." She turned to leave the room and halted quickly to prevent herself from colliding with her husband who had just walked in carrying a towel and sweats. Seeing Ryan put aside his unfounded jealousy and extend a friendly gesture toward Ethan surprised Amara and made her wish her boss hadn't shown up so they could finish what they'd started.

"Of course. It's not a problem," Ryan said, handing the towel and change of clothes to a confused Ethan. "I'll go make sure the guest room is ready while you get dry."

"I didn't think you were the type of woman to cheat on your husband. I'm disappointed."

"I really wish you were funny."

"I wasn't trying to be funny. That looked like Ryan, but he didn't punch me or anything. It must be his long lost twin."

"Go get changed."

"I will, but I need to get something out of the car first."

Ryan had finished preparing the spare bedroom for their guest and joined Amara, who was in the kitchen finishing dinner. He got another table setting out of the cabinet.

She watched him for a moment. "Thank you."

"I'm just setting the table."

She walked over to him and wrapped her arms around him. "You're not just setting the table. You're being hospitable to Ethan when we both know you don't really want to be."

"I told you he was going to be my best friend."

"You did, and I appreciate that you meant it. Especially since he interrupted our fun."

"Don't worry. It'll be just as much fun making you scream my name while he's trying to sleep in the room next door."

She looked up at him with narrowed eyes then smiled. "That sounds a lot like you trying to mark your territory."

"It sounds a lot like it because that's exactly what it is. It'll be easier to be his friend if I know that he knows you're mine."

He laughed, but she knew the statement was more truth than joke. Even still, she continued to smile up at him. "I'm mine, not yours. I'll be sure not to even whisper your name tonight."

"Challenge accepted." He bent down, kissing her on the collarbone.

Amara closed her eyes. Her teeth dug into the one side of her full bottom lip as she tried to suppress every pleasurable sound that wanted to come out. The more silent she remained, the harder he tried to make her moan.

"So my mom—" Ethan abruptly stopped both his words and his forward motion. "Sorry," he said backing out of the room.

"No, I'm sorry. For a second, I forgot we had company."

The devilish grin Ryan gave Amara confirmed that he'd not forgotten Ethan was here. "What were you saying Ethan? If you begin your sentence with so, I'll stab you with this knife," Amara said as she resumed cutting tomatoes for the salad.

"That seems awfully violent," Ryan said.

"It's my job to get him elected at any cost. Even if I have to stab him to get him to stop beginning sentences with so."

"Just let the man talk the way he actually talks."

Ethan looked at Ryan with the same look of confusion he'd regarded him with ever since entering the house. Amara narrowed her eyes at Ryan as she constructed an argument to silence him.

"We both know that people perceive those two little letters as a lack of confidence in what the speaker is saying. If the voters think he doesn't believe what he's saying, they won't believe it."

"You're absolutely right sweetheart," Ryan said, kissing the top of Amara's head. He turned to Ethan. "You were saying something about your mother."

Amara put a hand up to stop Ethan from speaking. "Is what you're about to say about the campaign or your father?"

"My father," Ethan answered.

"Proceed."

"So..." Ethan shook his head as if it would erase the word. "I was talking with my mother about the situations with my father."

"How did she react to the possibility of you having a half-brother?" Amara asked.

"Better than she did to him attacking you. She actually seemed to already know about the baby. She even gave me some things she thought might provide proof to back up Misti's claim. We can go through that after dinner," Ethan said.

"Me included, or just you and my wife?"

Amara reached for Ryan's hand and smiled. His question hadn't been asked with malice or animosity. She recognized he was trying to respect the blurred boundary lines between them. She wanted him to know his effort was appreciated.

"Neither of us can get the story out there," Ethan said, tilting his hand to indicate Amara. "We'll need you to do that."

"Are you sure you want to do this?" Ryan asked. "He is your father. I don't know if I would be able to put the screws to my father."

"I'm certain your father is a much better man than mine. He'd probably make a better governor too. My father is only interested in the kickbacks that come with the office. Every decision he makes is based on what he can get out of it."

"This will probably lose you the primary."

"I'm probably going to lose no matter which way it goes."

"Hey! Your campaign manager is both disheartened and offended that you feel that way," Amara interjected.

"You've gotten me further than I thought I could make it. Next time around, you'll be the reason I get elected. This time, Mrs. Layton's put too many obstacles in the way for even you to get me across the finish line first."

"I don't care about what that woman has or hasn't done. If you don't think you'll win, you won't."

"Is this where I'm supposed to start saying 'I think I can. I think I can.'?" Ethan said, thinking himself funny.

"Yes, because you're the little politician that could," Amara teased.

"Well, if you change your mind at any point, we don't have to go forward." Ryan extended his hand, and Ethan shook it.

Over the next hour, they ate, talked, and drank Copper Smith Brews.

After dinner, they began to go through the tote. Most of what was in it was not useful. But they went through everything thoroughly because they didn't want to miss something important. Ethan found a flash drive, and Ryan began to go through the documents on it. There were some old financial documents which Amara thought were probably irrelevant, but she forwarded them to her cousin Serenity.

They had gone all the way through the tote and much of what was there was old and not helpful in proving the governor was the father of Misti's baby. In fact, much of it was from before Ethan was even born. Some dated back to when his parents were in college.

"This was a waste of time," Ethan said, dumping his stack of files back into the tote. "I'm sorry, guys."

"It wasn't a total waste of time," Ryan said. "Those financial records on the flash drive might be helpful."

"This may not have helped much, but there's something out there. Your father isn't that careful," Amara said.

"I think I'm going to turn on the game. It's almost time for the tip-off. You like basketball?" Ryan addressed the question to Ethan.

"I'm a Pacers season ticket holder. My seats are right at center court." Ethan seemed proud of this fact.

Ryan shrugged. "I'm more of a Bulls fan."

"I'll have to take you to a game or two to convert you. You're in Pacers country now," Ethan said. "Do you play?"

"Of course." Ryan seemed almost offended by the question. "The question is, can *you* play?"

Both men got up from the dining room table. Ryan placed a quick kiss on Amara's smile. They continued to trash talk each other's games as they headed toward the family room. Amara heard Ryan offer Ethan a beer. Her smile grew because it sounded like they were actually becoming friends. She hoped they would and her husband would have somebody else to watch basketball with. She was tired of being forced to watch a game she neither cared about nor understood.

Amara organized the papers and files in the tote but left out the yearbooks. She didn't think she would find anything in them, but she wanted to look at them. Jacqueline Bedloe seemed like a lovely woman, and Amara was hoping to get a glimpse of why she might have been attracted to someone like her husband. Before Amara headed upstairs, she went to get a coffee. Most people couldn't do caffeine this close to bedtime, but Amara drank so much coffee her blood was fifty percent caffeine. She could hear the guys, and it sounded like they were arguing over who the best players were or sharing some kind of equally mundane sports talk.

"I'm going upstairs to look through the yearbooks," she told them. For the first time in what felt like forever, her life was good. She walked over to Ryan to whisper in his ear. "Don't spend too much time watching the game. I'm looking forward to your challenge." She stood back up and went to gather the yearbooks and her coffee. "Good night, Ethan."

"Good night, Amara. Thanks for letting me stay."

There was nothing in the first couple of yearbooks. She was able to find pictures of Jacqueline, Will, Catherine, and Robert, but not much more. It seemed that they weren't very active in campus life. Amara was about to give up and turn on the TV to channel surf when a picture caught her eye. She had no clue who the people in the picture were, but it wasn't them that piqued her curiosity. It was the couple locked in a passionate kiss in the background that had her fixated. The man looked a lot like Will Bedloe. And the woman? The woman wasn't Jacqueline. She knew this because she would recognize her mother-in-law anywhere.

Amara was shocked by what she had seen, and the book fell out of her hands. It lay there on the floor for a few moments as Amara tried to digest this new information. This at least explained why Catherine's attitude had changed when Amara asked if she'd known him in college. As Amara bent down to pick up the book, she noticed an envelope had fallen out.

She bent down to pick it up because she felt it was less threatening than picking the book back up. She thought wrong. The letter was from Jacqueline Bedloe to her father. Amara thought about not reading it, but Jacqueline wouldn't have given it to them if she hadn't expected them to read it. The flap wasn't sealed—it was just tucked in. Allowing curiosity to get the better of her, she opened it.

What she read inside made her heart constrict. She forgot how to breathe, only remembering to take a breath when she became lightheaded from the lack of oxygen. She sat there stunned, unable to move. For the first time, she understood Ryan's decision. When he had told her he was trying to protect her, she hadn't really believed him. Now she did. Now she could understand the need to keep a secret to protect the one you loved. But she also remembered the pain that had caused. The thing about secrets is they don't stay secrets forever. Which would be worse? Her telling him the secret, or him finding out she had known and didn't tell him once it came out? Neither scenario was good. But there was nothing she could do, so she took the letter and put it back into the envelope and back inside the yearbook and placed them in her laptop bag. She lay in bed, unable to fall asleep but praying she would so she wouldn't have to face her husband with this fresh secret. Her prayers were answered.

chapter 20

SOMEHOW AMARA HAD MANAGED TO not tell Ryan about what she had discovered. That was avoidance—she was up before him in the morning, got home from work after him, and was faking sleep in the bed before he got to bed. It also helped that he'd been traveling for the show. She used the impending primary as her excuse. While she had been diligently working on the campaign, she hadn't been working as closely with Ethan.

The secret that had created concealer-proof circles under her eyes impacted Ethan as well. While it was easier to be around him than Ryan, it still wasn't a piece of cake. And she knew cake—she'd been finding a sick kind of solace in a chocolate cake with whipped caramel icing she'd discovered at the grocery store bakery. She'd vowed that she'd have to quit the cake cold turkey since there was no twelve-step program for delicious cake addiction. But when Ryan and Ethan walked into the office together, she knew there was no way she'd be able to go cake-less tonight.

"There's my beautiful wife," Ryan said, scooping her into his embrace. "I've missed you."

Amara smiled through her fright. "I've missed you too." Which was both true and an unadulterated lie. She was glad that he had been away because every glance, or kiss, or touch, was fertilizer for the guilt growing inside her. On the other hand, she was a newlywed who was hopelessly in love again and still craved those kisses and touches.

"I thought you weren't due back until tonight."

He placed another kiss on her lips. "I really missed you, so I wrapped things up early to come home to you."

"Sometimes you're incredibly sweet."

"Not too sweet. I need to do some pre-taping work with Ethan."

"Oh, yeah, I forgot about that."

"How'd you forget when you're the one who put it on the calendar?" Ethan asked.

"You've been working her too hard. You should go easy on her."

"If you go easy on me on your show," Ethan countered.

"I may not feel compelled to punch you anymore, but there's no way I'm going to let you off for your record and platform," Ryan said.

"You can attack his record all you want, but I helped craft that platform. You attack it, and I may feel compelled to be stingy with my wifely duties."

He wrapped his other arm around her and pulled her close. She was smiling up at him. He bent down and kissed her. "We both know you find me highly irresistible."

"Do we really know that?" She reached her lips up to him for another kiss.

"Please get a room," Ethan begged.

Amara stepped out of her husband's arms. "Sorry, I guess that's not really professional of me," she said.

"Me, either," Ryan agreed, though he was still holding her hand. "I forgot I was here for work." He took his ringing phone out of his pocket and looked to see who the caller was. "I need to take this."

Ryan gave Amara a goodbye kiss on the cheek. As she watched him head out of her office, everything felt right in that moment. The moment didn't last long.

Ethan snapped his fingers and pointed at Amara. "I'd forgotten to ask you, did you find anything in those yearbooks?"

Dread kept the smile on her face. "Anything like what?" Amara knew exactly what he was asking, but she was taking her own advice, she wasn't going to divulge what she'd found unless he did. "Like bad 80s hair? I found a lot of that." Deflection, especially with a joke, was also a tactic she advised her candidates to use.

Ethan laughed but didn't stray from the original topic. "My mother said that there should have been something in those yearbooks. You're the only one who looked through them. Did you see anything?"

Amara glanced out her office door to make sure Ryan was still on the phone call. "I fell asleep before I could look through them all." Which was a partial truth, there were two that she had never cracked open after seeing that photo and letter. "I figured you and Ryan were right and that it was useless." There was no percentage of truth in that lie.

"It was weird. She didn't specify what, but she seemed to think there was something specific we should have found. Maybe she was mistaken. Even if you'd found something, I doubt it would have helped. My mother and I had a bit of miscommunication. While I was talking about my father having a child with Misti, my mother was talking about a baby she suspected he'd fathered and had aborted some time ago. What about your cousin? Did she find anything?"

"Though the flash drive was new, the files on it were over a couple of decades old. It looked like one of your grandfather's business accounts. There were some transfers to your father's account if that's of any help."

"You two ready?" Ryan asked, now off the phone.

"Actually, I'm really swamped. I was hoping that the two of you could do this on your own."

The two men agreed and left the office, chatting with each other. The sight of them being friendly should make her happy. A few weeks ago, her husband's jealousy and contentious relationship with her boss was her biggest concern. She was happy about it but wondered if their fledgling friendship would survive the truth. She was hoping that truth wouldn't come out until after the election.

For the second time today, her hopes were destroyed as soon as they were conceived. Within milliseconds of each other, her computer started sounding its new email notification chime, her cell phone started vibrating, and her desk phone started ringing. She picked up the desk phone first. Since only a few people even knew it existed, she figured it must be important.

"Misti! That—ooo— Be nice, Diane. Misti is an idiot," Diane said before Amara could even say hello. Or maybe she was talking to herself. It wasn't clear which as she continued to say incoherent things about Misti while telling herself to be nice. If what she was mumbling was supposed to be nice, then the thoughts she was having must have been downright evil.

Amara unlocked her computer from the screen saver. "What are you going on about? Did Misti try to seduce Jack?"

"I wish. That would have been better. You won't believe what she did. Misti—"

"Posted online that Will Bedloe is her 'deadbeat baby daddy'!" Amara yelled. She had set up Google alerts for any time either Will or Ethan was mentioned. That's what the dings on her computer had been. Misti's tweet had already been re-tweeted several times. "Will you represent me in her murder trial?"

"I can't—I'm going to be your co-defendant. Have you seen her Facebook post?"

"It's on Facebook too? I've only seen the tweet so far."

"Oh yeah, it's on Facebook and Instagram. I give it five minutes before it's on *TMZ* and *Buzz Feed* too. She named me as her attorney in the 'custody battle' and as the person to contact for interviews. My phone has already started ringing. She posted my personal cell number, Amara. My. Personal. Cell. Number. This woman is determined to send to me to an early grave—or at least early labor."

"Just turn it off and go to the farm. I'll call you there. I have to track down Ethan."

Amara wanted to scream, maybe throw a few things. This day was turning out to be the worst day of her life. It even topped the day she moved in with her husband, was betrayed by him, lost her job, and moved out of her husband's apartment. She took a deep breath and dialed Ethan.

"You and Ryan need to get back here immediately. Park in the alley and come in the back door."

"Why? What's wrong? Has something happened?"

"Misti has happened."

"What did she do?" Ethan asked.

"I don't have time to explain. This is a code red, all hands on deck, batten down the hatches situation. Just get back here."

Amara hung up without a response. She grabbed her purse from the desk drawer and pulled a couple of twenties from her wallet. "Who's over twenty-one or older?" she yelled from her office doorway. A couple of interns raised their hands. She called the one closest to her.

"Here," Amara said, putting the bills in the intern's hand, "take this and buy a chocolate cake with caramel whipped cream icing from Kroger. If they don't have one, drive around until you find one or have them make one. I don't care which, but don't think about coming back until you have one. I also need a chilled bottle of Riesling. It can be the cheap stuff—I don't care as long as it's cold. Got that?"

The intern nodded and left. Amara began making phone calls. First she called Serenity about the embezzled campaign funds that had magically reappeared. She also wanted to know how easily an outside source would be able to discover that they had ever been missing and if there were any way to prove Ethan wasn't complicit in the illegal activity.

She then tasked a couple of the interns with monitoring the social networks for comments on Misti's post, explaining to them what type of thing they should forward to her. She was just about to start drafting a press release when Jacqueline Bedloe walked through the front door and directly to Ethan's office.

"Hello, Mrs. Bedloe. What can I do for you?"

"You can call me anything but that. Please call me Jacqueline. I'll probably take my maiden name back after the divorce anyway."

"After what divorce?" Amara asked, hoping she'd misheard her.

"Mine. While my father was alive, I tolerated my husband's indiscretions because I didn't want to be disowned. That lowdown dog I made the mistake of marrying and I also had an agreement. He was supposed to be discreet. Well, my father's dead, and some piece of trash is publicizing the intimate details of her relationship with my husband all over the internet. I'm on my way to file and wanted Ethan to know I'm finally doing what he's been begging me to do for the last two years."

"Oh, okay," Amara repeated several times, too stunned and overwhelmed to say anything else. Then she added, "He should be back in a moment. Make yourself comfortable while you wait."

"Thank you. You're excellent with words. Do you think you can write my statement about the divorce?"

"I'll get right on that." She'd get right on it after figuring out how to salvage Ethan's campaign. Even though his father was the one with the questionable behavior, Ethan would be the one to pay the price. She shut the door behind her and leaned against it, taking deep breaths while trying to organize a game plan. She opened her eyes when she heard Ethan calling her name.

"Amara, Misti's timing for this couldn't be worse. We're a week away from the election," Ethan said.

"I know. We'll handle it. Your mom is in your office with some more news we'll have to handle."

She walked into her office and into the comforting arms of her husband. Ryan kissed the top of her head and rubbed her back. His arms had always been her place of comfort. Not being able to lean her head on his chest as she cried was one of the hardest parts of his betrayal. She wished she hadn't been too hurt to hear him out. After all, Ryan had been manipulated by Mrs. Layton too. She began to laugh.

"Am I missing something?" Ryan asked.

"I was just wishing I could be a fly on the wall when Mrs. Layton found out. She hitched her trailer to Will Bedloe, and now he's crashing and burning."

Ryan smiled down at her. "Isn't karma beautiful?"

"It certainly is. You want an exclusive?"

"Ethan?" Amara nodded. "I wanted to ask but didn't want to jeopardize us by asking that favor."

"It's no favor. This is mutually beneficial. A press conference would be too risky." She gave him one more kiss before going to her desk. "I'll have him at the studio in a couple of hours. By the time you get there, I'll have some questions I want you to ask him."

"No offense, Amara, but if you're giving me an exclusive, you need to let me do my job. I'm pretty good at it."

"I know you are, but so am I. There are just some points I need to be made, and the questions will help get them across. What's the benefit of an exclusive if I can't lead the interview a bit? I'm not asking this as a favor because you're my husband. It's a requirement that I would ask any journalist."

"You know you're really sexy when you're in political strategist genius mode."

"Well, the day is young, and by midnight I'll be the sexiest thing you've ever seen."

"You already are."

"You've already got an exclusive, flattery isn't necessary. Speaking of exclusives, you need to call your sister so you can get one with Misti."

Ryan took his phone out of his pocket.

"I may be able to get you an interview with the future ex-wife of the governor."

Ryan looked up from his phone with raised eyebrows. "Jacqueline Bedloe?"

"She's telling Ethan right now. She asked me to draft a press release for her."

"Way to bury the lead, Amara."

"Sorry, I didn't know that was the lead. Right now, I don't know up from down."

As Ryan left the office, the intern returned from her errand with the cake and wine in hand. "Is there anything else I can do for you, Ms. Adams?"

"Have you ever drafted a press release?"

"Only as a class assignment."

"Well, you're about to get some real world experience."

chapter 21

MISTI'S POSTS HAD GROWN LEGS fast. The selfies she'd taken with the governor were part of the reason. She'd even posted one with him groping her lace bra-clad breast. Within an hour, it had made national news. Somehow Ryan had been able to get promos on air for his exclusives with Ethan and Jacqueline. Amara had released official statements online for both Ethan and his mother. The one person who had remained quiet was the adulterer himself, Will Bedloe. Perhaps it was a strategy. Amara didn't see how, but maybe his people knew something she didn't know.

That wasn't the case. While his decades-long political career was being ambushed by a narcissist, he was having an afternoon delight. An industrious concierge at the downtown Conrad had conspired with one of the maids to get a photo of said afternoon delight. They would probably be unemployed by the end of the day, but there was no doubt *TMZ* paid them big bucks for those photos.

Catching a known womanizer with a woman other than his wife wasn't worth much, even if he was being touted as his party's front-runner for the next presidential election. What made the pictures valuable, however, was that the woman was the estranged wife a certain gay disgraced former senator from Illinois.

Amara wanted to print and frame those photos. Instead, she texted one to Ryan with a note that read simply "karma" with a smiley face. The woman who had tried to ruin her to get to the White House had just ruined herself for what Misti had described as the worst lay of her life. Actually, she'd said it was the worst lay in the history of lays.

A week later, Amara could count the number of hours of sleep on one hand and the number of cakes she'd eaten on both hands. Ethan's campaign had suffered. His platform didn't matter, and the fact that he had done nothing wrong didn't matter. The only thing that mattered was that he was a Bedloe. Her efforts to distance Ethan from his father were hindered by the fact that Will Bedloe strengthened their connection in every interview. He told Jacqueline that if she called off the divorce, he would stop sabotaging their son's campaign. He definitely wasn't going to win father of the year, but deadbeat of the year was his by a landslide. There were more baby mamas on the nightly news than on an episode of the Maury Povich show.

Most of the women came forward. Some wanted money. Some wanted their fifteen minutes of infamy.

Some wanted the money they thought they could get from the fifteen minutes of infamy. And there were those who only showed the palm of a hand in front of the camera, blocking it from capturing them on the screen as they hurried along, children in tow with hoods pulled over their faces. Investigative reporters had found those women. Ryan had even tracked down a few leads. That's what Amara was most stressed about. Even though she hadn't expected to lose this long-shot election this way, it hadn't bothered her. Her biggest concern was how close the entire world was getting to know a truth that Ryan had yet to find out.

All Amara wanted was a hot shower. That was a lie. What she really wanted was to lie in her husband's arm as she fell asleep, but she had to wash the grime of the past twenty-four hours off before she could do that. As she entered the house through the garage, she saw Ryan coming down the stairs.

"Good, you're home. I haven't been able to reach your phone for the past hour," Ryan said.

"Phone died, and I didn't charge it because I was sick of it ringing. Sorry I missed your calls. What's up?"

"Diane's in labor. She called me, her brother, after she couldn't get a hold of you. Come on, we need to get down there."

"But she's not due for like another two weeks. What's with the women in your family? Can't any of them go to their due date?"

THE NEARNESS OF YOU

"She's only a few days early. She's calling it stress labor and blaming it on Misti."

"Let me shower, and I'll be ready to go."

"We don't have time. I've already waited two hours just trying to reach you. I don't want to miss my first niece or nephew being born."

"It's sweet how excited you are to become an uncle. It makes me want to see you as the expectant father."

"We can work on me becoming a father right now," he said, grabbing her by the waist and pulling her in for a kiss.

She moved her head to the side. "If we have time for that, I have time for a shower," Amara said before heading to the bathroom.

The excitement had worn off after the third hour in the hospital with little progress toward the baby's arrival. Diane was sleeping—as best as a person can sleep with contractions every half hour—and Jack was right there, ready to hold her hand through every one. Noli was resting on the sleeping Cooper. Likewise, Amara was trying her best to sleep with her head resting on her husband and her body stretched across the uncomfortable waiting room chairs. She was roused out of her sleep by Ryan whispering in her ear. She didn't quite understand what he'd said.

"Is the baby here?" she asked.

"No, my parents are here."

She let out a sound that was more grunt than word. Nodding, she sat up long enough for him to stand. The next time Ryan whispered in her ear, the waiting room was awash in the soft glow of the early morning sun, and Diane had just given birth to her son.

"Wake up, beautiful. My nephew has made his debut," Ryan said in Amara's ear. "He takes after his uncle."

She stretched and worked the kinks out of her neck. "I thought you said he was handsome," she teased.

The delivery room was crowded. All four grandparents were standing around the bed, gushing over how beautiful the baby was. Rose Sloan, Jack's mother, had managed to move closer to her grandchild than her son was. Amara could tell that it took every bit of the woman's self-control not to snatch the baby out of Diane's arms.

"Amara, come see your nephew," Diane said, smiling down at the baby. She made a face at her slip of the tongue.

"Are you sure?" Amara asked, looking at Rose. She was afraid of coming between the woman and her first grandchild. Amara reached down and carefully gathered the swaddled baby into her arms. She raised the edge of the striped blue and pink cap he was wearing to see if he had any hair. "He's so beautiful, and he has so much hair."

"It was all the heartburn she had," Rose said.

Amara looked from Catherine to Robert and then down at the baby in her arms. She wondered if Robert had once held the baby Ryan in his arms, not knowing it wasn't his son. She remained lost in her thoughts and missed most of the conversation that occurred, but the elevated voices got her attention.

"What did I miss?" Amara said.

"You did not miss anything, but we missed your wedding to my son," Catherine said.

Amara looked at Diane. "Seriously?"

Diane raised and lowered her shoulder and flipped her hand through the air in an exaggerated gesture. "Like I told your husband when he asked me that two seconds ago, blame it on the Demerol or the epidural, but don't blame me."

"There is no need to blame it on medication when the only two people who should shoulder the blame are the two people who kept it a secret. How long have you been married?"

Amara squinted as she tried to calculate.

"The girl does not even know how long she has been married," Catherine said exasperatedly.

Ryan put an arm around Amara, kissed the top of her head, and smiled down at their nephew before saying, "About nineteen months."

"Why have you kept your marriage a secret for over a year and a half?" Catherine asked in a tone that commanded an answer.

"You know better than any of us that there are reasons to keep secrets." Amara held Catherine's glare with her own unwavering, cutting look.

"What exactly is that supposed to mean, young lady?"

Amara wondered if anyone else saw the hitching Catherine's breath. Perhaps she was the only one looking for it. When she saw it, she knew beyond a reasonable doubt that Ryan was not a Clark. She also knew that the other woman knew that Amara knew. She let out a breath to calm herself. This would be the worst possible place and time for Ryan to find out the truth. For his sake—and for Robert's sake if he didn't already know the truth—she would back down from this fight with Catherine.

"It means that I'm operating on about two hours' sleep and am too exhausted to have this conversation. We're here to celebrate the birth of your first grandchild. I suggest we do that," Amara said.

"I would like to speak with you outside." Catherine moved toward the door, not expecting to be denied. She only stopped when she saw a Ryan heading toward the door. "Not you, Ryan, just your...wife."

"Mother, I don't think—"

"It's okay, Ryan," Amara said. She was about to hand the baby to Diane, but Rose was there by her side to take him. Amara followed Catherine to a secluded area near Diane's room. "I shouldn't have said that."

"Your apology is not accepted," Catherine said.

"No apology was given. I literally meant I should not have said that. This is neither the time nor the place, and I am not the person to tell Ryan the truth."

"You are also not the person to decide if he needs to know the truth."

"You're right, I'm not, but at this point, neither are you. It's already been decided. The question isn't *if* you're going to tell him, it's *when* you're going to do it. If you don't tell him, I will."

"You will not tell him."

"I don't want to, but I will. I know how it feels to have your life destroyed on TV, and I won't let that happen to him. I love him too much for that. As his mother, you should love him enough to sacrifice him being mad at you for a while so that he can hear it from you, not me—and definitely not from a stranger."

"No one is going to find out."

"I found out, and I wasn't even trying to. Get your head out the sand. Five of his children from outside his marriage have already come to light, and people are digging for more. Is there a slim chance they won't find out? Yes, but it's not worth the risk to see if that happens. Jacqueline Bedloe knows he has a son older than Ethan because she got the check her father sent you to abort your child and go away. There's no telling who she's let that slip to. And if Will had any clue that Ryan was your son, he will put two and two together and not waste the chance to sell him up the river. At this point, that man is going down, and he's taking as many people with him as he can, so don't for a second think that he won't take you and Ryan along for the ride."

"Robert's name is on the birth certificate. There is no proof that he is not his father."

Amara shook her head. "Proof? What world do you live in that they have to have proof before they run with the story? Broadcast now, find proof later."

"It does not matter what you say. You do not scare me."

Amara turned at the sound of footsteps approaching. It was Jack. She hoped he hadn't overheard anything.

"Can you ladies have this conversation some other time? My wife is ready to get out of her hospital bed because she feels bad about you two fighting. So paste on a smile and get back in there before I'm the one you both have a problem with." Taking a page out of Catherine's book, Jack turned around and walked away, not expecting to be dismissed.

"Tell him," Amara said and followed Jack.

When she got back in the room, Diane mouthed the words 'I'm sorry' to Amara. She nodded and smiled. Ryan came to stand next to her and whispered an apology in her ear. She smiled at him and hoped her emotions were well-masked. She took his hand into hers. A few months ago, it had been difficult to be in the room with him, not wanting him near her, but faking the distance that day was equally as hard. It was comforting to not have the anger or the pretense of being just friends between them. It felt good to feel the warmth of his fingers laced between hers. It also frightened her because she knew it might not last much longer.

chapter 22

LITTLE DID SHE KNOW HOW soon the storm would come. Things began to go downhill rapidly. First, Will Bedloe was all over the TV, in handcuffs being arrested for misappropriation of campaign funds and various other offenses that could best be summarized as an abuse of power. It turned out Serenity was not the only one looking into the financial dealings of Will Bedloe—the federal government had been too. In all, there were twelve counts, and there would have been more if it weren't for the statute of limitations. He hadn't resigned yet, but there was no doubt that his time as governor would come to an early end. If he didn't resign, he'd be impeached.

Over the years and his various political offices, Will had awarded contracts to companies based on kickbacks and not qualifications. The company Jacqueline had inherited from her father was on the list several times. Though all of the shady dealings had taken place between

Will and Jacqueline's father, as the current CEO of the company and estranged wife of the indicted governor, she too was made into a pariah by the media. The value of the stock was free falling.

The cherry on top of it all was Misti's frequent interviews as a "Bedloe insider." She wouldn't have to worry about child support because Lifetime had offered her a movie deal. It was already in pre-production. While they didn't cast her to play herself, as she'd wanted, she was co-writer and co-producer. For a dumb blond, she was pretty smart.

With both parents in a negative spotlight, Ethan's support was disappearing. Interviewers wouldn't let him speak about anything else but his parents and the ever-increasing count of his half siblings. When Amara thought things couldn't get any worse, Will Bedloe gave a lie-ridden deposition that put the nail in the campaign's coffin and possibly Ethan's entire political career.

Ethan's uncharacteristic cursing echoed throughout the now sparsely populated campaign office and reverberated in Amara's office. Then there was a crashing sound. She hung up on the reporter on the other end of the phone without saying goodbye and ran to Ethan's office. Half the contents of his desk were on the floor, and paper was scattered everywhere. It was counter-intuitive, but his fit of uncontrolled rage made her respect him more. It was good to know he had some fight in him. He needed some fire to make it in this business.

Nice guys finish in the primaries. A nice guy with suppressed anger could win it all. The third US president from the state of Indiana was standing before her.

"He's claiming one of us took the funds from my campaign and he had nothing to do with it," Ethan said, answering her unasked question.

"What?" Somehow Amara was shocked by Will Bedloe's actions.

Ethan rewound the news back until his father's face appeared on the screen. "My accounting team managed my son's campaign funds, but the only two people who had access to the funds were Ethan and his campaign manager, Amara Adams. Any issue with his campaign funds can likely be traced back to her. Her less than ethical reputation precedes her. I would hate to think my son would do such a thing, but with the negative influence of his beguiling campaign manager, I can't say for sure he's not culpable. What I do know is that that's one crime that I am not involved in."

Ethan muted the TV when the reporting started speaking. "Why are you smiling?" he asked Amara.

"Because your daddy just gave an Emmy-worthy performance, but I'm about to give an Oscar-worthy one and teach him that he should make sure the fuse is good and long when he lights dynamite or it will blow up in his face."

"I don't understand."

Amara dialed a number on her phone and waited for an answer. "You don't have to," she said to Ethan. "Hello, Mr. Clark," she said into the phone.

"You know it turns me on when you call me Mr. Clark, Mrs. Clark."

"The purpose of this call is that another station just aired the exclusive footage from Will Bedloe's deposition."

"You also know that it turns me on when you're so professional."

Her husband could be incorrigible at times, and she liked to encourage him. "I'm going to take that as a yes, Mr. Clark. Would you like an exclusive response from Ethan and his campaign manager?"

"Of course. Can you be ready for a live shot in an hour?"

"We'll see you then."

"I'm glad I brought my glasses today."

"Are your contacts bothering you?" Ethan asked, returning to his normal concerned, nice guy self.

"No, but the cameras may not pick up my tears, so I need to draw attention to my uncontrollable emotions by taking my glasses off and wiping away my tears. Do you have a handkerchief?"

"Yes," he said, reaching into his pocket, not understanding what was going on.

"I don't need it now, but be a gentleman and hand it to me when I start crying during the interview."

"Amara, I'm confused."

"Don't worry, that's why I'm about to write your statement. This campaign may be a loss, but we're about to save your political career and distance you from your father."

AN HOUR LATER, ETHAN and Amara sat next to each other in front of an "Ethan for Senate" sign. Bright lights shined in their faces, and a camera was focused on them. Amara had changed into slacks and an off-white blouse. The pants were to prevent too much leg from showing while seated during the interview. The blouse was to conceal all hints of cleavage while also making her appear innocent. A few minutes before they went live, Amara emailed Ryan and his producer a video.

"Why didn't you send this to me an hour ago?" Ryan asked. I don't have time to review this before we air."

"Your producers do."

"What is this video?"

She paused long enough that the producers were telling Ryan in his ear piece that he was going live. Amara didn't have time to explain.

Ever the professional, Ryan smiled on cue. "Thank you Ericka. In a portion of Will Bedloe's deposition released today, he denies the allegations of misappropriation of funds. According to the disgraced governor, he had no involvement in the funds that magically disappeared and then, with the exception of $10,000, reappeared. I'm with Ethan Bedloe and Amara Adams at his campaign office to get their side of the story." The camera turned to Ethan and Amara. "I'll cut right to the chase—are either of you responsible for the missing money?" Ryan asked.

"Neither of us is responsible for the missing money," Ethan said, repeating the words Amara had written for him verbatim. "The only involvement we've had in this entire ordeal was trusting Will Bedloe and his finance team. I take full responsibility for that. When I hired Ms. Adams, she discovered the fraudulent activity and had an outside accounting firm verify it."

"Ms. Adams, why didn't you take the evidence directly to the authorities?"

"I had no way of proving that Ethan, or for that matter anyone directly involved with his campaign, had no involvement," Amara said.

"I had no incentive to commit such an act. When I turned thirty, I gained complete access to a sizable trust." Ethan said. "When my grandfather died, I inherited a considerable number of shares in Prescott Inc. I had no need to take the donations of the constituents who had found me worthy enough as a candidate to contribute their hard-earned money."

"Will Bedloe was bedding women high and bedding them low throughout the state," Amara said. "He needed money to do that. When his father-in-law died, he no longer had access to the Prescott's coffers. Jacqueline

Bedloe, his wife and the company's new CEO, would have discovered he was embezzling from the company, and her long-held suspicions of his infidelity would have been confirmed. In his mind, he had no option but to move to campaign funds. Since he was not running, the only choice he could make was to turn to his trusting son's campaign funds."

"Why are you coming forward now? What's changed?"

"After the activity was discovered, I confronted Will Bedloe directly. I had met him many times, but that was the first time I met the *real* Will Bedloe." Her voice took on a somber tone. "He admitted to having taken the money." She became silent for two heartbeats. When she spoke again, the crocodile tear she'd manufactured sat in the corner of her eye, ready to fall. She took a deep breath and continued. "Not only did he confess, he also accosted me with unwanted sexual advances." She took her glasses off to wipe the tear that was now falling down her face. Ryan reacted quicker than Ethan and handed her his handkerchief. "

"While I don't doubt your version of events, his alleged confession and attack are merely hearsay. It's nothing more than your word against his."

"I have photos taken of the black eye I received fighting him off."

A slide show of the photos she'd taken just in case displayed on the screen for the viewers at home.

"If these photos are to be believed, why didn't you go to the police and report the assault?"

"As you said, it was his word against mine."

"Then I have to ask you the same question I asked earlier. Why come forward now? What has changed?"

"I discovered a video on my phone where the meeting had accidentally been recorded."

"How do we know this video is authentic?" His voice may have sounded accusatory to the viewer, but it was laced with anger.

Amara kept her composure. Ryan had a right to be angry. She'd blindsided him with this video. She had been blindsided when she had discovered it. "Though a portion of the video's frame is obstructed by the back pocket of my purse, Will Bedloe can still be clearly seen and heard on the recording. It's also been explained to me that the metadata that is automatically stored on photos and videos taken with smartphones can verify the location and date of the video."

"It's difficult to believe that you went to confront the then governor of Indiana and accidentally recorded the meeting."

"I wish I could tell you I had been smart enough to purposely record the meeting, but I wasn't. The first few minutes of the video is, unfortunately, me singing quite off-key to the radio as I drove to see the governor."

"We will now play this video. Viewer discretion is advised. Some of the video is graphic in nature, but we

THE NEARNESS OF YOU

will air it in its entirety as it shows the actual acts of former Governor Will Bedloe."

They cut away from the live shot to the video, and Ryan and Ethan both stood to look at the small playback screen that showed what the viewers at home were seeing. Amara didn't bother to watch it again. When she'd discovered the recording and watched it, she had at first thought it was another funny accidental recording—the quick-record button she had set up to easily record on the campaign trail often recorded snippets of things. The actuality of what had happened was far worse than her memory. She'd must have instantly blocked out his hand on her breast and the fact he had managed to pry her knees apart and come to stand between her legs. Once was enough to see this. She'd never wanted to see it again, but now it would be everywhere.

His smug face on the TV earlier, blaming her and Ethan—the victims—had angered her into making a rash decision. She wanted him to pay. She'd been so enraged that revenge was all she could see and hadn't thought about what having her attack played over and over again would feel like. It was too late to turn back now. The bravado she'd had earlier was gone because she could still hear the audio in her earpiece. It sounded as bad as it looked. The tears that flowed down her cheeks were real. Ryan noticed, but the producers informed them that the shot was back on them, live.

Amara dabbed the tears from her face, praying that her waterproof makeup lived up to its name.

"Again, I apologize to the viewers at home for the graphic images and words of the video." Ryan, breaking from his journalistic professionalism to be a husband by taking his wife's hand said, "Amara, if you don't feel like continuing, we don't have to."

"Reliving that again was difficult, but I can continue," she said.

Ryan squeezed her hand before letting it go and resuming his role as a reporter. "Mr. Bedloe—"

"Please call me Ethan."

"Ethan, were you aware of this video?" Maybe he hadn't totally relinquished the role of husband. That question was more jealous husband wanting to know if his wife had shared something with another man that she had kept hidden from him than it was journalistic curiosity.

"I just saw that video for the first time just now, like everyone else," Ethan said.

"When I first saw the recording, I just wanted to forget it existed, much like I wanted to erase the memory of that evening from my mind. When I saw the former governor's statement an hour ago, I knew I had to speak up and tell the truth. Even then, I wasn't sure that I wanted to share the video. My decision to air it was not made until moments before we began the interview. I didn't have time to make Ethan aware of its existence."

"You didn't know about the video, but did you know about the attack?" Ryan asked.

"I was aware of it."

"Did you discourage Ms. Adams from reporting it to the police?"

"Not at all. I was insistent that she report it, the decision not to was hers. As she said, at the time, she believed it to be her word against his," Ethan said.

"Will you be pressing charges now?" Ryan asked.

"When it happened, he was still the powerful and well-respected governor of Indiana. I still bore the stigma of being the campaign manager wrongly accused of outing my boss, Senator Layton. Of course, now that I have proof, I will be contacting the police. I don't want Will Bedloe to ever again be in a position to assault another woman. My experience with him makes me wonder how many of his alleged mistresses were in consensual relationships with him."

Speculation was worse than actual facts and hard evidence. Amara wanted to not only nail Will Bedloe's coffin shut but lower it in the ground as well.

"Ms. Adams, you were wrongly accused of revealing Senator Layton's homosexuality? You were not the one who anonymously sent me those photos of the senator and his male lover?" Ryan asked.

Amara smiled, Ryan was getting retribution from Mrs. Layton while simultaneously putting the dirt on the grave of Will Bedloe's political career. "No, I was not your source. It was framed by Mrs. Layton."

"That's a pretty hefty allegation."

"It's not an allegation. She admitted as much in my office," Ethan said. "She knew a secret like that wouldn't remain hidden through the rigors of a presidential race, so she sabotaged Senator Layton so that her lover, my father, could become the front-runner."

"Is there an accidental video of this confession as well?"

"No, but there's plenty of evidence to support the accusation." And she would make sure that every news organization from CNN to *TMZ* had it.

"Ethan, voters have expressed concern that you are like your father."

"Many think I entered politics to follow in my father's footsteps. That is not true. I entered politics to be a public servant, to better the lives of the citizens of this state and hopefully this country. I didn't do it for the power, and honestly, I would make more money working for my mother. I do this because there are kids who have no dinner because their parents can't find a job. I'm in this because there are middle school kids who can't read. I became a public servant to change those things."

"This is what I know about Ethan. He is not his father," Amara said. "His father spent so much time philandering and embezzling money from the good people of Indiana that he didn't have time to raise his son. Outside of photo ops, Will Bedloe had little to do with Ethan. His mother Jacqueline, a remarkable woman, is single handedly responsible for the content of his character. Will Bedloe had as much to do with raising Ethan as he did with raising the many other children we now know he fathered. Being a member of the same household did not make Will Bedloe any less of a deadbeat dad to Ethan."

"With the Bedloe name being ruined, do you plan on retiring from politics?"

"As Amara pointed out, my mother practically raised me as a single mother. Today, my father demonstrated that the father and son relationship holds no value to him, as he was willing to perjure himself to try and bring me down with him. It is for this and many other, more personal, reasons that I will be legally changing my name to Ethan Prescott."

chapter 23

THE INTERVIEW HELPED BOOST ETHAN'S spirits and gave them hope for the next election, but he lost the current one by double digits. Even after the election, the media remained camped outside Ethan's house. The Will Bedloe news cycle had not ended yet. Amara sat on the edge of her bed, her cell phone still in her hands, after having finished a conversation with a journalist who wanted a statement from Ethan regarding a potential older half sibling that Will Bedloe had fathered while in law school. It was only a matter of time before that led to Ryan. Catherine had been quiet, making it clear that she was standing by her ill-advised decision not to tell the truth. She had ignored Amara's calls, and in uncharacteristic fashion, had not called her son a single time. She'd been left no choice but to be the bearer of bad news.

There was no telling how Ryan was going to react, but she doubted it would be positive. She opened the drawer on her nightstand and dug into her stash of caramel. The few that she ate brought no enjoyment or relief, so she slipped on her running clothes and running shoes. She needed to run off her nervousness and build up her nerves before talking to Ryan.

RYAN WAS EXCITED TO see Amara's car in the garage when he pulled up, even if she had prevented him from pulling in by parking slightly askew. A quick search of the house had him disappointed because she wasn't there. Ryan was bent over in the refrigerator looking for something to snack on when he heard Amara come home. As he suspected, she had been out running. She was drenched with sweat, which let him know it hadn't been a "stay healthy" run, but one of her runs where she was working through stress by pushing her body to the limit. He would much prefer she push the limits with him in bed, but she had chosen to run instead. It was a choice she'd made frequently since Ethan's campaign had started its downward spiral.

"You're home early."

Ryan looked at his watch. It was actually later than he had been getting home, but he didn't bother to point that out. She must have lost track of time. How long had her run been? "You want to go out for dinner tonight?"

"I'd rather stay in, but you don't have to cook. We can just order a pizza or Chinese. Whatever you want. I'm not really hungry."

Ryan put his hands on her waist. She pulled back and lost her balance, falling up the stairs. He put his hands in his pockets. "Are you okay?" he asked.

"I'm fine, just really sweaty."

"I'll order food while you shower."

Amara started up the stairs and stopped on the landing. "Did you get a call from a John Peterson today?"

"Who?" The concern he saw in her eyes dissipated.

"Never mind," she said and hurried up the stairs.

The loss had hit her harder than he expected. He'd thought she would be okay because she had known Ethan would lose. Ethan seemed to have taken the loss in stride. Maybe it was the fact that it was the second campaign in a row that she'd lost.

Initially, Ryan had been jealous of Ethan. It was only natural for an estranged husband to feel that way about a handsome, accomplished, and wealthy bachelor who spent more time with his wife than he. Then there was the misunderstanding over Amara's bruised and busted lip that had led to Ryan's regrettable actions. But once he got to know him and discovered how much they had in common, Ryan liked him and now considered him a friend. There was a good chance Ethan's lifetime membership at one of the best golf courses in the area would propel him right up to best friend status.

"Sorry."

Ryan was startled because he hadn't heard Amara come back downstairs. She was wearing his old sweatshirt again. She wore it frequently. Early on, that had given him hope that she would forgive him. Now it comforted him because it confirmed she loved him just as much as he loved her.

"Sorry for what?" he asked tossing the magazine, he'd been reading onto the coffee table.

"For wasting a year of our marriage on anger."

"It doesn't matter, we're past that now." His abandoned doubt found its way back home to the recesses of his mind. He knew Amara's many moods, but he didn't recognize the one was in at that moment. "We are past that, right?"

She bit her bottom lip and was wringing her hands. Then she began pacing. "My anger was justifiable after all—you lied to me."

He wasn't sure if she was talking to him or just talking out loud to herself. Either way, he didn't like the way the conversation was headed. "Lying to you was a mistake," he said, "and one you know I'll never make again."

"I don't know that, and neither do you. You lied to protect me. You may do that again. It's a hard decision to make. The truth is painful, but so is a lie in its own way."

"I really don't know where this is coming from," Ethan said. He couldn't sit any longer. He walked toward her, but she walked away and began pacing on the other side of the room. He heeded her nonverbal communication and began his own pacing, his hands buried deep in his pockets.

"It's coming from me lying because I wanted to protect you. I should have just told you. Maybe the truth is the best protection. This secret has been nibbling away at me from the inside out, and now I'm hollow. Just hollow."

She flopped down into a chair then immediately stood back up. She wasn't making eye contact with him or even looking in his general direction.

Her countenance had his doubt unpacking and reclaiming full residency in his mind. "Is this about Ethan?"

She drew her eyebrows together and nodded. "In a way it is."

"You two did have a relationship. You're trying to tell me it didn't stop when I came back. Or are you telling me you're choosing him?"

For the first time since the conversation began, she looked directly at him. "God no. I wouldn't do that. The only thing I've done is withhold information from you. I convinced myself it wasn't my place to tell you. Maybe I was really trying to protect myself. Maybe I didn't want to be the one to tell you because I didn't want you to hate the messenger."

"Amara, whatever you're about to say can't be that bad." He approached her slowly and took her into his arms. "I could never hate you."

She rested her head on his chest. "You may not hate me, but I predict you'll not like me much all the same."

He caressed her back and kissed her head. He took her chin between his fingers and tilted her head up. "I'll love you and like you. I promise." He pressed his lips to hers, kissing her long and slow until he felt her relax in his arms. She stayed there, pressed against him. He enjoyed her there, but he knew this was the calm of the eye of the storm, and the trailing winds would be worse.

"I love you, Ryan. Please remember that." She pulled away as if she would rather stay wrapped in his arms.

He watched as she walked out the room and returned with a book in hand. With deliberation, she turned to a page and slid the book in front of him. He looked at the two pages and failed to see what the big deal was. There was a picture of an intramural sports team on one page and various acappella groups on the other. Ryan looked at Amara with raised eyebrows and shook his head.

Amara pointed at a picture. She wasn't pointing at the two athletes with their arms wrapped around each other's shoulders but at the background. One glistening ruby red nail was all it took for his world to begin to unravel. Even with her head partially obscured by the person she was kissing, he could recognize his mother. The person she was kissing was not his father. His eyes wandered down the picture to the date underneath. It was less than nine months before his birth.

Ryan knew that he had been conceived before his parents graduated college and, more importantly, before they married. Simple math had revealed that secret to him when he was twelve. There was only six months between their graduation and his birth. Then they wed two weeks after receiving their diplomas. He'd always assumed they'd had a shotgun wedding because his dad was the type of man to take care of his responsibilities. Now he was wondering if his mother, well aware of Robert's character, had pinned the pregnancy on him.

He picked the yearbook back up and looked more closely at the photograph. "Why does this guy look familiar?"

"Because he's been all over the news lately." Her voice became really quiet. "That's Will Bedloe."

"This," he pointed at the photo, "this doesn't mean anything." He picked the book up and threw it across the room where its edge slammed into the wall with enough force to put a small dent in the painted drywall.

She placed a comforting hand on his back. He shot her a look that made her remove it.

"The picture alone doesn't prove a thing," Amara said. "It could've been just a kiss—a moment of passion— but this says otherwise." She slid an envelope in front of him.

He pulled the contents out. He picked up a check that fell out as he was unfolding the letter. It was made out to his mother, using her maiden name of Jefferson, in the amount of $5,000. He set it down and read the letter.

Dear Mr. Prescott,

Enclosed you will find the uncashed check you sent to me. I cannot accept your money as I will not honor your request to abort my child. However, I will use the utmost discretion by never sharing the fact that your new son-in-law, William Bedloe, is the father. There will be no public record as I have determined it would be prudent to list my fiancé on the birth certificate.

Furthermore, you should have no concern of my relationship with Mr. Bedloe becoming public knowledge. My misguided and unrequited feelings for him are something I would prefer to be forgotten by all parties involved. I wish the newlyweds many happy years of matrimony.

As you have my above assurance to never divulge my association with Mr. Bedloe, this should be the last communication between you and my family.

Sincerely,
Catherine Jefferson

Ryan folded the letter and placed it back in the envelope. His facial expression remained neutral, as if he'd just read a credit card pre-approval. The thoughts in his head, however, were not so calm and organized. Questions with no answers and epiphanies came in rapid succession. His sister was now his half-sister. His wife's boss, Ethan, was now his half-brother. He was no longer sure exactly who he was. So much of how he defined himself had changed. Now he knew he was biracial. He could no longer check "black" but had to check "other." He was no longer Ryan Clark. In an instant, he felt lost.

He studied every inch of the letter, including the frayed edges of the envelope, trying to distract himself from his thoughts. The crisp and neat letters on the envelope matched the letter, and it was easy for Ryan to recognize it as his mother's handwriting. The addressee was Jonathan Prescott. The return address read "Catherine Jefferson" at what must have been her college address. The stamp had Indiana at the top with a picture of a cardinal on the branch of a flower. The postmark over the cardinal on the stamp was in May of the same year as his birth.

Amara stood next to him. He could see her in his peripheral vision, glancing his way every now and then but otherwise not looking in his direction. He couldn't look at her, but it wasn't because he blamed her. True to his promise, how he felt about her hadn't changed. He was trying to distance her from this soul-wrenching moment as best he could. He didn't want to associate her with the betrayal and pain he was experiencing. He understood why she hadn't wanted to be the one who told him. Keeping this secret bottled up since the night of the storm must have killed her. He wished he could be of some comfort, but right now he was barely mustering up enough energy to stand.

The sound of the doorbell jarred him. "That must be the food. I'll get it."

chapter 24

"**H**ELLO? Is anyone else home?"

Confused, Amara walked to the front door to see the young delivery driver holding the greasy brown paper bags of Chinese food and a $50 bill, but no Ryan. She brushed past the young man in time to see Ryan's tail lights disappearing around the corner. She pulled out her cell phone to call her husband as she entered the house.

"Do you need change?"

"Sorry," Amara said, listening to the phone ringing unanswered. "Keep the change." When Ryan's voicemail picked up, she hung up and dialed again.

The delivery guy, a huge smile on his face for his big tip, tried to hand the food to Amara. When she didn't take it, he looked around for a place to set it. Not finding one, he put it on the floor and backed out the door, slowly pulling it closed behind him.

Amara continued to call for the next hour. When her call started going to voicemail after two rings, she knew

278

that he was okay because he was ignoring her. That made her both relieved and pissed. She stopped trying to get him on the phone and decided to find him. She drove to the indoor driving range to see if maybe he was hitting some golf balls. He sometimes did that when he was stressed. Of course, she wouldn't really know if he was stressed because he hadn't said anything. She had absolutely no clue what his state of mind was. Maybe he was drowning his sadness in beer and wings, but he wasn't at the pub that he swore had the best wings in town, and the toggle place he liked was closed. The security guard at the studio was nice enough to lumber down to Ryan's office to be sure he wasn't just ignoring the phone, but he was, in fact, not there.

There was a possibility he'd gone home to talk to his parents face to face. Enough time had passed that he would be there if that's where he'd gone, but she was already driving as a nervous wreck. She thought it best to wait until she got home to make that phone call. When she walked through the door, she was greeted by ants swarming all over the bag of Chinese food on the floor. Her husband was MIA. She was hungry but too stressed to eat. And even if she wanted to force food down, she couldn't because the ants had it. It was more than she could handle and she began to cry. Tears rolled down her face unhindered as she cleaned up the mess.

"Hi, Mr. Clark. Have you heard from Ryan?" Amara had tried to reach Catherine, but of course, she didn't answer.

"I've not talked to him for the last couple of days. You don't sound too good. Is everything okay?" Robert asked.

"No, Ryan left the house upset, and I haven't been able to reach him. Is your wife available?"

"What was he upset about?" Robert asked.

Having already made one Clark man aware of Ryan's true paternity with disastrous results, she didn't want to have to inform a second. "I just need to speak to Catherine, but she's not answering her phone. Can you please put her on the phone?"

There was a long pause. Amara thought he was taking the phone to Catherine, but Robert's voice came back on the line. "So he knows?"

Could he possibly know? Amara hadn't really thought about that possibility. She just assumed he didn't. Now that she was thinking about it, though, passing off a full-term baby as three months premature would be almost impossible. Then again, Catherine could have been a little loose in her youth and could have been sleeping with both men during the window of conception. "Knows what, sir?"

"That I'm not his father."

"How did...How long...Ryan," Amara said, finally able to get her brain to send her mouth a complete sentence.

"Why did you tell him?"

"Because I got a call today from a reporter who knew everything but Ryan's name."

"I guess it was best coming from you."

"It would've been better coming from your wife or you. Our marriage was already on thin ice, and I don't know if it'll survive this." In uncharacteristically rude fashion, Amara hung up on him.

AMARA BEGAN TO TRY Ryan again. At first, the phone just rang until voicemail picked up. Then it started going directly to voicemail. That intensified her anxiety. She dialed another number.

"Diane, is Ryan there?" Amara asked.

"Amara, what's going on?" Diane asked in response. "My father just called here and said that both you and Ryan hung up on him."

"Your father was able to get hold of him?" Amara said, feeling hope for the first time since he'd left.

"Please tell me what's going on. I'm starting to get worried."

"I'll call you back. I need to talk to your dad." Amara hung up and called Robert. "You talked to Ryan?"

"I did. It didn't go too well. He ended the call when I let it slip that I knew."

Had Ryan had done something irrational now that he knew both of his parents had lied to him his entire life? "Did you find out where he was?"

"From what I could tell, he was still in Indy. Catherine and I are on our way down."

Amara didn't know how to respond, so for the second time that night, she hung up on her father-in-law. It was becoming a bad habit.

Amara jumped when the phone rang. She hoped it was Ryan but feared it was the police with bad news. It was neither. It was Diane.

"Amara, tell me what's going on with my brother. My parents are giving me the runaround. I need a straight answer from you."

"He left the house upset a few hours ago."

"What was he upset about? Did you ask for a divorce? Are you leaving him for Ethan?"

"No, no. For the last time, Ethan and I are just colleagues and friends."

"For the last time? This is the first time I've said anything about you and Ethan. Ryan voiced his concern once, but I lied and told him he had nothing to worry about."

"That's not a lie," Amara said. "He has no reason to be concerned."

"Yes, he does. Ethan is handsome, really nice, and wealthy. If Jack wasn't my husband, and Will Bedloe wasn't his father, I would be interested." Amara began to cry again, and Diane stopped chuckling. "You are really starting to worry me. You're crying. You don't cry. What is going on?"

A loud sob exploded from Amara. Diane spoke soft, comforting words to try to comfort her friend as she continued to cry.

"Jack, come take the baby," Diane said away from the phone. Her husband could be heard in the background asking what was wrong. "I'm not sure. I think Amara needs me to go up there. Yes, I know it's late."

Amara sniffled and said, "He's right. It's too late for you to be driving up here, but I'd appreciate it if you came first thing in the morning."

"Of course. Do you think you're up to telling me what's going on right now, though?"

"I think it would be best to wait until the morning."

THE NEXT AFTERNOON, AMARA, Diane, and Robert and Catherine all sat in silence in various parts of the house. Amara had filled Diane in on Ryan's true paternity, and Diane refused to talk to either of them when they arrived. Out of respect, Amara didn't say anything either because none of the words she had for them would be pleasant. Amara sat in a chair in the living room where she could hear either door open. When the doorbell rang, she jumped up and was the first there, though the others weren't far behind.

"What are you doing here?"

"Ryan was supposed to meet me to play a round of golf today, but he didn't show up and I couldn't get him on his phone. I was checking to see if everything was okay, but I would guess no," Ethan said, taking in her appearance.

"Ryan's missing. No one has talked to him since last night."

"This is a family matter, Amara. There is no need to bring him into it," Catherine said.

"He is family," Amara said. Her eyes dared Catherine to rebut her. She didn't.

Amara took Ethan into the study and explained everything to him. The news was getting easier and easier to tell. Or maybe she was just numb. Ethan took it surprisingly well. Or maybe he too was numb. After the first five illegitimate half siblings popped up, the shock had probably worn off.

"One of the guys I hired as security is a former state police officer. I'll see if he has any connections that can help. Maybe he can issue an unofficial APB on his car."

Afternoon turned to evening and evening into night. Ryan hadn't called, and there would been no sightings of his car by the state police. He'd had preexisting plans to go out of town for business, but the airline wouldn't release any information, and he'd not checked into the hotel where he was supposed to stay. She hadn't wanted to alarm his producer or jeopardize his job, but after twenty-four hours, she called his boss. He hadn't heard from him, either, but he said that was normal. It was as if he'd disappeared from the face of the earth.

Amara suggested her in-laws stay at a hotel. If Ryan returned, it would be best that they weren't what he returned to. It took some convincing, but Amara finally talked Diane into going home to her baby and husband.

She agreed on the condition that Amara promised to call as soon as she heard anything. She also promised she'd be back first thing in the morning with Noli, who was upset Diane hadn't told her Ryan was missing so she could be there.

"You should go too," Amara said to Ethan after everyone else had gone.

"Okay, but call me after you call the rest of his family. You and he have both been there for me. Plus, I know some of what Ryan's going through. I've had my life turned upside down and have had to deal with siblings coming out of the woodwork. More importantly, I've had decades of living with the poisonous blood of Will Bedloe flowing through my veins, and it hasn't turned me into a super villain."

Amara cracked a small smile. "Who would you be? Lex Luthor? He did become president."

"I was thinking more Paste Pot Pete."

"Stop making stuff up."

He put a hand over his heart and one in the air. "I'm not making it up. He's a real, fictional super villain. Like you, he's from Gary, Indiana. Some mock him as one of the lamest characters to ever grace the pages of comic books, but I'd disagree. I've debated his qualities as a character online several times."

Amara just stared at him. "Please never let any of this come from your lips again. No one can ever know exactly how much of a fanboy you are."

He put his fist on his waist. "I am Fanboy. I use my vast knowledge of useless and obscure comic book and sci-fi facts to save the day."

Amara chuckled and smiled, shaking her head. "I don't see how that could save the day."

"It just did. I put a smile on the face of a damsel in distress. You're probably going to search the web for Paste Pot Pete to see if you need to expunge any nerdy arguments I've gotten into with anonymous strangers. But don't you worry, I don't use my real name. I'm SuperHoosier415."

He was right—it was indeed a super power. For the first time in almost two days, she smiled. In those wee hours when she was wide awake with worry, she would probably Google Paste Pot Pete to see if he was a real super villain just to get her mind off things.

chapter 25

THE SUN HAD JUST STARTED to peek over the horizon, bringing enough light that shapes could be distinguished in the pitch darkness. Amara was on the couch, willing herself to go back to sleep. After two sleepless nights, Amara was exhausted, but every time she fell to sleep, thoughts and dreams of Ryan being hurt somewhere woke her. The alarm's notification that the door from the garage was ajar sounded. As she had done countless times over the last couple of days, Amara hopped up.

"Ryan!"

Sheer joy at seeing Ryan propelled her forward. She wrapped her arms around him with such force that he would have choked had he not wrapped his arms around her and picked her up off her feet. She was crying into his neck, and he could feel her heart pounding against his chest. This was not the reaction he had expected to his return. He'd thought he was taking a huge risk by not wearing a bulletproof vest and a protective cup.

"I'm sorry, Amara," he said, burying his face in her hair.

She let go and pushed out of his arms. She wiped her tears with the palm of her hand. "You should be. I'm so relieved to see you, but I have half a mind to kick you out." She poked a finger into his chest. "You promised me you wouldn't hate me."

"I don't hate you. You were on my mind the entire time. I just needed time to myself to think. I needed to figure things out on my own." His voice was low and raspy.

"That's fine, but you could have called or sent a text message, updated your Facebook status, tweeted, sent a telegram or a pony express or a smoke signal. Something!" She punctuated each word with a punch to his chest. "I wouldn't have cared if you sent it down the mountain with Moses as long as I knew you weren't dead on the side of the road."

"I'm sorry."

"Seriously? Sorry? You think sorry cuts it? You left without a word. You went to pay for the food, and then you were gone."

"When I picked up my wallet to pay, I saw my keys, and I just had to go." His hands were in his pockets, and he was avoiding eye contact with her.

"Where were you?"

"Georgia. I tried to get some work done."

"I contacted the hotel there. You hadn't checked in."

"I arrived a day early, and the hotel was full, so I stayed at a different one."

"Was the interview so urgent you had to leave early without telling me?"

He shook his head. "After talking to my father...to Robert, I needed...I...I didn't want you to see me in the state I was in."

"You'd rather have me worried to death about you than let me see that you're not invulnerable? I already knew that. I knew that this would hit you hard. I've been going out of my mind because I didn't know your state of mind. You could have let me know *something*. No one has heard from you in two days. *Two days*, Ryan! Two! Days!"

Amara pushed him to emphasize how upset she was. Then she started to cry again. He pulled her into his arms to comfort her and to prevent her from seeing him crying. He'd come home because he thought he was all cried out, but he wasn't. Finding out his mother had lied about who his father was had pushed him to the edge, but then the discovery that Robert was just as culpable in the lie had sent him right over that edge.

"Amara, please don't be mad right now because I really need you," he whispered into her hair. "I don't know, Amara, I just don't know."

His body leaned into her so that she was supporting some of his weight. He was sharing the weight he was feeling with her because he couldn't carry the burden alone anymore.

She pulled her head back and looked up at him. "You don't know what?"

"I don't know who I am. I don't know what to do. I just don't know anything. I can't wrap my head around it all."

"The way I see it, there isn't much to wrap your head around. You're still Ryan Clark. You are still the son of Robert Clark. For better and mostly for worse, you are still the son of Catherine Clark. And you are still the brother of Diane and cousin of Noli." She cradled his face in her hands. "The most important thing for you to understand is that you are still my husband, and you're stuck with me as your wife. You don't need to figure anything out on your own. We—you and me—are in this together. You just need to let me do it because I got this, even if you don't."

He leaned into her and rested his forehead on hers. "I'm not stuck with you. You're stuck with me. I'm fortunate to have you. I love you."

She rubbed her nose against his. "You are very fortunate, blessed even, because I love you too."

"Do you really 'got this'?"

"Of course I do. I am Amara Adams-Clark. I don't say I got it unless I got it. Let me get some coffee started, and I'll tell you the strategy I planned on telling you two days ago."

"I'll start the coffee. You should go wash the dried tears and crust from your eyes."

Her hands flew to her face, and she ran to the half bath to check herself in the mirror.

AFTER SEEING WHAT APPEARED to be a Halloween mask reflecting back at her in the mirror, Amara ran upstairs to wash her face, brush her teeth, and fix her hair. Ryan must really, truly love her if he had an entire conversation with her looking this run-down. She put a bit of concealer under her eyes and a tinted moisturizer all over. She wasn't a vain woman, but she looked like "who did that to you and why," never an acceptable way to look.

"You've made me a liquid apology." She pointed at a giant-sized mug of coffee covered with a mountain of whipped cream, drizzled with caramel, and sprinkled with mini chocolate chips. She took a moment to savor that first delicious sip. "I need to call everyone to let them know you're home, unless you want to."

"I'm not ready for that yet."

She made the first call to Diane, who volunteered to call the rest of her family and hold them off from coming to the house until the afternoon. Her second call was to Ethan. He asked if it was okay if he came by later or if it was just family only. Amara reminded him that he was now family too. Ryan sat and watched her through both calls.

"I have way more than one sibling. Now that's a change," Ryan said.

"It is, but you get to choose how much of a relationship you have with them. While I hope you're accepting of them, it's understandable if you're not."

"Are we supposed to all sit down for Thanksgiving dinner with Will at the head of the table carving the turkey?"

"Not at all. I wouldn't recommend being in the same room with him holding a knife. You don't want him in your life, and I don't think he wants any of you in his. I will never consider him to be my father-in-law. That title is designated for Robert, your father. You have to understand that everything he did was out of love. He loved your mother and you enough that he married her and claimed you as his own. He's a pretty amazing guy, and he raised you to be just like him."

"I should just ignore the fact that he lied to me my entire life?"

"Ryan, lying and protecting are occasional bedfellows. You know that firsthand. All Robert and Catherine tried to do was protect you because they love you."

"Catherine did to avoid the embarrassment of being an unwed, single mother."

"That's not true. Your father is the one who insisted on the marriage. She was prepared to raise you on her own."

He looked at her with furrowed brows. "What?"

"They explained everything while you were on your vision quest."

He tried not to chuckle but did. "You're not going to let it go, are you?"

"You were gone two days. You asked me not to be mad right now, and I can see you're in turmoil, so I'm saving the mad for later. When you're in a better place, I'm going to rip you a new one."

"That's fine, but my apology will come in the form of makeup sex." He dodged the throw pillow she threw at him. "Will you tell me what they told you? I'd rather hear it from you. It'll make seeing them more palatable."

"Your mother had taken extra classes during the summer session, and the campus was mostly empty, so she kept running into Will Bedloe. He struck up a friendship with her, and they started dating. They dated most of the first semester of her senior year until she discovered he was also dating Jacqueline. When your mother confronted him, he told her she was the type of girl a guy like him had fun with but didn't marry. He told her he had political aspirations, and she was crazy for thinking she was anything more than a 'fine piece of chocolate.'" She paused. "You know, I'd never heard your mother curse until yesterday when she quoted Will Bedloe. At any rate, Will had been a distraction from her schoolwork, and she was barely passing calculus. Robert was a friend who had tutored her before in high school, so she went to him for help. He'd had a crush on her since ninth grade, but he knew her strict father didn't allow her to date. Seeing graduation on the horizon, and knowing he may never see her again, he asked her out. They'd known each other for so long that it was no surprise when they fell head over heels in love right away."

"Kind of like us? We kind of skipped most of the dating part and got married."

"We could have dated if you hadn't been so noble and wanted to wait. Anyway...back to your parents. When she discovered she was pregnant, she told Will and tried to break things off with your father. By that time, Will's engagement and first political candidacy had already been announced. It's only speculation, but that's likely the reason Jacqueline's father put up the money to have you aborted and keep Catherine quiet. When she finally explained to your father that she didn't want to burden him with another man's child and that she would be fine raising you alone, he told her their love was more important than your paternity. Between him finding so much to love about your mother and saying stuff like that, I'm certain he was heavy into drugs back then."

"I've always thought it was either drugs or witchcraft that made him marry her."

"They are the only logical explanations. He was so in love with her that he insisted on marrying her and claiming you as his. Then one day she got a letter from your grandfather that included the letter and check forwarded from Johnathan Prescott. Your grandfather wrote that it didn't matter if she kept or aborted the baby, that she was no longer his daughter. Her roommate called your father because your mother was inconsolable. He finally convinced her to marry him that night."

"She never thought about aborting me? Even before Robert stepped up, she was going to keep me?"

Amara nodded. "She has always loved you, Ryan. She's an absolute piece of work, but she loves you. The biggest part of why she kept this a secret was because she never wanted you to know that your biological father wished you were never born. True, there was a part of her that was glad to not have to deal with the embarrassment, but for the most part, it was her trying to protect you."

Amara let Ryan contemplate that for a minute. She also needed more coffee. His parents' story was kind of sweet. Their love was something that no one outside the two of them understood, but the two of them got it. Robert was the only person who understood Catherine. And Catherine only let her guard down for Robert.

"What's your plan to deal with this?"

"Simple—if you're in front of the story, you control the story. Contact the network and see if they're interested in doing a special edition of your show. Will Bedloe was the undeclared front-runner for the presidential bid, so they should be. If not, you'll get it up online, and I can get it on *Huffington*, *BuzzFeed*, or *UpWorthy*. I really don't think that'll be necessary though. Your station will want this because they won't want to get scooped on a story about one of their own."

"It'll be a half hour of me talking to the camera."

"That would be stupid, and no one will watch. It'll be an interview with you and some of your siblings."

"Half siblings."

"If that's how you choose to see them. They only share half of your DNA, but the same will be true for the children we'll have someday, will you call them your half children?"

"Of course not. But calling Ethan my half-brother is weird enough. Calling him my brother is..."

"Just think about him and the eight other as family if you can't call them siblings just yet."

"Interviewing my...family has already been done."

"It has, but most of the emphasis has been on Will, not the experience of the woman and children. Do you think you're the only one who had an identity crisis when finding out who your biological father was? Catherine wasn't the only one who tried to sweep it under the rug. Ethan gives the appearance of having this all under control, but he's struggling with his own issues. Finding out about you was different. Even when the sister who was less than nine months younger than him was found, he was still holding on to some belief that his father had originally loved his mother and then went astray afterward. You're proof that his mother was just a means to an end, and in a way so was Ethan. That's why Jacqueline never told her father or husband about Catherine returning the check. She didn't want her son to ever feel anything other than wanted and loved."

"I hadn't considered how Ethan was dealing with this," Ryan said.

"Most of the media hasn't. There've been questions shouted at a six-year-old and his mother as she tried to hustle him from his kindergarten class to her minivan while cradling her two-month-old. They've sat in judgment of these women for having a relationship with a married man. They revealed to a woman who had never known who her father was that he was alive and well just days after she lost her mother to cancer."

"That must be tough." He ran his hand back and forth over the crown of his head as he sank back into the chair. "How do you know all this about her?"

"She and I had a chat. She talked with Ethan too."

"She'd be willing to do an interview?"

"She would, but only if you go to Kentucky. She's graduating from the University of Kentucky." Amara watched him process it all. It was apparent that something was bothering him. "Ryan, what's going on in that handsome head of yours? Talk to me. Remember, we're in this together."

"Your plan is good. It's actually brilliant. I just don't think I could do it. I don't know if I'm ready for it. I can't objectively interview someone else dealing with the emotional fallout of Hurricane Bedloe."

Amara nodded. She understood that it was easier for her since she was looking from the outside in. The advice she was giving was good, but she didn't know how likely she would be to follow it if the situation were reversed.

"As a journalist, you're too close. What if you didn't do the interviews? You can do the segments in between. They could even interview you."

"Will you do it?"

"Do what?"

"The interviews. Half of your double major was journalism."

It wasn't a horrible idea. She had already built a rapport with a couple of the adult children and the mom of the six-year-old. There was also Ethan and perhaps Jacqueline. "If you can get the station to go for it. And by go for it, I mean pay me. My most recent campaigns have gone down in flames. I may not be working anytime soon, at least not using the political science part of my degree."

Ryan went to his producer, and the network's news director loved the idea. They replaced a rerun of their normal prime time hour news show with a special edition of Ryan's show and agreed to pay Amara enough to keep her in caramel, coffee, and clothes for a while. The doorbell rang, reminding them that before they could tackle putting together the interviews and segments of the show, they had to tackle talking with his family in the aftermath of the revelations.

chapter 26

RYAN STARTED TO GET UP when the doorbell rang, but Amara blocked his way.

"I will answer the door. You're not allowed to answer the door until I'm confident you won't pull another runner," she said, gesturing for him to stay put on the sofa.

Ethan was the first to arrive. He hadn't been the first person Amara had notified about Ryan's return, but logistically it made sense that he was the first to arrive.

"Sorry it took so long, but I stopped to pick up a few pizzas. I figured people would be hungry." He carried the food into the kitchen and gave Ryan a head nod to say hello. "Welcome back. I got a tee time later if you want to unwind with a round of golf."

"Golf? You see Ryan for the first time since finding out he's your half-brother and you talk about a tee time?" Amara said.

Ethan glanced at Amara with his usual look of incomprehension at her question. "He's like the millionth half sibling I've found out about this week. I can fake being shocked, but genuine astonishment is long gone. You want me to hug him and cry on his shoulder while proclaiming he's the brother I always wanted and never had? Like I said, brothers are popping up like dandelions. Ryan's my half-brother. So what. Nothing's changed. He's still the less handsome yet more stylish guy who won the awesome girl but can't beat me at golf."

"I disagree with your statement that nothing's changed," Amara said.

"I disagree with your statement that I'm less handsome," Ryan said.

"I think you're more handsome," Amara said to Ryan with a smile.

"Stay out of our sibling rivalry," Ethan said to Amara.

Ryan grunted a laugh. "A rivalry would imply we were in the same league. You're like a bench-warmer on a peewee team, and I'm an All-Pro in the big leagues."

"We'll see how big league you are on the golf course with no Mulligans," Ethan said.

"It was just the one, and I got distracted," Ryan said.

"You're right. Things haven't changed at all. You two are still arguing about golf," Amara said.

"Things have changed. Our first meeting began not with a handshake but with his fist greeting my stomach at a high velocity. Then we became friends. Now we're family. I'm actually kind of glad to have another adult sibling to help me navigate this mess and lament about having the worst father in the world," Ethan said. "More importantly, you need me to help you deal with the sudden notoriety that comes along with being Will Bedloe's son. While you were away, did you figure out what you're going to do?"

"No, but Amara did," Ryan said.

"Of course she did," Ethan said, taking a bite of pizza.

"What does that mean?" Amara asked.

Ethan covered his mouth as he finished chewing. "That no matter the situation, you can spin your way through it."

"This time I'm not spinning." Amara wrapped her arms around Ryan and laid her head on his chest. "I'm just trying to make this less painful for my husband."

Ryan took her chin between his fingers and tipped her chin up. He smiled at her before kissing her. Amara turned in his arms and kissed him as passionately as she'd made love to him after returning home.

"I'm trying to eat here," Ethan said.

"If we gross you out, feel free to leave," Ryan said then gave his wife another brief kiss.

"Are you kicking me out?"

"He didn't kick you out. He gave you an invitation to leave at your discretion."

"Maybe I should go before your family gets here."

"You're just trying to leave before Catherine gets her and tries to kick you out again," Amara said.

"Exactly, I don't want to be in the way of you discussing family matters," Ethan said.

"This is our home, and you are family. We want you to stay," Amara said. "As far as I'm concerned, you're more welcome here than Catherine."

The doorbell rang again. "Showtime," Ryan said, looking at Amara for support.

"It's going to be fine."

"Can I invite them to leave whenever I want?"

"Just as long as you don't leave all of a sudden again."

There was more impatient ringing of the doorbell.

"That's definitely not my mother. A lady such as herself would never exhibit such a display of impatience."

The alarm notification that the front door was open sounded.

"I tried being patient," said a voice from the living room, "but I still have a key to this house."

"And didn't see why we should wait," said Diane as she and Noli entered the kitchen. Noli dropped the keys on the counter and hugged Amara then scowled at Ryan. "Rule number one of running away from your problems is that you contact at least one person to let them know you're alive," she said to him.

"How is he?" Diane asked, hugging Amara.

"I'm right here. Why are you asking her?" Ryan asked.

"Can you tell your husband I haven't calmed down enough after what he put us through the last couple of days to talk to him rationally?" Diane said to Amara.

"And how is my replacement brother doing?" she asked Ethan as she gave him a hug.

"Amara laid into me enough for everyone."

Diane spun around. "You seem to be in perfect physical condition, so she didn't do a good enough job for me." Her eyes glistened with tears as she took a deep breath. "I was really worried that something had happened to you."

He forced his sister into a hug and kissed the top of her head. "I know it's not enough, but I am sorry. You have to forgive me, though. All those times I wished I was adopted, it was never Robert that I was wishing I wasn't related to."

Diane let out a weak laugh. She dabbed at her tears with the scarf she was wearing. "I guess you're right." She gave him one last squeeze and stepped out of the embrace. "Do you think you're going to get away with calling him Robert?"

"No, but calling him Dad seems almost wrong now."

"I thought we settled this already. Does calling Will Bedloe Dad seem right?" Amara interjected.

"No, but—"

"There is no but." She took Ryan's hand into hers and gave it a squeeze. "Robert Clark is and has always been your dad."

"He must have forgotten that one time when he was sixteen and feeling all grown and called Dad Bobby," Diane said.

Ryan shook his head. "We don't need to bring that up."

"Yes, we do. I don't know this story. What did he do?" Amara

"It was the one and only time I've ever seen my father get physically violent," Diane said. "He punched Ryan hard in the stomach. As my brother was doubled over in pain, my dad said 'Next time you call me anything but Dad, I'll make you really hurt.'"

"He is your dad because you inherited the sucker punch to the gut from him," Ethan said.

"Ryan is the man he is because of Robert Clark. I don't know why he's not grasping that," Amara said.

"I get that. I do. I'm just struggling to make it fit with this new reality."

"I know your reality has changed. Your biological family has changed. I've learned biology doesn't mean everything. If Uncle Robert isn't your family because you don't share his DNA, then I'm not your family, and I don't accept that. You are my cousin. You tormented me by tearing the heads off my dolls when I was little. You helped your father plan my parents'," Noli closed her eyes to keep the tears there, "funeral when I couldn't. You were even willing to fight a man twice your size when you thought he'd broken my heart. So if you say you're not my family, I will be really pissed because," she sniffed and dried her eyes, "I really loved those dolls."

Ryan laughed as he locked Noli into a bear hug. "And I love my cousin."

"As your cousin, you should trust me when I say avoiding and running away won't help," she said. "Your issues will just wait there for you to face them. And by issues, I mean Catherine and Uncle Robert. And by face them, I mean talk to them."

"What she lacks in subtlety, she makes up for in accuracy," Diane said. "Maybe it's time you call them and ask them over."

"They're waiting for an invitation?"

"I told them you were home but not ready for visitors, and they should wait until you call."

"Speaking of invitations, when will you be sending out yours?" Noli asked Amara.

"Invitation for what?"

"Your wedding, of course."

"What wedding?" Amara held up her left hand and wiggled her fingers. "I'm already married. I've already had my wedding."

"No, what you had was a legal transaction in front of Elvis, not a wedding," Diane said. "And according to your mother, what happens in Vegas stays in Vegas, so it's probably not even legal."

"Diane, you're a lawyer, and you're listening to my mom? She's just upset she didn't get to be mother of the bride."

"And I'm just upset I didn't get to be bridesmaid," Diane said.

"Exactly," Noli said. "You stood as a bridesmaid at both of our weddings, not disclosing the fact we had missed the opportunity to be bridesmaids at yours. So you have to have a wedding."

"I'll tell you what I told my mother—I'm already married and feel no need to waste money on a ceremony." Amara wrapped her arms around Ryan and kissed him. "Isn't that right?"

"Actually, after all we've been through since that day, it would be nice to exchange vows again in a more elaborate ceremony. Plus I get to see you in a wedding dress." Brian bent down to whisper in her ear, "And take it off of you."

"Do you really want a wedding?" Amara asked, looking up into Ryan's eyes.

"Mainly because it's followed by a honeymoon."

"I have these friends that got married at the city's county office then had an elaborate jumping the broom ceremony," Ethan said.

Everyone in the room turned toward Ethan. "What do you know about jumping the broom?" Amara asked the question on everyone's mind.

"Just because I'm a wealthy white guy doesn't mean that all my friends are wealthy white guys. My friends are from various backgrounds, all different races and economic and educational levels."

"Apparently, so are our siblings," Ryan said. His tone was flat and his eyes were pensive. When he noticed Amara analyzing him, he put on a smile.

Amara smiled a big, genuine smile right back at him. "I saw a dress that's the perfect amount of formal and casual for a jumping the broom ceremony and reception." She leaned into Ryan, letting her lips brush across his earlobe before whispering, "And the perfect lingerie to wear underneath it."

"That's a very compelling argument," Ryan said to Amara before kissing her.

"I have an even more compelling argument," Amara said with a husky voice.

"Really? What's that?" he asked, looking into her eyes as if they were the only two in the room.

"How about we call your mom now so we can get this over with and get all these people out of our house so we can do a little honeymoon planning."

Anxiety waged a fierce battle with desire in the depths of his brown eyes before conceding. Ryan wanted his Amara more than he feared confronting his mother. Knowing his wife would be by his side made the impending conversation with his parents less intimidating. He nodded.

THE TENSION IN THE room was as crushing as the pressure in the depths of the ocean. A few words of greeting were exchanged, but Ryan had not spoken to or even looked at his parents. Catherine and Robert sat on the sofa next to each other, looking at their son. Ryan sat in the chair, staring at the floor, then his hands, then back at the floor. Amara sat on the arm of the chair, with one foot on the floor and the other swinging back and forth nervously. One hand rested gently on Ryan's back. Diane, Ethan, and Noli sat on the stools at the kitchen island, staring uncomfortably at each other and the light fixtures.

Amara was the one to take the thousand pound bull in the room by the horns. "Ryan, do you have any questions for your parents beyond the information I've already relayed to you?"

He looked at her. It was easier to direct his questions to her than to his parents. "I was wondering if they had ever planned on telling me the truth, or were they hoping of getting away with lying to me for my entire life?"

"Ryan, we never fathomed that man being your biological father would come to light."

"You planned on lying then?"

"Why would we have told you the truth? Better yet, *when* would we have told you the truth? You're in your thirties, and you responded by running away for two days. If we had told you earlier, your face would have been on the side of a milk carton," said Robert.

"Robert, we agreed you would not get upset because it will not help," Catherine said softly with pleading eyes.

"I'm not getting upset. I'm already there. This boy is acting like we've somehow wronged him by loving him and raising him." Robert was looking at Ryan as if he wanted to slap some sense into him.

"Ryan is having a difficult time adjusting to the news, but he doesn't feel you've wronged him," Amara said.

"Don't try sidestepping the truth with us, Amara. He just called us liars, and he's sitting there sulking. He's angry with us, and he has no right to be."

"You're right, he is angry with you, or at least he thinks he is. I know from personal experience that when you're upset about circumstances that are outside of your control to change or fix, it's easier to focus your anger on someone than to live with that feeling of helplessness."

"What circumstances need to be controlled? Who his father is? I'm his father. I don't care what a DNA test will say. His birth certificate says I'm his father. Over thirty years of loving him says I'm his father. The hundreds of thousands of dollars I've spent keeping a roof over his head, putting braces on his teeth, and paying for his fancy private university degree says I'm his father. If he wants to change that fact, then I owe him an apology because somewhere along the way, I messed up and raised a fool." Robert stood and looked at his wife. "Catherine, I'll be waiting in the car if you want to stay and beg him to forgive you for loving him, but I refuse to entertain his childish behavior any longer."

Robert didn't glance or hesitate as he walked by Ryan. He kissed his daughter and niece on the cheek and shook Ethan's hand to say good-bye. Diane began to follow him, but Noli gestured for her to stay as she followed her uncle to the car. No one spoke. The uncomfortable silence stretched on for several minutes until Catherine began to speak in a meek voice that seemed foreign coming from her.

"When I first found out I was pregnant with you, I thought I had failed myself." Catherine sat, her hands folded on her lap and her legs crossed at her ankles. Her eyes were fixed on no physical thing, only on the past. "I had made a promise to myself to get my degree and finally not be my father's greatest disappointment. I was going to be an unwed mother, and that made me feel like an absolute failure. But the love I felt for you, Ryan, was greater than that feeling of failure.

"When your father—I am speaking of Robert—told me he loved me unconditionally and would raise you as his own, I felt disappointment in myself. I was disappointed that I had not seen Will or Robert for the men they were. I was disappointed because I did not recognize my feelings for Will were nothing more than infatuation with a charming, yet substance-less man or that I was in love with my quiet and shy friend. I am sure you think I married him because I did not want to be a single mother. That is not true. I married him because I loved him. How could I not? In my entire life, he was the only person besides my late mother who accepted me as I was."

Catherine finally looked at her son, who had finally focused his attention on her. "We were married, and a few short months later, we welcomed you into the world. A year or so after that, I was pregnant again, and I miscarried. It was my first of three. Robert told me we should stop trying because his son was more than enough. We stopped trying, but were still blessed with

Diane." Catherine glanced at her daughter. Diane's eyes were filled with tears, and Catherine smiled to comfort her.

"Ryan, I never mentioned your biological father, not because I was lying to you, but because no thought of the mistake named Will Bedloe crossed my mind for years. That remained the case until his first gubernatorial race. We discussed telling you the truth, but considering he thought I had aborted you upon his request, I felt it was in no one's best interest. If you want to be angry with me because you disagree with that decision, then so be it, but you have no right to be mad at Robert. I can't stand by and tolerate your disrespectful behavior toward your father." Catherine stood and smoothed nonexistent wrinkles from her skirt. "Your father and I will be home—or, if she will have us, we will be at Diane's—whenever you are ready to apologize to your father because you do owe him one."

Ryan sat with his elbows resting on his knees and his hands grasping the back of his head. Amara had left his side and was apologetically trying to convince Catherine to stay. When she insisted on going, Amara hugged her mother-in-law, and she hugged back. Catherine made arrangements to visit with Diane after retrieving their belongings from the hotel. She even voiced kind words of salutation to Ethan before showing herself out.

"Ryan, are you seriously about to let them leave?" Ethan said with all the authority of a seasoned politician. "If you must be angry at anyone, be angry at the man who didn't even want to give you a chance at life. If Robert Clark were my father, I would be begging for forgiveness and thanking both of them for saving me from a life with Will Bedloe. Now stop brooding and go catch them before any more damage is done to your relationship."

Ryan jumped up and ran out the door, just in time to stop his parents from pulling out of the driveway.

epilogue

"ONE MINUTE," A PRODUCER said into Ryan and and Amara's earpieces.

"Are you nervous?" Ryan asked Amara as the makeup artist retouched her lip gloss.

"Not at all," she said, looking around at all the cameras and people on the station's sound stage.

"You're lying."

"No, I'm trying to convince myself it's the truth."

"You'll be great."

"Thank you," she said, smiling at him. "Are you nervous about being the story instead of just reporting it?"

"If you weren't by my side, I would be."

"I would kiss you, but there wouldn't be time to fix my lipstick again."

"There will be plenty of time for that afterward."

"You mean after we have dinner with your parents?"

"I was thinking a little before and a little later. Maybe a quickie in the bathroom during," Ryan said nonchalantly.

"Five. Four. Three. Two. One," the producer counted down in their ears before Amara could respond.

"Good evening, I'm Ryan Clark."

"I'm Amara Adams-Clark, and this is a special edition of *What Matters to You*."

"I perceived it to be my job to track down the children of Governor William Bedloe. As a journalist, we soothe our souls by saying we're just doing our jobs by seeking the truth. My colleagues and I saw these children and their parents not as people, but as just another nail in Will Bedloe's political coffin. I never considered what it must feel like to have your truth become a lie. That is, until I discovered I was the product of a failed college romance between my mother and Will Bedloe. For a few days, my entire life became a lie. My wife, being far more intelligent than me, reasoned that the only thing that had changed was that my family had grown. I had more siblings, including one of my good friends. My father was still the man who had loved and raised me. Tonight we are going to look at this from the perspective of my new extended family and not as a story about a promiscuous politician."

Ryan spoke directly into the camera, like he had done so many times in his career, but this was more important than any of those times. His appearance of having it together was just that—an appearance. Though he was no longer in shock, he was still raw and emotionally drained from the fallout of the revelation of his true paternity. It was not hyperbole when he told Amara he couldn't do this without her next to him.

He already knew that when it came to working the media, his wife was a master. That evening, there was a part of him that was afraid because of how good she was. She was far better than he was. Amara was like Barbara Walters, and most of her interviews resulted in tears. She was so gentle and understanding that the interviewees couldn't help but expose their souls for her. The icing on top of that was that the camera loved her almost as much as he did.

"I've never been so nervous," Ryan said once all the cameras and bright lights were turned off and most of the crew had left the studio.

"You said you weren't nervous. I know you were part of the story, but you've done this hundreds of times and there was nothing for you to be nervous about. Me, on the other hand, I just hope how anxious I was didn't show up on camera," Amara said.

"You were perfect. You are perfect. That's what made me so nervous."

"What are you talking about?"

"You are an amazing woman. You are the kindest, most intelligent woman I know and there's no woman in the world more beautiful than you." Ryan dropped to one knee. The few remaining people in the studio went silent and all their attention was turned to the couple. He pulled a ring out of his pocket. "Amara, will you marry me?"

Amara looked at her husband confused. She leaned in and said, "Ryan, we're already married."

He smiled. "I know, but that was a spur of the moment decision in Vegas. I'm doing it right this time. I want to declare my love for you in front of our friends and family. I'm asking you if you choose me to be your lover, friend, and partner for life."

"I chose you in Vegas."

"I know, but things happened. I want—I need to know if you *still* choose me because Amara, I chose you then, I'm choosing you now, and I'll choose you every morning for the rest of our lives. If I make it to heaven before you I'll be the first face you see. I love you. Amara, will you marry me again?"

She blinked back her tears of joy. With shaking hands, she took the band off her left hand and put it on her right hand. "Yes. Again and again, yes."

The onlookers in the studio burst into applause. Ryan slipped the ring on her finger then pulled her onto his leg and kissed her.

acknowledgments

Thank you to all the readers who enjoyed Jack and Diane and someone to love. It's been a long wait for Ryan and Amara's story. Thank you for your support and patience.

Thank you, Mary. You weren't very patient in waiting for this book and I'm grateful for it. Your notes on the rough draft proved quite valuable as I made revisions. Thank you for all your support not just of my writing, but of me.

To my sister thanks for being my unpaid assistant. If it weren't for you taking on some other tasks I would have never been able to get this finished. Thanks for being my sounding board as I worked through the plot. I promise you I'll write Misty's hot mess of a story even if it's just for you.

To my two children, thank you so very much for giving me time to do "book stuff". You are my inspiration.

Thank you to all my friends and family who continue to encourage and support me. Some of you even buy my books just because I wrote them and have no intention of ever reading them. That's love.

To Carlton, this isn't a thank you, this is a challenge. I really need to see my name in your acknowledgments, so get to writing.

Most importantly, thank you God for your grace, love, and your forgiveness. You gave me this talent and I hope I'm not wasting it.

about the author

Lena is a lifelong Hoosier who recently moved to the high desert of New Mexico. Storytelling and romance are the loves of her life. From a very early age, she created meet-cutes with her Barbies and made up her own bedtime stories. Her love of love grew by reading Sweet Valley High and watching classic black and white movies starring her favorites Carey Grant and Audrey Hepburn. The Nearness of You is her third novel.

a note from the author

Thank you so much for reading my book! I hope you enjoyed reading it as much as I enjoyed telling it. If you did enjoy it, please leave a review. Even a short review is a great way to support me and help others enjoy Ryan and Amara's story.

Love,
Lena

Find Lena across the web:

Website: indewstyle.com
Email: dew@indewstyle.com
Instagram: indewstyle

also by Lena Hampton

Jack & Diane

Diane is months away from a law degree, her dream job in Chicago, and a wedding to a doctor.

Jack is on the verge of inheriting his family's farm when his dad retires.

Their worlds collide when Jack comes along on the deserted road where Diane's car died after racing away from her philandering fiance. The moment Jack sees Diane's warm brown eyes he knows he met the woman of his dreams. Diane finds herself falling in love with Jack, but loving him would mean letting go of her dreams.

Can they somehow make both their dreams come true?

Someone to Love

She's afraid of love and he doesn't believe in it.

Magnolia Freeman travels the world trying to outrun the pain of her parents' sudden deaths. As much as Magnolia dreads returning home she can't deny her favorite cousin's requests to help plan her wedding.

Cooper Smith believes no good can come from love. As far as he's concerned a "relationship" shouldn't last more than a night—or two nights if it's a holiday weekend. Despite his skepticism about love he volunteers his restaurant for his best friend's wedding.

Magnolia and Cooper give in to their attraction since neither of them are looking for anything serious. When their fling turns into something more Magnolia leaves but can't get the heartbroken Cooper out of her mind or her heart, especially when there's a permanent reminder of him growing inside her.

Can Magnolia and Cooper get beyond their fears to find someone to love?

other titles from inDEWstyle

Whiskey Kisses by Dan. Elizabeth

A wild celebrity meets a serene accountant.

Wilder Mann is accustomed to sneaking out on groupies before they wake up, not chasing them down the hotel hall barefoot in his boxers to keep them from leaving with a part of his heart. Then again, Serenity is no groupie. She's not even a fan.

Despite her best efforts Serenity Breedlove can't resist Wilder's charm and falls for the caring and vulnerable man behind the country singer's bad-boy swagger. But she learns dating a star has its pitfalls when her weight becomes the topic of national discussion. While Serenity loves Wilder the man, she is not a fan of Wilder the persona.

Can their love survive his fame?

Made in the USA
Columbia, SC
01 November 2024